CHASING WILD

THE WILDS OF MONTANA

KRISTEN PROBY

&

AMPERSAND

PUBLISHING, INC.

Chasing Wild

A Wilds of Montana Novel

By

Kristen Proby

CHASING WILD

A Wilds of Montana Novel

Kristen Proby

This one is for the characters in this book. Chase and Summer were relentless in their need to have their story told, and they consumed me. I hope they're as pleased as I am with their happily ever after.

PROLOGUE
SUMMER

Five Years Ago

I'm *so* freaking tired. Working two jobs, back-to-back, on the same day will do that to a girl. Especially when said girl hates said jobs with every fiber of her being.

I didn't bust my ass through college to get a degree in political science to then turn around after graduation and work as a retail clerk *and* a bartender.

Not because there's anything wrong with those vocations; I simply suck at both of them.

And the truth is, I don't want to be an attorney, either. My parents think I should head off to law school next and follow my father's footsteps into politics, but that's never been *my* ambition.

I don't even know what my dream is because I've

been busy chasing someone else's aspirations. Sitting in an office for the rest of my life, buried under papers, or addressing crowds of people and kissing strangers' babies sounds like prison to me.

But after two months of working in retail and at the bar, I can safely say that neither of those things is what I'm meant to be doing either.

I should head back to the apartment that I share with my best friend, Lyla, but I think she planned on having a party tonight, and after a full evening of dealing with drunk college students at the bar, I'm not up for dealing with it at my own home. I want peace and quiet.

So, I head over to Dennis's place. He's been my boyfriend for three years. My parents introduced me to him at a gala event I was required to attend, and I actually ended up liking him, which doesn't usually happen. Dennis wasn't just handsome; he made me laugh, and it was easy to be with him from the moment I met him. Sure, he can be pushy and a little selfish, but who can't, right? Lately, despite his badgering me, I haven't been ready to live with him yet, so we've maintained our separate apartments. But tonight, I want to sleep for a solid ten hours.

I pad up the stairs of Dennis's apartment building. The dark quiet of the warm summer night makes my eyes heavier, and I'm *so* excited to slip into bed and fall blissfully into sleep.

I use my key to unlock his door and soundlessly slip inside but notice that the lamp is still on in the living room. He doesn't usually leave that on unless he knows that I'll be coming here after work, but I didn't text him before I headed this way. Maybe he's still awake?

There's a bowl of half-eaten popcorn on the coffee table and two bottles of beer, mostly gone.

Something has the hair on the back of my neck prickling, and everything in me goes cold.

With a frown, I cross to the short hallway that leads to his bedroom and notice a T-shirt and a sundress tossed carelessly on the floor. Closer to the bedroom door are pants, boxers, and panties.

And when I reach the doorway of Dennis's bedroom, I find the man himself sleeping soundly in the bed, with my *best friend*, Lyla, wrapped around him, also sleeping.

I stay perfectly quiet as I watch them for a moment and wonder how long this has been going on. Is it new? Has it been going on the whole time that Dennis and I have been together?

And then it occurs to me that I just don't give a shit. As I watch them sleep, I don't feel much of anything at all.

I return to the living room, take his key off of my keyring, and set it on the small kitchen counter. I don't care if I recover the few pieces of my clothing in his bedroom, and when I glance around, I realize that there's nothing else in this apartment that belongs to me. We had mediocre sex on that couch too many times to count. I worked extra shifts and bought him the TV for Christmas because his old one died on him in the middle of a video game challenge. He cooked me dinner in this kitchen every Sunday night. But aside from memories, there's nothing here for me. So, I walk out, down the steps, and out to my car, where I sit for about five minutes, trying to gauge how I feel about this new development.

Shouldn't I be crying? Should I have yelled and thrown things and screamed at the two people who I'm supposed to trust the most in the world? Because, in the moment, none of that occurred to me.

"I really don't care," I mutter, shaking my head as I lean my head against the seat. "I don't want this life. I don't want him, and I obviously don't want Lyla either. *None* of this is what I would have chosen for myself if I'd been given the chance to choose after high school."

Starting the car, I head for my apartment just a mile away and immediately begin to pack my things. I fill my two big suitcases full of my clothes and three totes with the few kitchen items, linens, and personal items I don't want to leave behind.

The rest of it, the furniture, belongs to Lyla. Her parents outfitted this apartment our junior year in college, and I moved in and paid half the rent. So, packing up my belongings and stuffing them into my Chevy Equinox doesn't take long at all.

I take one last pass through the apartment to make sure I have everything and grab a computer charger from the living room that belongs to me, along with a magnet off the fridge that my aunt gave me for Valentine's Day last year. Content that I've remembered everything, I take one more key off of my key ring and leave it on the kitchen counter.

I don't write a note or send a text or anything cliché like that.

I simply leave.

And I know *exactly* what I'm going to do.

I'm going to start living the life *I* want to live.

CHAPTER ONE
SUMMER

"I'm so sorry, baby girl," I croon to my French Bulldog as more fireworks are let off outside, in the middle of the street, in my little neighborhood in Bitterroot Valley. "I know you hate them so much. I do, too. But it's just noise; it's not going to hurt you."

Lily stares up at me with scared eyes and cowers against me, and I fold her into my arms, holding on tightly. I've tried *everything* I could think of to mitigate the noise for her. The TV volume is up, I gave her a Benadryl to try to make her sleepy, and I even wrapped her tightly in a blanket, but she hated that and scooted right out of it. She's agitated and scared, and it breaks my heart. Lily is a rescue, and loud noises like this frighten her.

"I thought it was illegal to let off fireworks in town," I grumble, tempted to call the police, but I don't want to be *that* neighbor. It's not like this happens every day.

"They should be calming down now. It's getting late, and most kids should be going to bed."

I wish Lily could understand me, but I keep my voice calm and soothing and rub her soft, fawn-colored fur gently while kissing her sweet little head.

I rescued Lily last year, and we immediately fell in love with each other. She comes with me to the flower shop that I own pretty much every day, so we're together most of the time.

And that's good, because she's definitely a Velcro dog. She prefers to be with her person, and when she can't be with me, she goes to my aunt Paula's house, where she's spoiled and coddled, which suits Lily just fine.

I breathe a sigh of relief when it starts to sound like I'm right about the fireworks calming down. The loud pops are starting to be farther and farther apart, so I lower the volume on the TV a bit, testing it out. There are a few loud bangs here and there, but they're farther away, and Lily lowers her head to my lap and falls instantly asleep.

"Holy shit, I'm glad that's over," I breathe, resting my own head back on the couch with exhaustion. I'd be perfectly fine if we just did away with fireworks altogether. If my little dog, who knows she's completely safe with me, reacts like this, then I can only imagine the fear this holiday puts into the wildlife around here.

"I think we deserve some ice cream," I whisper, thinking about the pint of peanut butter-chocolate currently sitting in my freezer. "Of course, I don't want to move you now that you're settling down."

Considering this new challenge, I hear someone jiggling my front door handle.

Lily's head immediately comes up, and she growls as she stares at the door.

"Who's there?" I call out as Lily moves off my lap, and I stand, but there's no answer, and the jiggling stops.

I hurry back to my bedroom, open the bedside table drawer, pull out the one gun that I own, and rush back to the living room, where Lily's still on high alert.

"Who's there?" I call out again, louder this time.

The jiggling starts once more, and that just pisses me off.

"Listen here, asshole. I have a fucking gun, and I'm not afraid to use it. I'm calling the cops."

It stops, and I can hear footsteps running down my sidewalk as I pick up my phone and dial 9-1-1.

"9-1-1, what is your emergency?"

"Someone just tried to break into my house." I hear the tremor in my voice now. "I think they ran away, but I want someone to come over here, please. I live at four-three-three Sixth Street."

"I'm sending someone right now. What's your name?"

"Summer." I lick my lips and run my hand down Lily's back. Her fur is still standing on end. "I'm Summer Quinn."

"Okay, Summer, I just called someone, and they should be there in less than five minutes. Are you safe?"

"Yes." I look around, listening. "Yes, I don't think anyone is here now."

"Okay, good. I'm just going to hang out with you until our officer arrives, okay?"

"Thanks." I rub Lily's head and then pace in front of the couch as I wait. "I'm sure you guys are busy tonight, and I'm sorr—"

"Don't apologize," she interrupts, immediately making me feel a little better. "This is what we're here for, even on a holiday. The officer should be pulling up now."

"I just heard the car door," I confirm and run to look through my peephole. "Yes, I see him coming this way. Thank you for your help."

"You're welcome. I'm hanging up now."

I end the call and open the door when the doorbell rings and find Chase Wild on the other side.

"Oh, God, Chase." I sniff and realize that I have tears rolling out of my eyes. "Someone tried to break into my house."

"Tell me what happened." His handsome face is hard and sober, and I'm just *so* relieved that he's here.

"I heard someone jiggling my door handle." I gesture to the door. "So, I grabbed my gun and yelled at them."

His eyes widen. "Wait, you *what*?"

"I'm no victim." I firm my chin and shake my head, so mad all over again. "I scared them right off."

"Do you have any video of your front porch?"

"No." Damn it, I *need* to do that. "I'll get it installed in the morning, for sure. It's probably just kids, right?

Because Bitterroot Valley is so safe. I've never heard of anyone breaking and entering around here, and I've been here for almost five years."

"It doesn't happen often," he confirms. "And yeah, probably kids."

Why does he look like he wants to say something else?

"Are you okay to stay here tonight? I'll dust for fingerprints and look around outside, but without video, I don't know how much I can do."

I swallow hard and nod. "I can stay with a friend tonight."

I'll take Lily to my aunt Paula's house. That isn't a problem. I'm absolutely *not* staying here until I beef up the security and get some cameras installed. And it pisses me off that I suddenly don't feel safe in my own home. I *love* my little house.

"Don't worry," he assures me with a soft smile. God, he's handsome. I've always thought Chase was an attractive man, even more so when he's in uniform. He's tall and broad, with dark hair and the most gorgeous hazel eyes. That jawline is chiseled and, well...wow. "It's going to be okay."

"I'm sure."

He pats my shoulder, but I pull away from him. I don't know why I did that, and I immediately mentally kick myself.

Why did I do that? But he doesn't even blink an eye.

"You get your things," he suggests. "I'll get those prints."

"Thank you." I sniff once more, wanting to apologize for pulling away from him, but I decide against it. "Thanks."

I smile and turn to Lily, who's been waiting patiently on the couch for me. I have to pack my things, along with hers, and get ready to go. I want to leave when Chase does so I'm not here alone.

It doesn't take me long to fill a duffel with a couple of days' worth of clothes and toiletries, and then I pack up Lily's food, her dishes, and her favorite bed, along with my pillow, and take those out to my car in the garage. I call Aunt Paula really quick and fill her in, and she assures me that I should, in fact, get out to her place, *pronto*.

Just when I come back inside, Chase is finishing with his fingerprinting kit.

"I'll take these in tonight to run them," he assures me. "Are you all set?"

"Yeah, we're ready to go. I don't know if you've met Lily."

"Sure, I have," he says as he crouches down to pet my girl. "She's usually in your shop with you. Hey there, Lily."

She sniffs his hand and then licks it, which makes us both smile.

"She was scared tonight, with all the fireworks."

"Damn Fourth of July," he says with a sigh, and I notice for the first time that he looks tired around the eyes. "People don't seem to care about fireworks ordinances around here. It's late enough now that it should slow down."

"I'm taking Lily to my aunt Paula's house," I tell him. "She lives out of town, so there isn't much noise out there."

"Miss Paula is a gem," he says with a grin. "I'm glad that's where you're headed. Do you want me to help coordinate the installation of the security for you?"

I blink at him and frown. "Well, I guess I'm not sure who to call, but I can google it and figure it out."

"I can do it for you."

That makes me pause.

"Why would you offer to do that? I'm sure you're exhausted and busy, and I don't want to put you out."

"It's not a problem," he says with a shrug. "I'll have my brother, Brady, help me, and we'll have it done in less than an hour. We just did something similar, on a bigger scale, of course, out at the family ranch, so it's in our wheelhouse right now."

"Honestly, that would be an amazing help." I smile up at him, relieved that he offered. "I'm swamped at the shop right now because we're smack dab in the middle of both tourist *and* wedding season. So, if you have the time and the will to do it, I won't say no. Just let me know how much to reimburse you."

"Deal." He bends down to pet Lily once more and then grins at me. "I'll wait outside for you to lock up before I go."

"Oh, you don't have to wait for us. I'm sure it's fine."

His face hardens just a little. "I'll wait," he says again,

more firm now, and that sends a little thrill down my spine. "You're scared, Summer. There's no need for you to be here alone for even a minute."

"Thanks."

"You're welcome." He nods and turns to leave, and I lock up behind him, then get Lily and myself situated in the car before pulling out of the garage.

True to his word, Chase is waiting in his squad car as I push the button to lower the garage door, and then I pull the car away from the house, and Chase eases onto the road behind me.

Yeah, Chase is a nice guy, with the looks to match and an amazing family. If I were looking for a relationship, which I'm *not*, he would be at the top of my possibility list.

"You like him, don't you?" I ask Lily, who's panting and watching her dark surroundings. She loves car rides, but today has been rough on her, and now we're out late at night, and that's way outside of her routine. "Don't worry, we're going to Aunt Paula's house. You love it out there."

I see that all the lights are on in Aunt Paula's little house when I come to a stop in the driveway, and as I carry Lily up the walkway, the front door opens. Chase pulls in behind me, waves out his window, and then pulls out to head back to town.

"Oh, darling," Aunt Paula says with a worried frown on her pretty face, "you two get in here. What a horrible experience, and so unlike Bitterroot Valley."

"That's what I said to Chase," I reply as I follow her into the house.

"Chase was on duty?" she asks as she gets two mugs for tea out of her cabinet. Lily is off sniffing around the house, trying to find Baby, Aunt Paula's old Siamese cat. "I'm glad. I sure do like him. And the two of you have been dancing around your feelings for years."

I don't acknowledge that last comment. What am I supposed to say? That I have a massive crush on the man but have been too scared to act on it? I'm not saying that out loud. "He was honestly great tonight, and he's going to install the new security at my place tomorrow, with his brother Brady's help."

"A girl could do far worse than to have the Wild brothers helping her out," Aunt Paula says with a wink. "I might be a little jealous. Maybe I should stage a break-in of my own."

I chuckle and dip my tea bag in and out of the hot water.

"I think the police are busy enough as it is. Thanks for letting us crash here for a couple of days."

We hear the sound of an angry hiss, and then Lily barks.

"Those two." I shake my head. "Lily wants Baby to like her so bad."

"Baby will come around," Aunt Paula says. "It just takes him a little time."

"It's been almost a year since I rescued Lily."

"Baby's set in his ways." She shrugs. "And, of course,

you can come here whenever you need. If I had my way, you'd still be living here with me."

"I'm not too far away," I remind her. "Besides, you needed the space here for all your crafts and paintings. You're an artist; you have to spread out."

It's the truth. My Aunt Paula isn't just an amazing florist. She paints and sews, knits and embroiders, and she can make *anything* grow. Her little house is like a fairy cottage in the woods, with so many flowers and herbs and vegetables growing in every available piece of dirt. Not to mention the bread she bakes fresh every week, and all the projects she always has going.

She's wonderful.

"I loved nothing more than spending my summers here," I say with a happy sigh as I look around the space that looks so much like it did when I was a kid. "It's always been my safe place, and I know it's here when I need it. But I'm happy in town, too, Aunt Paula. I like being able to walk to work when the weather's nice, and I have great neighbors."

"It's good for young people to be where the action is," she agrees. "But yes, you're *always* welcome here."

"I know."

She welcomed me with open arms five years ago when I left the life I hated in Missoula. And she helped me start the life I love now, here in Bitterroot Valley.

I always knew I belonged here.

Lily whines, and I know that it's time that we go to bed.

"Thank you for everything. I'm going to head to bed.

We've been so busy at the shop, and I'll need to get an early start."

"Okay, darlin'. I'm going to finish a sewing project I started earlier today, so if the light bothers you, just let me know."

"It won't." I cross over and kiss Aunt Paula on the head. "Love you."

"I love you, too."

Lily and I make our way back to our bedroom. The bed is made fresh for us, and Lily immediately hops up, turns in a circle, and lies down.

I take my time washing my face and getting into pajamas before sliding in next to her.

No, the light doesn't bother us at all, and the rhythmic whirring of the sewing machine is the perfect white noise to send me off to sleep.

———

"CAN we take another wedding in August?" Ida, with the phone held against her shoulder, asks me from across the shop.

"What date?" I ask as I arrange the last of the local lilacs I have in a vase. It's always so sad to me when lilac season is over. They smell amazing.

"What date?" Ida asks the person on the line. "Okay, let me ask the boss. Hold, please."

She presses the phone against her shoulder again and looks up at me.

"The fifteenth?"

"No, ma'am, that's the Wild wedding, and I'll need all hands on deck for that one." I add some baby's breath to the bouquet as Ida relays the bad news to the potential customer, and then she hangs up and walks over to resume working on her own bouquet.

"The calls just keep coming in, even though the website clearly states that we're full for the season." Ida huffs and reaches for a bucket of yellow roses for the bridesmaids' bouquets for this Saturday.

"I guess they figure that if they call and ask, they can talk us into fitting them in," Sharla, another of my employees, says.

"Aunt Paula always says, 'It never hurts to ask.' However, the calls are getting annoying." I sigh and stare at the arrangement, wondering what it's missing. "I think I'll add a message before it rings through, reiterating that we're not taking any more weddings until November. It's really not a bad problem to have as a business owner, but the calls are taking up a lot of our time."

"Not a bad problem at all," Sharla agrees. "You know, some pink baby roses would look sweet in that."

"Oh, you're right." I rush off to the cooler and pull some out and bring them back. "It adds just the right pop of color. Good idea, Shar."

The bell above the door jingles cheerfully, pulling Lily out of a dead sleep in her bed in the corner.

"Well, hello, boys," Ida says as Chase and Brady Wild saunter into the shop.

"Ma'am," Brady says with a nod. "It always smells good in here."

"Flowers." I grin at him. "They always do the trick. How's it going, guys?"

"Great," Chase replies as he picks Lily up into his arms and is attacked with kisses. I think this could be the first time since I brought her home from the shelter that I feel a little jealous of my dog. "We got the cameras and the smart doorbell installed. We went ahead and put a camera on the back door and the garage door, too."

"Good," Ida says, giving me a stern eye. "Our girl is alone too much in that house, and sure, it's a safe town, but we need to keep an eye on her. We can't be too careful."

"Too bad you're not a guard dog," Brady says as he takes his turn loving on Lily. "You're just a lover, aren't you?"

"She'll growl and sometimes bark if someone's at the door, but no. She's not a guard dog."

I laugh when Lily drives that point home by kissing Brady square on the mouth.

"You can just download the app onto your phone," Chase continues, "and it'll show you whenever someone or something trips the sensors."

"So, it doesn't know the difference between a deer and a person?" I ask.

"It's not *that* smart," he says with a wink. "Here, I'll walk you through it."

I pull out my phone, and Chase helps me, standing just behind my right shoulder. I can feel the heat coming off him against my skin, and I can even smell the soap from his shower. My body practically hums whenever he's close to me.

Yeah, I'm definitely attracted to him.

"There, you're all logged in," he says and reaches around me to point at my screen. "See, there's the front door, and if you touch here, you can see the back door and yard."

I nod, following his direction, and grin up at him. "Is it weird that I'm excited about this?"

"No." He smiles back at me. He's so close, he could just lean in and plant those lips on my forehead.

And for a heartbeat, it looks like he might do just that. I don't even feel an urge to back away from him. Not at all.

But then he pulls away, and I slip my phone back into my pocket.

"How much do I owe you guys for all of this?"

"I saved the receipts," Brady says and pulls them out of his back pocket, then passes them to me.

"And for labor?"

"We're not charging you for that," Brady replies before Chase can as both men shake their heads. "It took an hour. Don't worry about it."

"Okay, how about some flowers, then?" I walk to the cooler and pull out two sweet little bunches of wild roses. "Thanks, guys. I really appreciate it."

"I don't think anyone has given me flowers before." Brady sniffs his. It's kind of cute to see the handsome cowboy bury his nose in a flower. "Nice, thanks."

"Thank you," Chase echoes. "Now, how about the shop? Do you have decent security here?"

I bite my lip, and Brady laughs.

"I'm going to take that as a no," Brady says.

"I'll call a company."

"We'll see to it," Chase counters and sends his brother a look. Brady nods. "I'll take care of it before the end of the day today."

"Seriously, Chase, I know you're busy. I can hire a company for this."

His gorgeous hazel eyes narrow on me, and I can't help but lick my lips. "Do you think I do much in this life that I don't want to do?"

"Probably not."

"He doesn't," Brady says helpfully. "Just let him do it. It's faster that way."

"I don't want to take advantage of you, that's all."

"You're not," he replies simply. "I'll be back later with the supplies and tools. For now, we'll let you ladies get back to it. I know you're busy."

"Brides will be the death of us," Sharla says and wipes her brow with the back of her hand. "But they pay my salary, so I really can't complain."

"Are your brother and Erin getting ready for the wedding next month?" I ask him, not quite ready for him to go.

"They're excited," he confirms. "They wanted to have that barn completely renovated and ready to go, but that's pretty ambitious for just a couple months of work. They'll make do, though, because my brother isn't willing to wait another year to marry her. Hell, he doesn't want to wait another *day*."

"Something tells me it's going to be a bit more involved than *making it work*," I reply.

"Sure, that's simplifying it down a bit," Chase agrees with a nod. "It's going to be a lot of work. We're all spending pretty much every extra minute out there helping out, but like I said, my brother won't wait. He's impatient when it comes to Erin."

"That's so *romantic*," Sharla says with a dreamy sigh. "They're great together. I love seeing them when they come to town."

"I won't disagree with you there. They are pretty great," Brady says. "And we don't mind helping."

"Summer, if you need anything or have questions, don't hesitate to call me." Chase drops his business card onto the counter and offers me a smile. "That's my cell number. And I'll be back later."

"Thanks. I really do appreciate both of your help."

"See you later," Brady says with a wave, and then they're off again, and Lily makes her way back to her little bed to settle in for another nap.

"Well, then," Ida says, her lips pursed as she watches me.

"What?"

"Oh, please," Sharla says with a laugh. "It's written all over your face that you have a crush on that sexy policeman. And who can blame you? He's one fine specimen of a man."

"What? I do not." I focus on fussing with the booms in my hands. "You two are a couple of busybodies."

"Uh-huh," Sharla says, her tongue in her cheek. "Sure. Well, I sure hope you find a reason to use that phone number. It would be a shame to let a man like that go to waste."

"If you're not going to use it, I will," Ida adds with a sassy wink.

"You could be his *mother*."

"But I'm *not* his mother, honey," Ida retorts. "Not even a little bit."

I smirk and carry the finished bouquet of lilacs to the cooler.

I have no plans to use that phone number. But, I can admit to myself, I'm not sorry that he's coming back later to work on the security here at the shop.

CHAPTER TWO
CHASE

I set up a makeshift shop on the family ranch the day after Erin, my soon-to-be sister-in-law, asked me to make her an arbor for her wedding. She wants it made out of some of the recycled wood from the old barn on the property that she's going to have rebuilt and converted into an event space to rent out for weddings and parties, so the arbor would be a piece that the business offers guests to use for their events.

The whole family agrees that the new business venture is a great idea, and I especially love that she wants to reuse as much of the old wood as possible. The barn collapsed in on itself long before I was born, and it's just sat there, in the middle of a grazing field for cattle. There are several other smaller buildings, also no longer in use, around it. We never considered using any of it for anything. In fact, when we were kids, Dad thought about tearing it all down but never did.

Erin saw it this past spring and had the great idea of

turning it into a business. With the gorgeous views of the mountains as the backdrop, I have a feeling that the space will be booked solid year-round.

My brother, Remington, mentioned to his fiancée during one of our family dinners that I like to build things in my spare time, and Erin batted her green eyes at me and talked me into building her pretty much whatever she wanted for the wedding. She's been amazing for my brother and his kids, and I adore her. She knows that she has me wrapped around her tiny little finger.

No, the event space definitely won't be ready in time for next month's nuptials, but that doesn't mean that we can't make it work with a tent, and we can bring in whatever Erin wants to make it pretty for her.

Right now, I have to build this arbor, which is a fun project. Or would be, if I had the right shop to do it in.

I have a small woodworking space in the two-car garage at the house I rent in town, but it's nowhere near big enough for this project. Plus, the wood I'll use is on the property. It doesn't make sense to move all of it into town and then move it back out here again.

So, I took over my brother's garage.

Remington and Erin, along with his two kids, live in the big farmhouse on the ranch. The same one that our parents owned and raised all five of us kids in. Remington took over the ranch from our dad a few years ago, and when our parents built a smaller, more manageable house for themselves on the property, Remington moved his family into the farmhouse.

But for now, I'm using his garage.

And even that isn't really big enough for what I need.

"How's it going out here?"

I turn to see Rem standing just outside the open garage door, his thumbs in his pockets, watching me work.

"Slower than I'd like."

"Why is that?" He saunters in, picks up a hammer, and flips it around in his hand as he watches me measure a board and mark it with my pencil.

"Because I don't have enough space." I glance up at him and see his shit-eating grin. "Why are you so fucking chipper?"

"Life is damn good right now, that's all."

I shake my head and measure again. "I'm happy for you, Rem. I really am. Erin's the best."

"She's worried that we won't get it all done and thinks we should move the date out until spring so we have more time to do everything."

"I figured," I reply with a nod. "I was just talking about that with Summer at the flower shop yesterday. I also told her that there's no way in hell you'd go for that."

"Fuck no," he confirms, his voice mild. "I'm marrying her next month. Whether it's in a field of grass or at the courthouse, I don't care."

"*She* cares," I remind him. "And all of her family's coming in from Seattle. All of her *very* famous family. So, we'd like to give them something pretty to look at while they're here."

"The mountains are just fine," he grumbles and then

shrugs. "Anyway, you said you need more space to work in? This garage isn't tiny."

"This arbor is going to be big. The bar she wants me to build is also good-sized. And who knows what other odds and ends she'll want. So, yeah, I need more space, but this is bigger than my shop in town, so I'll make do. I'll have to run home later to get more tools and bring them out here."

"You could probably use Dad's garage, too," he offers, thinking it over, "but it's just a two-car."

"I might have to store some things in there," I reply with a nod. "Good idea. Hey, I've been thinking." I lean against the board that I still haven't cut and hold Rem's gaze with my own. "I think it's time that I built a place out here. The ranch belongs to *you*, but all five of us siblings have acreage."

"You haven't decided which acres you want, but yeah, there's definitely a place for you out here. You don't want to be in town anymore? You always said before that you liked being close to the station in case you were needed at work for an emergency. Being this far out of town isn't convenient for that."

"I can make it into town within twenty minutes," I reply. "And yeah, I liked being closer to the action in the beginning, but people have started stopping by the house when I'm there to ask questions or to try to get me to do them a favor."

"What kind of questions and favors?" he asks, narrowing his eyes.

"The usual shit. *Can you tell my neighbor to cut his tree*

down, or *can't you get me out of this ticket?* It's a small town, and you know that I love it, but it comes with small-town politics and attitudes. People think they can call me on my day off, and I don't like that. I'm ready to come back home. I love it out here. And I need to build a big fucking shop so I have the space I need for wood-working projects. In fact, I'd likely build the shop first and go from there."

"Fine by me," he replies with a nod. "I'd love to have you out here more often. Might put you to work some-times. You're damn good on a horse. What part of the property were you thinking?"

"On the lake." I grin over at him, as just the thought of it makes me happy. "I'm surprised no one else has built there."

"It's not a big lake," Rem reminds me.

"Big enough to put a little dock on and fish in the summer. The sunsets are pretty out there, too."

"You already have it mapped out in your head."

"Yeah, I do. And I'll build it myself."

That makes him pause and frown over at me. "*All* of it?"

"I can't do the electrical and plumbing, but the rest? Yeah. I can do that. And I want to build my place with my own two hands. It's kind of a family tradition out here."

"I don't think there were construction companies in this valley a hundred years ago, so building things them-selves was kind of a given. I didn't know that building your own place was a dream of yours, man."

"I didn't either, until recently. I'm not in a rush. We'll

get through this wedding, and then I'll start digging into what it'll take. I'll have to get the land surveyed to make sure that it's stable enough for a house and a big shop. It won't happen overnight, and that's okay with me."

"No, but it's damn exciting to think about. Just let me know what you need from me, and I'll make it happen."

That's Rem. Always ready to jump in and help. Always the big brother.

"Thanks."

He pauses. "Do you want to go have a look now?"

"Actually, yeah, I do."

Rem laughs as we walk out of the garage and over to his Jeep. We hop in, and it only takes us about five minutes to make our way over to the lake. He's right, it's not a big lake, definitely not big enough for motorized boats, but it's not tiny. We've spent many a summer canoeing and paddleboarding out here. Swimming and fishing. Hell, we'd camp out here as teenagers, sometimes for a week at a time.

"Not only is it a pretty spot," I say as Rem comes to a stop, "but it's not part of your grazing land. It won't interfere at all with the business."

"That makes it a win-win, then," he replies. "Point out where you're thinking, and I'll drive us over."

I point to the other end of the lake, and Rem turns to me in surprise.

"All the way over there?"

"That's right."

"Okay, then, hold on. It's going to be a bumpy ride."

He puts the Jeep in gear. He's not wrong; it's a rough

ride through the brush and trees, but we eventually make our way to the other side of the lake.

"Right here," I murmur and climb out of the Jeep, taking a deep breath of clean air. "I want the shop here. Four bays wide and two stories tall."

"Nice," Rem says with a nod, scanning the land. "And the house?"

"About forty yards that way, closer to the shoreline. It'll also have an attached garage so it's easier in the winter. Not a huge house, about two thousand square feet, all one story."

"I already like it," he says, surveying the area, and I can tell he's picturing it all in his head.

"I do, too." I can imagine the wraparound porch, my truck in the driveway, and a dock on the water. I want to fish out here in the summer, maybe with a couple of kids and a pretty wife. I don't just want this for now. I want it forever. This is my place.

"I know we need to get through the wedding to really wade into the project, but why don't you go ahead and get the surveyor on the schedule? They might be booked out a bit, and this way you're on top of it. Have plans drawn up."

"Plans are drawn."

"I should have known," he says with a rueful laugh. "It may be a newer idea, but once you get your mind set on something, it's full speed ahead."

I simply grin over at him. "No sense in moving slow."

"No, God forbid we move slow." He snickers. "Come on, we'd better get back."

But I stop, just for a minute, and look back at my place. I belong here. I'm ready to plant my roots in this spot.

"If she had any issues, she'd have called me already," I mutter to myself as I park my truck in front of Paula's Poseys and cut the engine. "And she likely doesn't want my mom's cookies. This is lame."

I've wanted to see Summer all week since the incident at her place on the Fourth. Yeah, I want to check in to see how her new security systems are working out, but more than that, I just want to look at her. Make her smile that big smile that lights up the goddamn room. Bonus points if she laughs because Summer has the best laugh I've ever heard.

"You're a sap," I whisper as I push out of the truck and, with a plate of cookies in hand, walk to the door of the flower shop. The bell rings as I push in, and I hear Summer laugh and then see her pat a tall man on the shoulder.

"Oh, stop it, Evan. He didn't say that."

"Swear to God," Evan says, his right hand in the air as if he's swearing on the witness stand.

Both sets of eyes turn to me. Summer's expression warms, and if I'm not mistaken, her smile brightens.

Evan's eyes narrow. I keep my face passive but quirk an eyebrow.

This idiot can fuck right off.

"Well, hey there," Summer says. "It's good to see you, Chase."

"Hey. My mother swears she baked too many of her famous peanut butter cookies, and I can't eat two dozen by myself, so I thought I'd stop in to share with you. Also, I wanted to see how your security systems are working out."

"First of all, I *never* turn down a cookie," Summer says and accepts the plate from me just as Lily the dog hops out of her bed to come and greet me. "And second, everything is working great. I think I've finally got the hang of checking the app, and I love being able to see both places when I'm not there."

"You got a security system?" Evan asks.

"I did," she confirms. "Both here and at home. I'm sorry, Evan, I assume you know Chase Wild?"

"Sure," I say with a nod to the other man. "How's it going, Evan?"

"I'm great," he says and turns back to Summer. "Why do you need a security system?"

"Oh, I had some kids try to break into my house on the Fourth," she says, waving it off. "Chase and Brady installed it for me."

"Well, that was...nice," Evan says with a forced smile. "You're okay?"

Summer bites into a cookie and closes her eyes with a groan.

Jesus Christ, I want to make her groan like that for completely different, more primal reasons.

"These are seriously *so good*. Tell your mama I want the recipe, Chase."

"You're okay?" Evan repeats, clearly irritated that he's being ignored for cookies.

"Oh, yeah. Totally fine now." She waves him off and takes another bite of cookie.

"Well, you know you can always call me. I'm just down the street. I'm pretty sure I can be at your place in just a few seconds."

"I appreciate it," she says to him. "Chase arrived and saved the day, and now I feel a lot safer. You should try one of these cookies."

"I'm allergic to peanuts." His voice is tight as he shakes his head. "I'd better go back to the office for my next appointment."

He nods at me, then looks longingly at Summer before walking out the door.

Looks like Evan Spencer, Attorney at Law, has a crush on the florist.

And he's going to be damn disappointed if I have anything to say about it.

"Seriously," Summer says as she chews another cookie. "Do these have crack in them or something? Because holy moly, they're addicting. Ida, come eat some cookies before I eat them all myself."

She breaks off a tiny piece of her cookie and offers it to Lily, who's sitting patiently like a good girl.

"I'm glad you like them," I say with a chuckle. "They were always a hit when we were kids."

"They'll go right to my already too-wide hips," Summer says with a shrug. "But I don't seem to care."

"Nothing wrong with your hips."

I *love* her curves. She has a phenomenal body. Today, her long blonde hair is down around her shoulders, wavy and begging for my fingers. She's in jeans that hug those curves perfectly, and a green T-shirt that shows off breasts that would make any red-blooded man sit up and beg.

Summer Quinn is a gorgeous woman, and I've been attracted to her since the first day I laid eyes on her years ago.

Summer smirks at my hips comment and pops the last of a cookie into her mouth. "Thanks for that snack. I was hungrier than I thought. I guess I forgot to eat lunch."

"What do you normally eat for lunch?"

"Oh, I just grab a sandwich from the deli or something. With it being the busy season, I eat while I work."

"She works too much," Ida says as she comes out of the back and snags a cookie.

"Where are the other girls?" I ask, looking around. "It's quiet in here."

"Sharla and Margie are both out on deliveries," Summer replies. "And my new gal, Vickie, is working over at Charlie Lexington's office on a wedding we're doing in early September."

"You know better than to mention a Lexington when a Wild is around," Ida reminds Summer, whose eyes widen.

"Oops, sorry."

I laugh at that and shake my head. "The family rivalry isn't *that* bad."

"Oh, yeah, it is," Ida disagrees. "I went to school with your father, and let me just tell you that it's worse than that."

"For the older generations," I reply with a shrug. "They may not be my favorite people in town, but you can speak about them in my presence. It's fine. I'm not going to pull out my gun or anything."

"I wonder if Erin would hire Charlie for their wedding. She's the best event planner there is," Summer wonders, and that makes me bust up laughing.

"Okay, that might be a line that we wouldn't cross."

"But why? Charlie is the best in this part of the state. She's super organized and listens and works so well with all the local vendors. I was just talking with Erin yesterday, and she's so overwhelmed. She needs the help, Chase. More than Millie or even I can give her. It's a big wedding, with really famous people coming, and her family lives far away."

"Well, when you put it like that," I mutter, thinking it over. "I just don't think that Rem will go for it. We've mellowed out a bit where the Lexingtons are concerned, but hiring them? That's altogether different."

"Mention it," Ida suggests. "Just don't mention it to your father. I think there are a few other wedding coordinators in town, but none hold a candle to Charlie. That girl can work magic out of a dandelion and a paperclip."

"So, she's the MacGyver of weddings?" I laugh at

their nods and then reach down to pet Lily, who's still hoping for more pieces of cookie. "I'll mention it. None of us wants Erin to be under too much stress. This should be fun for her."

"Ha," Ida says, shaking her head. "Says a man who's never had a wedding. Of *course,* she's stressed out, honey. But Charlie can at least help."

"Good to know." I glance back at Summer. "What kind of sandwich?"

"Huh?" She blinks those blue eyes at me.

"What kind of sandwich do you order from the deli?"

"Turkey on rye with mustard."

I wink at her and turn to leave. "Good to know. Enjoy the rest of your day."

"Bye, Chase."

CHAPTER THREE
SUMMER

"You know," Ida says thoughtfully as she reaches for another delicious peanut butter cookie that I swear is laced with an addictive, possibly illegal substance, "I used to be squarely in the Team Evan category."

"I didn't realize there were teams." My voice is dry as I cross my arms over my chest, wondering where she's going with this.

"Well, he's a nice kid. Definitely has the tall, dark, and handsome thing down, and he's *so* charming. Not to mention, we all know that Evan has political aspirations, and you know all about that life."

Yeah, and I have no intention of ever being with anyone who reminds me of my father.

"Evan is just a friend," I remind her. "I've never said anything different, especially to him."

"Oh, I'm not insinuating that you're a tease, honey," Ida continues, munching on the delicious cookie. "Not at

all. I just like him. But you don't look at Evan the way
that you look at Chase."

"And how is that?"

"Like he's a big piece of chocolate cake, and you'd like
to eat him alive."

I smirk and shake my head. "No, I don't."

I hope I don't, anyway, because how embarrassing is
that?

"It's not obvious," Ida continues, reassuring me.
"You're not all gooey and ridiculous about it, as if you
were a teenager, but I see the spark in your eyes when he
walks through that door, and that spark definitely isn't
there when you're talking with Evan."

"Thank you for the play-by-play," I retort. I don't
really know what else to say to that, so I start unpacking
new plants that just came in.

"And it's new," she continues, clearly on a roll. "Not
that Chase spends a lot of time in here, but I can't say
that it's something I've noticed before."

"Ida?"

"Yes, honey?"

"Let's not talk about this anymore, okay?"

"You're the boss."

———

"I NEED THAT DRINK," I announce to my best friend, Polly,
as I sit in the booth across from her at The Wolf Den, our
favorite bar in town. "Thanks for ordering ahead."

I sip the huckleberry margarita and sigh in happiness.

"Bad day?" Polly asks with a laugh.

"Not *bad*," I reply and sip again. "But man, it's been busy. I bet your shop's busy, too."

Polly owns the best dress boutique I've ever been in. A Pocket Full of Polly continues to grow in popularity, and she's expanding to online sales, which is super exciting.

"Crazy season," she confirms and holds her glass up to cheers with mine. "And God bless it; it keeps us afloat in the lean months."

"I know," I concede, "but man, I feel like I can't catch my breath this week."

A shadow falls over the table, and I look up, surprised to see Evan there.

"Hello, ladies," he says with a smile.

"Don't tell me you're working as a server part time," Polly says.

"No, ma'am, I'm here with a colleague and thought I'd swing by and say hello. How are you two?"

"Great," I reply with a smile. "Glad the work day is over."

"I hear that. You two have fun." He knocks on the table and then walks away, and I look over at my best friend.

"Don't tell me that you think I should date Evan."

Polly scowls. "Hell no. Evan is absolutely *not* your type."

"Thank you." I sigh in relief and have another sip of my drink. "The ladies at work seem to think Evan *is* my type, and I've always made it clear to him that he's just a friend."

"I mean, sure, he's handsome, but knowing your history with politics, I know you don't want any part of that scene," Polly says, shaking her head.

"I do have a confession." I take another sip of my drink, needing the courage.

"Did you sleep with Evan?" she asks, her eyes widening.

"No! Hell no." I scrunch up my nose. "Just, no. I think I might have a crush on Chase Wild."

Polly stares at me for five seconds and then busts up laughing.

"What's so funny?"

"Of *course,* you do, honey. Have you seen that man? Holy shit, Summer, he's hot as the sun, and I think you should chase him down—see what I did there?"

"Har har."

"Chase that man down and ride him like the cowboy he is."

"*Polly.*"

"What? You should. You haven't dated in five freaking years. It's time to move on from those assholes and get laid, girlfriend."

"Hi, Pot, I'm Kettle. I don't see you dating and getting laid."

"I'm focusing on my career right now."

I tilt my head to the side. "Yeah? Me, too."

"Seriously, Summer," Polly continues. "You told me that Chase asked you out years ago."

"He did, but I wasn't ready for anything then. I was too...numb."

"I get that. But you're not numb now."

"No, I'm not. He was so sweet when he came to my place on the Fourth, and he pops in now and then to see how I am. He even brought me cookies today because he said his mom made too many."

"Okay, that's sweet. And a total excuse to get to see you."

"You think?"

"Hell yes. If he had *extra* cookies, he could have taken them to work or something. He wanted to see you. He's hot, Summer. Do it. Go for it."

"I don't know."

Polly rolls her eyes. "Okay, now you're annoying me. You don't have anything to lose. Do the hot Wild brother so you can report back and tell me all about it."

"I don't know if that's a good reason to have sex," I say, considering. "Also, I didn't even say anything about sex to begin with. I was thinking about just dating him."

"Do both," Polly suggests with a wink. "And tell me all about it."

"You've lived here all your life," I reply, and lean back when our food is delivered. Polly ordered this for us, too. "God, I love tacos."

"Me, too," Polly says. "Sure, I've lived here forever. What do you want to know?"

"What do you know about the Wild family as a whole?"

"Aside from the fact that they breed hot men?" She pops a chip into her mouth and shrugs. "They were one of the founding families of Bitterroot Valley, so they go way back. Rem runs the ranch now. Chase is the cop. Brady rides rodeo every chance he gets, and he's damn good at it."

"Doesn't he win awards and stuff?"

"Oh, yeah, that man is damn good on a bull. Ryan's the second oldest." She twists her lips before taking a bite of her taco. "He left for a long time, worked in the city. I think he was in New York, but I'm not sure. Something to do with finance."

"I've seen him around town recently."

"Rumor has it that he's back for a while. He has a good-sized ranch of his own, and he bought some horses recently. My brother's been helping him with them. Ryan rescued them from a pretty bad situation."

"Okay, that's kind of sexy, a man who rescues horses."

Polly chuckles and nods.

"Does your brother know him well?"

"Oh, yeah, Mac and Ryan have been best friends since they were kids. And then Millie is the youngest Wild sibling."

"I love Millie," I reply and scoop a heap of guac onto my chip and take a bite. "She's the best."

"Totally agree." Polly nods. "Chase is the middle kid. Smack in the middle. I like him."

"I think I like him, too." I finish my taco and drain the last of my margarita. "I mean, I already knew that I liked him well enough as a person, but I'm attracted to him. So, I think I'll consider a date with him."

"Oh, great," Polly says with fake enthusiasm. "At the rate you move, you'll date him when you're at retirement age."

"You're a riot."

With a smirk, Polly also finishes her meal, and we decide to call it a night. We pay the bill and walk out of the bar to our vehicles.

"Next week, same time, same place?" I ask her.

"Unless you have a hot date with the cop, yes," she replies and leans in to hug me. "Seriously, go on a date with him."

"I don't even know if he wants to," I remind her.

"He does." She winks at me and gets into her car. "I'll wait for you to get in yours before I pull away."

I wave and then unlock my own car, get inside, and start the engine, and then Polly drives off, headed for home.

After putting the car in reverse, my car starts to move, but I realize immediately that something isn't right.

"What in the hell?" I put it back in park and get out, circle the car, and realize that I have a flat tire on the passenger side. "Well, shit."

The door of the bar opens, and Evan strolls out, tilts his head when he sees me, and hurries over. "Are you okay, Summer?"

"Flat tire," I reply with a sigh. "Just my luck."

He scowls and walks around to see for himself, and kicks it. "Yep, that's flat. Come on, I'll give you a lift home, and we can call Brooks to come take care of this."

"Thanks." I follow him over to his BMW and sit in the passenger seat after he holds the door for me. "I'm sorry about this, but I'm grateful for the ride home."

"It's definitely not your fault," he replies immediately and fastens his seat belt. "You probably ran over a nail or something somewhere along the way."

"I just replaced those tires, too," I grumble with a huff. "Figures, right?"

"They'll fix it," he assures me as he drives us into our neighborhood. "Did you and Polly have fun?"

"We always have fun," I reply with a smile. "I feel like we've been friends since we were kids. Aunt Paula says we're two peas in a pod."

"I like her a lot," he says with a nod. "She's a good businesswoman. Her boutique seems to be doing really well."

"She's smart about what she brings in to sell," I agree. "Tourists and locals alike love it, and I think that's really smart."

"I agree."

"You should date her."

Evan glances my way, an amused look on his handsome face. "I like her, but not like that."

"Your loss, I guess." Evan pulls up to my house. "Thanks a lot for the ride. I appreciate it."

"No problem. Do you want me to walk you in?"

"Nah, I've had my eye on the security app, and there hasn't been anything going on. I'm good. Thanks for coming to my rescue."

"Anytime. Have a good night." He waves to me, offers me that charming smile, and then drives off toward his own house just down the street.

It's too bad that Evan isn't interested in Polly *that way* because I think they'd make a cute couple.

Lily is excited to see me when I walk in the door. She does her zoomies through the house and then runs out to the yard to do her business as I put a load of laundry into the wash and unload the dishwasher. By the time that's done, she's ready to come back in, and I give her dinner.

"I know you hate these evenings when you're here by yourself." I scratch her behind the ears. "But I deserve to have a social life, too, you know."

She doesn't reply, just leans into my hand as I continue to scratch her in her favorite spot.

"Come on. Let's go watch some TV."

"WHEN DID YOU GET HERE?" Sharla asks me with a frown. She glances at her watch. "I thought *I* was early, and it's seven in the damn morning."

"I was here at six," I reply without looking up from the bridal bouquet I'm working on. "This is a busy weekend."

"They're all busy this time of year." Sharla loops her apron over her head and immediately strides into the cooler to fetch what she needs for the orders she's working on today. Before long, Ida and Vickie arrive, ready to dig into work.

"Margie's sick today," I inform the others, who all pause what they're doing and stare at me. "That's all I know. So, Vickie, you'll be delivering by yourself today. I'm sorry."

"It's okay," Vickie says, waving me off. "I've got this. Don't worry about it. If I have to, I can stay late."

"Thank you," I reply, relieved that the conversation went way better than expected. Not that Vickie's ever given me trouble, but I was worried that she'd tell me she couldn't stay later than scheduled. "I owe you."

"You owe me nothing," Vickie says with a wink. "We've got this."

The morning flies by, and when the bell above the door sounds, my eyes are glassy, and my brain is foggy as I look up and see Chase walking through the door.

"Good afternoon, ladies," he says with that handsome grin, looking delicious in his uniform.

"Afternoon?" I repeat and check the time. "Wow, I didn't realize it was so late."

"I take that to mean that you haven't eaten," he guesses and sets a brown paper bag on the glass counter. "One turkey on rye with mustard. Just for you."

My stomach growls.

"You should go sit outside in the fresh air and eat that," Ida suggests. "Take twenty minutes."

"I shouldn't," I reply as I untie my apron and pull it

over my head. "But I'm going to. Do you have time to join me?"

"You bet."

I gesture for Chase to follow me, and we walk outside and across the street to the park in the town center. We find a bench and sit, and when I unwrap the sandwich, I sigh in happiness and pass Chase half.

"Eat with me."

"I won't pass it up."

We take a bite in companionable silence, watching people pass by, and I tip my head up as I chew, enjoying the way the sunshine feels on my face.

"I love summertime," I murmur before I open my eyes and take another bite. "I used to *live* for it. Every year, I got to come here to Bitterroot Valley and spend a couple of months with Aunt Paula, help her in the shop, and run around her property. I still say that summer here in Bitterroot Valley is the absolute *best*, but now I can't help but wonder why she would agree to let me come stay with her every year."

"Why do you say that?" he asks.

"Because now I know how busy she was. It's the craziest time of year for the business, yet she never said no to having me underfoot for several months at a time."

"She probably enjoyed it as much as you did."

"I think so, too, but she must have been swamped."

"What did your parents do while you were here for the summer?"

I clear my throat and shrug a shoulder. "The same thing they did when I was home. My parents are in politics, so they traveled a lot. It felt like they were constantly campaigning and running off somewhere. When Dad was in DC, Mom would go with him. I swear, they're attached at the hip. He's retired now, but they still like to schmooze with the who's who of politics. They weren't thrilled that I didn't follow in their footsteps."

"They wanted you to?"

"Of course. I was supposed to be the first woman governor of Montana. But I did not want to go to law school, and the political life didn't interest me. They supported me through college, but once I'd graduated, I told them to stop sending money. I just wanted to be separate from them, in every way."

"That's a very different family life than what I grew up with," he considers and watches and someone jaywalk across the street.

"Is that really illegal?" I shield my eyes from the sun with my hand.

"Yep," he says with a sigh. "Walking outside of a designated crosswalk is a violation, and I can write a ticket for it."

"Do you?"

"Not often," he says with a shrug. "I don't have time. But I have in the past, and I likely will again. Usually when it's dangerous and the jaywalker is being stupid."

"Makes sense." I nod and can't help but smile, remembering all the times I've done it myself. "I have to confess, I'm guilty of jaywalking."

"I'll cuff you and take you in."

The idea of Chase *cuffing* me makes my mouth go dry,

and I can't help but look over at his mouth. It's full and sexy, and he's likely good at using it.

"For the first time in my life, I wish I could read minds."

That pulls me right out of my reverie, and I laugh nervously. "And I'm glad that you can't. Thank you for lunch. It was really nice of you."

"I feel bad that I ate half of it."

"Don't. I offered." I smile over at him, and he reaches out and tucks my hair behind my ear.

"I think we should hang out sometime, Blondie."

"You do? Also, did you just call me *Blondie*?"

"It suits you." His lips twitch with humor. "And yes, I do. What do you say? I mean, we're friends, right? And friends hang out together."

As friends. Well, that's disappointing, but I nod slowly. "Sure. They do. That would be fun. How are things going out at the ranch for the wedding?"

"It's busy out there," he says. "In fact, I'll be headed there in a little while when I get off work. I'm building the arbor, bar, and a few other things for Erin, and I spend my days off out at the ranch, working on those projects."

"I didn't know that you built stuff."

"It's a hobby." He lifts a shoulder. "It takes my mind off things."

"That's how I feel when I'm designing flowers," I agree. "I can just zone out. It's my favorite part of the business."

"Not all the taxes and math?"

"No. That's definitely not my favorite. What else have you built?"

"All kinds of things. My dining room table, a chair for my mom, a wishing well birdbath that a friend asked me to make his wife for her birthday."

"That sounds super cool. Do you have a picture?"

"As a matter of fact." He pulls his phone out of his pocket and scrolls through photos, then turns it to me, and I feel my jaw drop.

"Chase, that's *gorgeous.*"

"It turned out sharp," he agrees. "Here's hoping everything that Erin wants works out, as well. Some of the wood from the old barn is too rotten, so it's been a pain in the ass. What are some of your hobbies?"

"I like to paint. I don't do it often, but I enjoy it. Mostly watercolors, but sometimes I'll draw with charcoal." I watch a little boy riding his bike on the sidewalk alongside his mom, who's pushing a stroller. "I should do more of that. Paint, that is."

"If it makes you happy, then yeah, you should." The radio on Chase's belt signals, and he grins over at me ruefully. "I have to get back to work."

"Me, too," I say as we stand. "Thanks again for lunch and the break. It was nice."

"I'll see you soon," he says, but stays put.

"Don't you have to go?"

"Not until you're safely back inside your shop."

I frown and glance around. "It's the middle of the day. I'll be fine."

Chase crosses his arms over his chest, showing off

sculpted biceps, and doesn't move, waiting for me to go inside. "I'll make sure you're back safely, Blondie."

"Okay, stubborn man, I'm going. Don't work too hard."

"Take your own advice," he suggests with a wink before I turn to walk away. I can feel his eyes on me as I cross the street and even as I walk back into my shop.

Yeah, I would spend more time with Chase, even if it is just as friends.

CHAPTER FOUR
CHASE

"You must have worked the early shift today," Erin says as she walks toward the garage where I'm putting the finishing touches on the arbor.

"I did." I grin over at her, happy to see her. Although I've known her for less than a year, my brother's fiancée has quickly become one of my favorite people. "And you have good timing because I'm about finished with this. I need you to put your stamp of approval on it before I move on to the bar."

Erin's green eyes shine as she looks it over. "Oh, Chase, it's *so beautiful*. And I know that it'll be great for not only *my* wedding but also for so many others who want to have their special day out here on the ranch. It's exactly what I wanted."

"Thank fuck," I mutter and close my eyes, propping my hands on my hips. "You have no idea how much pressure this was. I didn't want to have to tear it apart and start over again."

"No, you did a great job." She tilts her head to the side and taps her lips, examining it. "I wonder..."

"Wonder what? If you want something changed, now's the time to say something."

"No, not changed. It's exactly what I asked for. I just wonder if Summer will be able to hang the flowers on it the way we discussed in her shop, or if I'll have to change my mind on some of those decisions."

"Nope, no changing your mind on your wedding vision." I shake my head, and Erin laughs.

"I can compromise," she says.

"No. You want it a certain way, and that's how you'll have it. I'll get with Summer about it and make sure it all works out for you."

"I can't even tell you how grateful I am for that."

"For what?" Rem asks as he joins us, looping his arm around Erin's shoulders and kissing the top of her head.

"I'm going to take point on speaking to Summer about the flowers on the arbor," I fill him in. "So Erin doesn't have to worry about it. She has enough to figure out."

"Appreciate it," Rem says with a nod, admiring my handiwork. "You did a hell of a job there, Chase."

I look up at the arched arbor and nod in agreement. This might be one of my best pieces to date. "Thanks. I'm happy with it, but I'm just glad that Erin likes it."

"*Love*," she says. "I *love* it."

"Hey, I have a question." I turn to both of them and scratch the back of my neck. "I was in the flower shop the other day, and the ladies there mentioned that

Charlie Lexington is the best wedding planner in the valley."

Rem's eyes narrow. "And?"

"And...have you considered hiring her to help you out?"

"I have," Erin confirms and side-eyes her fiancé, "but Remington shot it down. Rival family, and all that ridiculousness."

"It's not ridiculous," Rem insists, but I shake my head.

"Maybe it is, just a little," I reply, and Rem turns his eyes back to me. "We don't have beef with the Lexington siblings, Rem. Our parents had beef with *their* parents."

"I still have beef with their dad," Rem says, shaking his head. "He's an asshat when it comes to property lines. Nothing has changed there. I caught a fence that was moved just last week."

"That's not Charlie's fault," Erin reminds him. "And yeah, I could use the help. Look, my aunt used to be the best event planner in Seattle, and she volunteered to come out here to help, but there's no need for her to fly back and forth if there's already someone who lives right here who's just as good. Charlie has relationships with the vendors and knows all the ins and outs of this place. My aunt Alecia doesn't."

"You two are ganging up on me," Rem says.

"Nope." I grin at him. "I had no idea that Erin was already thinking about it. Talk about it some more. Maybe Charlie won't take the job, but it might be worth the ask. Anyway, I have to go figure out this arbor situation with Summer."

Erin bounces over to me and pulls me down to her so she can kiss me on the cheek. "You're the best almost-brother-in-law ever."

"I'm going to tell Brady and Ryan you said that. No take-backs."

I laugh as they walk away, and then I pull my phone out and call Paula's Poseys, smiling when Summer herself answers the phone.

"Hey there, Blondie, this is Chase. How do you feel about a field trip?"

"A *field trip*?" I can all but hear her frown on the other end of the line. "I have several hours left of work here, Chase. I'm sorry, I can't just leave. I wish I could, though."

"Yes, she can," Sharla calls out.

"Honey, you *need* to get out of here for a while. Go hang out with the handsome cowboy," comes Ida's voice.

"It's actually work related," I put in and explain the situation with the arbor. "I'd like to come pick you up and bring you out here so you can look at it in case you need to change anything for the wedding."

"Hmm." She sighs on the other end of the line. "Okay. I can be ready to go by the time you get here. I'd like to see the arbor."

"Great, I'll be there in thirty. See you soon."

Immediately after ending that call, I place another to Old Town Pizza and put in an order for carryout, then get into my truck and head for town.

The pizza's ready for me when I get there, and when I pull up in front of the floral shop, Summer's waiting out on the sidewalk.

"They kicked me out," she says as she hops up into the truck. "Like, physically shooed me right out of my own business. But Ida's going to take Lily home for me, so that's nice of her. You got pizza?"

"I did," I reply with a grin, and I can't help but reach over and tuck her hair behind her ear the way I did earlier today. Keeping my hands to myself is proving to be harder and harder, and thankfully, she doesn't seem to mind. "It's good to see you, Blondie."

Summer grins and then wrinkles her nose. "You saw me just a few hours ago, at lunchtime."

"Still good to see you." I pull away from the curb and head back for the ranch. "How was your day?"

"I sound like a broken record, and I know it's annoying, but it was busy," she says with a half laugh. "Do you care if I roll the window down for fresh air?"

"Not at all." I actually prefer to ride with the windows down in the summertime, so I roll mine down, too, and smile over at Summer, who's letting her hair fly all over the place, with her eyes closed and a small smile on her delectable, plump lips.

God, she's fucking gorgeous, with all that golden hair and smooth skin. I want to pull over to the side of the road, pull her into my lap, and kiss the fuck out of her for hours.

But she made it clear long ago that she's not interested in that.

And it just might kill me.

I turn off the highway onto the ranch road, and before long, we're parked in front of the garage.

"God, it's gorgeous out here," Summer says, surprise hanging heavily in her voice.

"Haven't you ever been out here before?"

"No, Erin and I did all of our planning in my shop. Look at that view of the mountains." She stands, hands on hips, staring at the mountains with awe written all over her face. "You know, I was born and raised in Montana, and it runs through my blood, but I never get tired of looking at the mountains."

"I couldn't agree more." After a moment, I gesture to the garage. "It's in here."

"Oh, right. Sorry, I got distracted. This is amazing, Chase. You *built* this?"

"With my own two hands," I confirm. "But Erin is concerned that you won't be able to hang the flowers the way you discussed."

Summer taps her finger on her lips, the same way Erin did earlier, as she examines the arbor. "Yeah, we can do it. I'll have you add a few discreet hooks here and there, and it'll be totally fine. We can also use zip ties and twine. I can hang flowers on just about anything."

She turns to me and narrows her eyes. "Chase Wild, you could have shown me this over a FaceTime call, and it would have been a lot faster. I feel bad that you came all the way into town to get me, when I could have saved you the trouble."

"But then I wouldn't have the pleasure of showing you around the ranch, would I?"

She gazes longingly at the mountains. "Well, I would like to see it. And you have pizza."

"Pizza and a tour sounds like a good deal to me." I hold her door open for her, then round the front of the truck and climb into the driver's seat. "We'll keep these windows down and eat on the way, if that's okay."

"Are you kidding? I can eat pizza anywhere." She opens the box and takes out a slice, passes it to me, then takes one for herself. "I do notice, however, that you're always feeding me."

I glance her way, and my breath catches in my throat. Christ, she looks good on my ranch, the sun shining through her blonde hair, watching me with happy blue eyes as she munches on her pizza.

"Why do you think that is?" she continues.

"We have to eat," I reply with a shrug. And I love watching this woman eat. The way she eats is sexy as fuck, and she's unapologetic about enjoying every bite.

"Plus," I continue, "I like spending time with you. Two birds, one stone."

She glances my way and then back out the window. "So, what was it like to grow up out here?"

"Heaven." I finish my pizza and move to get another slice, but Summer's already holding it out for me. "Thanks. Growing up here was the best there is. We were hardly ever inside, unless there was a blizzard. We spent most of our time with our dad in the barn or on horseback."

"I've never ridden a horse," she mutters, and I frown over at her. "What? I may have grown up in Montana, but my dad was a senator. I lived in the city."

"Well, we're going to change that and get you on a horse in the near future."

"Maybe," is all she says as she chews on her pizza. "That barn is *big*."

I grin and nod as we approach the barn. Lucky and Bruiser, two of the ranch hands, are just walking outside.

"Hey there," I say to the men. "This is Summer Quinn. She owns the floral shop."

"We've met," Bruiser says with a nod. "Hello, ma'am."

"Hi," Summer says with a smile.

"How was your niece's recital?" I ask the big man, whose eyes go gooey at the mention of his niece.

"She was the star of the show," he says proudly. "I'll show you pictures tomorrow."

"Can't wait."

"How far out are you goin'?" Lucky asks. "There's a grizzly in the north pasture."

"Holy shit," Summer breathes next to me.

"I wasn't planning on going that far. I'll show her where the new event venue will be, and then we're headed back over by the lake."

"Good idea," Lucky says with a nod. "Have fun, you two."

I nod and pull away from them and feel Summer watching me.

"What's up, Blondie?"

"I have so many questions. First of all, how old is Lucky? He looks *really* old."

"He is." I smile and then shrug. "I have no idea how old he is. He was old when my dad was a kid. But that might be all the time he's spent in the sun showing. What other questions do you have?"

"You know about Bruiser's niece's recital?"

"Sure. They might be employees, but they're family, too. We have to trust them with the most important thing in our lives: our home."

"I like that," Summer says slowly. "That's actually really sweet. And finally, *grizzly bears*?"

"You're not new to this area. Bears are a fact of life."

"I can honestly say that in my almost thirty years of living in Montana, I've never seen a griz in the wild."

"Wow." I blink at that. "Well, maybe someday, you will."

"I'm fine. I don't need to see them."

"They're not scary if you aren't being an idiot. Just don't try to pet them."

"Still don't need to see them." She shakes her head adamantly, making us both laugh. "No way. I'm good. Oh, is that where it's going to be?"

I nod when she points straight ahead. "Yeah, the old barn has been dismantled piece by piece. The concrete slab is down, but I think they're going to hold off on construction until after the wedding so the ceremony's not in the middle of a construction zone."

"Oh, I like that idea," Summer says with a nod. "This is absolutely...I can't catch my breath."

She covers her chest with her hand, and I slam the truck into park, all of my attention immediately focused on her.

"What's wrong? Shit, are you allergic to something?"

"No, it's not that." She takes a long, deep breath and then turns to me. "It's just so *pretty*."

She pushes out of the truck, and I take my own breath, calming my racing heart. Jesus, she scared the shit out of me.

"That view in the background," she says, turning a circle to take it all in. "That's priceless, Chase. Erin's photos are going to be spectacular."

"I hope so because they'll be splashed in every magazine and gossip site on the planet," I reply. "Her father is an uber-famous football hero, and don't even get me started on the celebrity roster of the rest of her family. It's mind-blowing."

"I'd heard that Erin was related to a lot of famous people," she murmurs.

"Leo Nash is her uncle."

That stops her in her tracks. "*What*?"

"Yeah. And you know the country singer, Sidney Sterling?"

"Who doesn't? She's my favorite."

"Married to her cousin."

"Stop lying."

I cross my fingers over my heart. "I wouldn't lie to you, sugar. So, yeah, we want this to be just perfect, not only for them, but for our girl, as well."

"Well, in my personal and professional opinion, it doesn't get any better than this. Wow."

Summer crosses her arms over her chest and just stands there, gazing at the mountains. There are cows out in the field, grazing. We can hear the buzz of bees, and a bird chirps overhead as it flies by.

It's about as serene as it gets.

"Come on, we have more to see."

Reluctantly, Summer hops back into the truck and grabs another slice of pepperoni as I drive us back the way we came, and then around to where the lake is.

"You have a whole *lake* on this property?"

"Yes, ma'am."

"Ever gone skinny-dipping?" She quirks an eyebrow at me, and the thought of swimming naked with this woman immediately takes up residence in my brain.

"More times than I can count."

"Fun." She hops a little in her seat, and then I make my way around to where I want to build, and before I can say anything, Summer holds up her hand. "Stop. Oh, God, stop right here."

For the second time, I throw it into park, and Summer hops out of the truck.

"What is it?"

But she doesn't answer. She walks slowly over to the water's edge, then turns and surveys the area.

"There should be a dock right here," she begins. "A place to fish, maybe. And a house, right there, with a view of the lake from the kitchen window."

The sunlight, beginning to fade now, dances on the

crown of her head, and as she turns to me, those deep blue eyes are full of wonder.

And it's right here, in this moment, that I know without a doubt that I'm going to spend as much time as humanly possible with Summer Quinn.

"Why hasn't anyone put a house here?" she demands, frowning.

"I'm getting to it," I finally reply.

A slow smile spreads over her gorgeous, plump lips. "Are you really?"

"Yeah, really." God, my heart, and other key parts of my anatomy, aches. "I've already had the plans drawn up and everything. I'm just waiting to get past the wedding to move forward with it."

"Thank God," she says with a sigh. "Because this spot, right here, *needs* a home. It's absolutely perfect. Tell me all your plans. I want to know."

"Really?"

"Oh, absolutely. Spill it."

I nod slowly, resisting the urge to pull her to me and kiss her. I've been so fucking attracted to this woman since the moment she moved to town, and now here she is, daydreaming about my house with me. "Well, you're right on the placement of the dock and the house. Single story, with a wraparound porch. I want to screen in part of it so I can sit out on warm summer nights like this and not get eaten alive by mosquitos."

"Smart," she says with a nod. "Go on."

"I want a big shop over there." I point to the spot I showed Remington. "With lots of space for any project I might dream up. But there will still be an attached garage on the house."

"You need a greenhouse," she says, pointing to the west. "There's not going to be a lot of shade there, and it would be perfect for a greenhouse. You can plant vegetables, flowers, you name it."

"I hadn't thought of a greenhouse, but I do want some killer landscaping." I rub my chin, watching her. "What else would you do?"

"I'd have a regular outdoor garden next to it, and probably flower beds all around the house. Flowering trees and bushes, too. Although there are already so many gorgeous wildflowers in the woods, you really don't need them. You'd want a birdbath and a bird feeder. Maybe a little water feature to add the sound of running water. It's so soothing."

Did this woman climb inside my brain and look at all my plans for this place? Because that's what it feels like. I feel naked as I stand here with her, and she lays out for me exactly what I want for this property.

"I'm sorry," she says, shaking her head with a little laugh. "I totally got carried away. This is such a great spot. I couldn't help but daydream a bit. You're going to have a gorgeous home here, Chase."

"Look." I take her shoulders in my hands, relieved when she doesn't flinch or back away from me, and turn her so she can see the sunset on the other side of the lake. "This is another reason why I want this spot."

"Oh, Chase." She brings a hand up to cover mine and,

to my surprise, leans back against me. "That is just...amazing."

Yeah. It's fucking amazing.

When the sun has set, and the sky begins to darken, Summer turns to me with a grin.

"Thank you for sharing this with me. I needed that."

"You're welcome. Should we head back?"

"Yeah, probably. Ida took Lily home and fed her, but I don't like to leave her home alone for too long."

We climb back into the truck, and with the windows rolled up now, we make our way back to the highway and into town.

When I park in front of her house, Summer turns to me. "I think we should go out on a date. Not as friends."

I quirk up a brow, and her eyes widen right before she slams her hand over her mouth. Her cheeks redden, and she shakes her head. "Oh, God, I can't believe I said that out loud. I meant to say *thanks for a nice evening.*"

She stares at me, and I feel the smile spread over my lips.

"And you're not saying anything. You know what, I think I'll just go now, before I embarrass myself more."

"Whoa." I reach out and snatch up her hand, keeping her where she is. "I think I was stunned speechless. You absolutely *should* have said that out loud, sugar. I don't know what you want if you don't say it."

"I could have been more eloquent," she mutters.

I grin and pull her hand up to my lips. "Nah, I think you did just fine."

CHAPTER FIVE
SUMMER

He's not laughing or scowling. In fact, he's perfectly calm as he smiles over at me with those sweet hazel eyes.

"I think," he continues, "that maybe we're finally on the same page. Or maybe just in the same chapter. And that's a good place to start."

"You mentioned being friends this afternoon—"

"Well, yeah, because you already turned me down once a while ago, and I'm not in the habit of harassing women who aren't interested."

"It's not that I wasn't interested before; it's that I wasn't *ready*. But I'm ready now." I take a long, deep breath and let it out slowly, willing the butterflies to calm the hell down. "And that makes me nervous."

"Why?" He squeezes my hand once. "I'd never do anything to intentionally hurt you, Summer."

"I know." I shake my head and turn in the seat to face him. "I know that about you, and I don't even know you all that well. I feel safe with you, and I enjoy spending time with you, too."

His eyes narrow. "I don't see the problem."

I can't help but let out a short laugh. "It's just me and my odd insecurities. I haven't dated anyone in, well, a long time. For...reasons."

"Reasons that you don't have to go into." He tucks my hair behind my ear, which makes me tingle in all the right places. "How about tomorrow night? We'll keep it casual. How does The Wolf Den for dinner sound?"

"Did someone tell you that it's one of my favorite places?"

"No, but that's handy because it's one of mine, too." He smiles again. "Tomorrow night?"

"I'd like that."

"Me, too." He climbs out of the truck and makes his way around to let me out of the passenger side, and then he walks me to my door. I kind of love how chivalrous he is.

"Thank you for showing me your home," I say after I unlock the door and turn to him. "It's really beautiful out there on the ranch. The spot you have picked for your house is unbelievable."

"It was fun," he agrees. He leans in, and just when I think he's going to kiss me, he simply presses his warm lips to my forehead, sending even more tingles—tingles on steroids—all the way down my body to the tips of my toes. "Have a good night, Blondie."

"Thanks." I walk inside and close the door and immediately pull up my phone and the video app so I can watch Chase. He pauses, still facing the door, and then he shoves his hand through his hair and turns to walk down to his truck. I can see him glance this way once more before he starts it up and drives away.

Lily's sitting in her bed, giving me the side-eye.

"Wow." I swallow, then toss my handbag onto the table by the door and kick off my shoes. "Like, *wow*. If having his lips just on my forehead can make me feel like *that*, I can only imagine what will happen if he ever kisses me for real. Now, don't pout, Lil. I know that you were fed and loved on, and Ida texted to let me know that she left here thirty minutes ago. You weren't alone for long."

My eyes are heavy as I walk through the house to the bedroom and continue to my bathroom, where I start the shower.

Yeah, starting something with Chase is a little scary, and not because I think he would hurt me. I know he wouldn't, like I told him in the truck. I'm just not used to dating someone who likes me for *me*, and not what my father's political connections can get them. Sure, I was attracted to Dennis, but it wasn't lost on me that he wanted to have a career in politics someday.

I've heard through the grapevine that he's already being groomed for exactly that.

I don't trust people easily. I grew up in a fake world, where I was expected to smile whether I felt like it or not, and where I learned early that most people can't be trusted.

I stick mostly to myself, aside from the girls at work

and Polly. And, of course, Aunt Paula. Evan has wanted to be in my circle, in my *life*, for several years, and he's a friend.

But that's all he'll be.

And now, I find that I *want* to open myself up to Chase in ways that I don't think I ever have before. I've always held a piece of myself back from everyone, kept that wall up so I didn't get too hurt.

I found my best friend and my boyfriend in bed together, and I didn't even shed a tear, for fuck's sake.

But I think things would be different if I let myself get attached to the hot cowboy cop. And that's exactly what he is: a cowboy cop. He's sexier than sin in his uniform, but then seeing him in tight jeans and a black T-shirt with a cowboy hat knocked me off my axis. Chase Wild is *sexy* with a capital S.

He's also kind and smart, and he lets me ramble about things. I've always been a chatterbox, much to my mother's horror. And I know that I can let my excitement get away from me, like when I saw that place by the lake. I saw the house so clearly in my mind, I just couldn't help but talk about it, couldn't help but be *excited* about it. And Chase didn't seem to mind at all.

I like that about him. Dennis used to tell me that the motor on my mouth was running away from me and to rein it in.

I can't imagine Chase saying that to me or anyone else.

With a towel wrapped around me, I step out of the

shower and walk into the bedroom and stop, frowning at the window.

"Lil?" Lily, who hopped up onto the bed while I was in the shower, lifts her head. "Is there someone at the window?"

My heartbeat quickens. I could *swear* I saw a shadow behind my blinds. But there's nothing moving—now.

I reach for my phone and check my security app. There's no one on any of the live videos. No animals or movement of any kind. Of course, this window is in a blind spot, but if someone was walking here, they'd have to pass by the front or rear camera.

"Nope," I mutter, staring at it, watching carefully. "Nothing going on."

I shake my head and set the phone down.

"I'm just tired. Getting up at five in the morning to be at work by six is early for this girl," I say to Lily, who's laid her head down again, but continues to watch me as I dry off and pull on some shorts and a tank top. "I'm too much of a night owl. But that's okay. In a few months, I'll have a quarter of the work, and I'll be complaining about that."

I climb into the bed beside my dog and kiss her head.

"How was your day? It was nice of Marion from the coffee shop to bring you some treats." Lily licks my face. "No, I don't have any for you. It's time for bed."

We snuggle down, and I open up my iPad so I can read for a while, and, before long, Lily is snoring happily beside me.

I hear the slightest thump outside my window, and I

sit very still, listening. It happens again, and without another pause, I reach for my phone and call Chase.

"Hey there, Blondie," he says, and his voice immediately calms my hammering heart. "You okay?"

"I think someone is outside of my house," I reply, not bothering to whisper, as I don't move my eyes from that window. "There's nothing on my cameras, but I can hear someone outside my bedroom window. I should have called 9-1-1. I'm sorry, Chase—"

"Be there in five."

He hangs up, and Lily doesn't even stir as I get out of bed and wait, listening. Chase and Brady were right: Lily is *not* a home protector.

There's another small noise, and I shake my head. There's *something* out there. Maybe it's a critter. That would make sense. It's summertime, so it could be a raccoon or a cat. Anything, really.

My phone pings with a text.

Chase: I'm going to walk around your house before I knock on the door.

I reply with, *Okay, thank you.*

I watch him on the app. I can see him on the video as he walks around the side of the house, and then he disappears from my view. I switch to the backyard, and a few seconds later, he appears. Every muscle in his body is on high alert, and he's not skulking around. He's walking with authority, and it's not just reassuring. It's *sexy.*

But there's nothing and no one else in view.

I see him walking back toward the front door, so I

hurry through the house and meet him there, opening the door before he can ring the bell.

"I'm sorry," I begin, shaking my head as he steps inside, and I close the door behind him. "I absolutely should *not* have called you."

"Yes, you absolutely should have," he replies easily as his eyes skim down my body. He clears his throat. "I walked around and didn't see anyone. There aren't any footprints under the window, but it's been dry lately, so they might not have shown up. Nothing on the cameras?"

"No, nothing. It's probably my overactive imagination. Or an animal."

"Could be an animal," he agrees with a nod.

"It was just so weird because I could have sworn there was a shadow or something through the closed blinds. But I suppose that could have been headlights from a car."

He nods, thinking it over. "Do you want me to stay for a while?"

"No." I frown and then shake my head with certainty. "No, I'm really okay. I'm so sorry that I made you come all the way back over here. I just wasn't thinking clearly, and you were the first person who came to mind to call."

"I like that." Chase pulls me into his arms and hugs me close. I'm so surprised that I don't return the hug for a nanosecond, but then I wrap my arms around his waist and lean into him. He rocks us back and forth and presses his lips to the top of my head. "I'm glad you called me, Blondie."

His voice is soft, and I feel like, for the first time in a long damn time, I can exhale.

"Thanks." I don't want to move yet, so I don't. It feels good to soak him in. "This is really nice."

"Sometimes, a person just needs a hug." I feel him grin against my head.

I don't remember the last time someone other than Aunt Paula hugged me. I never really thought of it.

"I hope I didn't get you out of bed." His heart beats steadily next to my ear, and his chest is firm under his soft T-shirt.

"Nope." He stops rocking. "Where's Lily?"

"Asleep on the bed. Snoring."

"Definitely not a guard dog."

I chuckle and pull back, smiling up at him. "No, she's not. I'm sorry for the false alarm, but I'm definitely not sorry for the hug."

"I don't like that you were scared." He reaches up and tucks my hair behind my ear in that way he does that sends little zings down my arm. "Out of curiosity, is that what you sleep in?"

"Huh?" I drop my gaze to take in my tank and shorts. "Oh, yeah. Not terribly sexy, I know."

"Right. Sure." Chase shakes his head and chuckles. "Okay, I'd better head out, unless you want me to stay."

"There's no need. Thanks again for coming all this way."

"I'm only four blocks away, you know. It's a small town." He winks, and then he's out the door and headed down to his truck.

Well, now I know that I'm *not* irresistible. He had me in his arms, mostly naked, and didn't make a move to even kiss me.

With a shrug, I lock the door and head back to bed. Lily's exactly where I thought she would be, in the middle of the bed, sprawled on her back, snoring happily. I usually put her down in her own dog bed on the floor at night, but she can stay up here with me tonight.

I want to snuggle.

I DIDN'T TELL anyone that I was going on this date with Chase tonight because they'd hype it up and make me even more nervous than I already am.

I don't need any help in that arena.

Since we're going to have dinner and drinks at the bar, I decided to keep it casual, with a simple blue sundress and sandals. And when I open the door to Chase, who insisted on picking me up, I see I made the right choice because he's in those delicious jeans that hug his ass in just the right way, and a green Henley.

"Wow," he says. "You look amazing."

"Aw, thanks. So do you." I step out with him and walk beside him down the sidewalk to his truck. "What did you do today? Did you work?"

"I have a few days off, so I got started on Erin's bar for the wedding. Helped Remington with some work on the ranch and played with the kids for a while. How was work for you today? No, wait." He opens the door for me, then circles around to the other side. "Let me guess. It was busy."

"Extra busy today," I reply with a nod. "Half of the order I placed for a wedding on Saturday didn't come in. So, I had to call around frantically to find the flowers we need, have them overnighted, and pray they all arrive in one piece."

"Damn, that sucks."

"Big time. It's wedding season. And this bride wanted a whole bunch of freesia."

"I don't even know what that looks like," Chase admits, making me laugh.

"They're a pretty purple flower. Delicate. And they smell good. But they're not as easy to get in as quickly as, say, roses. But we'll make it work. I have some ideas up my sleeve if the flowers don't arrive in time."

He parks in front of The Wolf Den, and Chase escorts me inside where a Sidney Sterling song—my favorite country artist—is playing through the speakers, and plenty of the tables are already taken.

I like the atmosphere in here. It's laid-back, but it's not a dive. The food's good, and it's clean, with fun, old-timey photos on the walls from days in Bitterroot Valley long ago.

"I'm seating you at your grandpa's table," the hostess informs Chase. "He'll be watching you, so be good."

"Great," Chase says with a laugh, and we slide into opposite sides of a booth. On the wall is a picture of a man with a rifle and a big, dead bear.

"Is that your grandfather?" I ask him, gesturing to the photo.

"Yep. That's him. It was taken on the ranch a long time ago."

"Hey there, what can I get you to drink?" our server, Pete, asks as he places two coasters on the table and winks at me. "Huck margarita for you, Summer?"

"I'm really predictable," I say with a laugh and then shrug. "Yes, please, because they're delicious."

"I'll just take a beer," Chase replies. "Blue Moon, if you have it."

"Sure thing. Do you need a minute with the menus?"

Chase looks at me, raising an eyebrow.

"I always know what I want because it never changes, but I can wait if you're still deciding."

"I know what I want, too," Chase says. "You go ahead, sugar."

I order the tacos with extra chips, and Chase gets himself a burger with fries, and finally, we're alone.

"Did you hear any more noises last night after I left?"

"Are you kidding?" I smirk and shake my head. "No. I sleep like the dead once I finally fall asleep. The house could be falling down around me and I'd sleep through it."

"Lily gets it from you."

"Yeah." I laugh again. I laugh a lot when I'm with this man, and it's nice to feel so comfortable. "Yeah, she does. I still feel silly for overreacting last night, Chase."

"Don't. I'd rather double-check that it's nothing than ignore it and it be *something*."

Pete sets our drinks on the table, and then he's off again, and I lift my glass, but before I can sip, Chase holds his up to mine in a toast.

"To first dates," he says.

"I can toast to that." I clink my glass to his and then take a drink. "They make really good drinks here."

"I've never been a liquor guy," he says, shaking his head. "It gives me a headache."

"You're missing out on this one. I'm not usually a fan of tequila, but this is a masterpiece. Hey, have you tried that new restaurant down the street? Ciao?"

"Not yet," he says. "I hear it's good, though. We should go there next time."

I grin over at him. "So, there's going to be a next time?"

"Oh, for sure. There's going to be a next time. As soon as possible." He winks at me, and butterflies erupt into a cha-cha in my belly.

"Hey, Summer." I glance up at Brooks, surprised to see him approach the table.

"Well, hi. How's it going?"

"Great, thanks. Sorry to interrupt. I was going to call you in the morning, but since you're here, I'll just let you know now that your car will be ready by the end of the day tomorrow. I'm sorry I didn't have the right tire in stock for you, but it arrived this afternoon."

"It's no problem." I shake my head at him. "I appreciate it. At least the weather's been nice, and I don't mind the walk to work. I'll be by before you close tomorrow."

"See you then." He nods at Chase. "Hey, Chase."

"Brooks. Have a good evening."

The man walks away, and I happily sip my drink.

"Did you have car trouble?" Chase asks.

"My tire was slashed," I reply and take another sip. Is it just me, or are the drinks *extra* delicious tonight? "Here, actually, last weekend when I was here with Polly for our girls' night out."

"Wait, *what*?" Chase is scowling at me now. "It was *slashed*?"

"Yeah, but I didn't know it at the time. I left here, and when I tried to drive away, it was all wonky, so I got out to check, and sure enough, flat tire. I thought I might have just driven over a nail or something, but nope. Someone cut it. Thank goodness Evan was here that night, and he drove me home."

His face tightens, and I tilt my head to the side. "What's wrong?"

"You didn't tell me this before now."

"No, I didn't. I guess it didn't occur to me."

"Someone slashed your tire." He's definitely irritated with me. "And you didn't tell me."

"I can't prove who did it, so there was no reason to call the police," I point out. "It was probably a random hit by some stupid kids. Brooks didn't have my model of tire in stock and had to order it. I don't mind walking, but I admit, I'm glad it'll be ready for me tomorrow. I prefer driving when it's hot like it's been, especially for Lily's sake."

"There *was* a point in calling the police, Summer. We could have requested the security cam footage from the parking lot, so if it was kids, or some weirdo, we would have found them."

"I didn't think of that." I frown down into my drink. "I've been so preoccupied with work, I just wanted to get the tire fixed. And I didn't know it was vandalized on purpose until Brooks called me the next day."

"You should have called me," he says again, his voice hard. "I'd have driven you to work and back."

I frown over at him. "Why are you so upset about this?"

"Because you've been walking to work after someone slashed your tire, *alone*, and I could have driven you."

"Okay. But it's fine. *I'm* fine."

Our food arrives, but I don't dig in like I normally would. I hold Chase's gaze with my own.

"You know, this is our *first* date. And sure, we've seen each other quite a bit over the past couple of weeks, but... this is our first date, Chase."

"I get it." He sighs, wiping his hand over his forehead. "Yeah, I get it. Sorry, I just don't like the idea of you out there before the sun comes up, walking to work with Lily."

"It's okay. Obviously, I called you last night when I was scared. The other stuff? The tire and the walking? It didn't scare me." I shrug and pick up my taco.

"Another drink?" Pete asks.

"One more," I agree.

"I'm good. I could use some water," Chase says and turns back to me. "Okay, let's start over at the beginning and get back to first date conversation. What brings you to Bitterroot Valley, Miss Quinn?"

I chew, considering what to tell him. The tequila, God love it, is already starting to go to my head, and it's a pleasant little buzz that gives me a boost of courage.

"Well, my aunt Paula, you know her"—he nods—"has lived here forever. Now that I think about it, I don't know why she moved here. That's something I'll have to ask her. Anyway, like I told you before, I used to spend the summers here with her when I was a kid, and I loved it. I didn't enjoy living in Helena."

"Why not?"

"My parents aren't bad people, but they're not great parents, either. Dad was always campaigning, and Mom was obsessed with being the wife of a senator. They travel, they host parties and go to dinners, and I'm just... there. Or, I was. Anyway, I went to college, and I was expected to go into law. So, I got a political science degree."

"Wow," he says, winging up an eyebrow. "Where did you go?"

"University of Montana in Missoula. My parents introduced me to a guy they knew, Dennis, at a gala. He was also going to school in Missoula, and he was...nice." I shrug a shoulder and pick up my new drink when it's delivered. "He was handsome and made me laugh. Of course, he wanted my father's political connections, and I knew that, but I didn't let it bother me much."

I take another drink and eat a chip, eyeing Chase through blurry eyes, thanks to the alcohol. He's listening to every word I'm saying. I have his *full* attention, and I admit, I like that a *lot*.

"This is really a lot of information. Is this a first date conversation?"

"I don't see why not," he says and pops a fry into his mouth. "I asked. Go ahead."

"Okay, well, I dated Dennis through college. I never moved in with him, though. He wanted to, but I liked having my own place. I shared an apartment with my best friend, Lyla. And trust me, this is working its way back around to what brought me to live here full time."

"I'm riveted." He chuckles and sips his water. "Seriously. Keep talking."

"It's a juicy story." I waggle my eyebrows and sip my margarita. "So, we graduated from college, and I was kind of lost. Now that I look back on it, that's exactly what I was. Lost. I didn't want to go to law school. I was working in retail during the day and as a bartender at night. It was long hours, sometimes eighteen-hour days."

I stop to think about that.

"Actually, I'm not going to complain about my long hours at the flower shop anymore because it's way better than that."

"It sounds challenging."

"It was horrible. I'm not afraid of work if I enjoy the job, but those two jobs were not fun. Anyway, after one particularly grueling shift at the bar, I decided that I didn't want to go straight home. Lyla told me she was going to host a party at our apartment, and I'd just finished serving drunk college kids all evening, you know?"

"Sure. You don't want to deal with that when you just want to crash."

"Exactly. So, I went to Dennis's apartment. Figured I'd crash at his place. I was so tired." I frown, remembering that night. "I knew when I walked in that something was...different. I just had a feeling in my gut. And then I found clothes in the hallway, and when I got to the bedroom—"

"Oh, no." He shakes his head ruefully.

"They weren't having sex," I reply, remembering it through my foggy memory. "They were sleeping. Out cold. Dennis and Lyla."

"The *best friend*?"

"The same one. I stood there for a few minutes, just looking at them, and I was numb. I left the key to his apartment on the kitchen counter and went home. I packed my things, loaded up my car, left *that* key on the kitchen counter, and decided that I didn't want that life. I didn't want *them*. Bitterroot Valley was always home for me, so I came here with Aunt Paula, and she took me in without a moment of hesitation. I've been here ever since."

"Did you ever speak to the two assholes again?"

"Nope." I drain the last of my drink. "I ghosted them."

He lifts a sexy eyebrow. "Really?"

"Really. They tried to call or text to see what was up. Especially Dennis, because he wanted those political connections, but I never replied." I frown. "I shouldn't have had that second drink. It's a truth serum, and that's not good."

"It's pretty good from where I'm sitting." He smiles, and I lean my chin on my hand, gazing over at him.

"You're pretty." My voice sounds all dreamy and soft.

"Yep, that second drink is kicking in."

"I would probably tell you that if I was sober, too, so I'm not embarrassed. And I'm not *that* tipsy."

I take a deep breath, and we chat for a few more minutes. Chase pays the bill, and then we're back in his truck and headed for my house.

"It occurs to me," I say as we reach my front door, "that we talked all about me tonight. You didn't tell me about *your* sordid past and the girl you found in bed with your best friend."

He smirks and tucks my hair behind my ear. "Thankfully, that didn't happen, but I have other tales to tell on the next date when I take you to Ciao."

"That's a deal, then."

I really, *really* want him to kiss me. But he doesn't. He leans in and presses his lips to my forehead again, and when he pulls away, I frown up at him.

"Am I repulsive to you?"

"Excuse me?"

"The kissing thing. Don't get me wrong, the forehead kisses are nice, and something out of a movie, but you haven't actually"—I gesture between the two of us—"kissed me."

"Are you repulsive?" he asks, shaking his head. "Fuck

no. It was all I could do to walk away from you last night."

"Oh, good, because I thought maybe the bedtime outfit was a turnoff."

He blinks in surprise and then blows out a breath. "No. No, it wasn't. I haven't kissed you," he says, stepping just a smidge closer to me, "because once I start, I won't stop until I kiss every inch of your amazing body, and you're not ready for that yet. So, we'll take our time. I'm okay with that."

"Wow. Are your panties wet, or is that just me?"

The laugh that bubbles out of him is one of surprise and delight, and he kisses my forehead again.

"My pants might be a little tight," he confesses. "Now, I'm going to be a gentleman and walk away, as long as you can get inside okay."

"Pfft." I wave him off. "Of course, I can. It's *right there*. Next time, we can do the kissing thing."

"That's a promise."

CHAPTER SIX
CHASE

How could she think that she's repulsive? What kind of a complete fucking asshole would have put that thought in her gorgeous little head? Because Summer Quinn is *anything* but repulsive. Jesus, she stars in all of my fantasies, whether I'm sleeping or awake.

I left here hard as fuck last night, and thanks to the conversation on her porch, I'm leaving in the same condition tonight. I glance over to her front porch and watch her open the door and stumble inside, closing it behind her after she blows me a big kiss.

Summer's funny when she's a little tipsy. I like that she's more outspoken and comfortable talking to me, even if it took a little liquid courage to get us there. I hope that we've crossed a line tonight and that she stays comfortable with me.

I start the engine, but before I can pull away from the curb, my baby sister texts me.

Millie: Whatcha doing?

I grin and call her.

"Why are you calling me?" she asks. "You're supposed to text."

"I'm driving," I reply easily. "What's up?"

"I was bored and thought I'd come hang at your pad for a while, but if you're out and about, it's all good."

"I'm headed home now." I can hear something in her voice that isn't usually there, and it has me curious. "Meet me there. I'm two minutes out."

"Okay. See you soon."

She hangs up, and I drive home, park in the driveway, and walk inside. My rental is bigger than I need, and I don't have a ton of furniture, so I've closed off the rooms I don't use. I've just kicked my boots off when there's a quick knock on the door, and then Millie strides right in, grinning at me.

"Hey," she says. "Where were you tonight?"

"I had a date," I reply easily. I know that she's going to dig for information, and she'll likely tease me about this for the foreseeable future, but I don't really give a shit. "With Summer Quinn."

Millie stops in her tracks and stares at me. "Seriously? You finally asked her out?"

"And she actually said yes." I offer her a bottle of water, toss it to her when she nods, and join her in the living room. Millie stretches out on my couch, so I sit on the floor on the other side of the coffee table with my back against a chair.

"And how did it go?" Millie asks with a sly smile. "I like her a lot, by the way."

"I do, too. It was great. The conversation is easy, and I like being around her. It doesn't hurt that she's the prettiest girl I've ever seen."

"Well, cheers to that." She holds the bottle up and then takes a drink. "Good for you. Will you see her again?"

"That's the plan." I stretch my legs out and cross them at the ankles. "What's going on, Mill? You don't usually want to just hang out and chat."

"Maybe I *should* want to," she says. "I mean, you're my brother, and we're friends. We can hang."

"Okay, sure." I watch her quietly, patiently waiting for her to get around to what brought her over here. Millie's close to all of us brothers, but she and I have always had a special connection. And I know that it takes her a while to speak about what's on her mind, so I'm patient.

"Where did you and Summer go?" she asks.

"The Wolf Den."

She nods, as if she's thinking that over. "Cool, cool. No sexy time?"

"I absolutely refuse to speak to my baby sister about my sex life."

Millie rolls her eyes at that. "Oh, come on. If Brady asked, you'd tell him."

"No, I don't think I would." I lean back on my hands. "How's work going at the coffee shop?"

"I've been there for a long time," she says and plucks at her lower lip. "Five years this week. I *love* it there, Chase."

"I know you do. And you're damn good at what you do."

"It's just making coffee. I'm not saving lives or anything."

"It isn't *just* anything. I can't make coffee with that monster you use there, and it's more than that. You're good with the customers. You're excellent at banter, and if someone's giving you a hard time, you can stick up for yourself and diffuse a situation."

"It doesn't hurt that my brother is a cop and only a phone call away."

"If that makes you feel better, I'm glad, but don't sell yourself short, cupcake. You don't take shit from anyone."

"It comes with the territory when you have four older brothers." She grins over at me, but then the smile falls, and she looks worried. "Marion wants to sell me the business."

And there it is. The reason she's here.

"Owning the coffee shop and working there are two very different things," she continues. "And I have to wonder if it's financially feasible."

"You know you can take a loan from the ranch. Remington would back you in a heartbeat. Hell, Ryan would *give* you the money without a thought."

"I know." Tears spring to her eyes, and before I can jump up to hug her, she holds her hand up to stop me. "I'm okay. I think I'm just tired. I haven't slept in a few days because all I can think about is this. I mean, I'm *honored* that Marion came to me and asked me if I wanted the opportunity."

"Marion seems too young to retire," I reply, frowning. "Why does she want to sell?"

"She wants to open a catering business and doesn't feel like she can do both. I understand that. Passions change with time. She opened Bitterroot Valley Coffee Co, so she's owned it for a long time."

"I guess what it boils down to is, do *you* want it?"

"Yeah." Her pretty hazel eyes find mine, lighting up with excitement. "Yeah, I do. Am I too young to own a business?"

"You're almost twenty-six," I remind her.

"Am I smart enough?"

I narrow my eyes at her. "Start saying shit about my sister and I'll kick your ass."

That makes her snort out a laugh. "You know what I mean. I can't do taxes and bookkeeping and stuff. Payroll scares me."

"Honey, you hire a bookkeeper for that. Erin took over the ranch's books, and I bet she'd do yours, too. Or use whomever Marion has used all these years."

"Marion *likes* math," Millie says, wrinkling her nose. "She does her own books. But you're right, I could talk to Erin about it, but not until after the wedding and their honeymoon. I don't want to add any more to her plate."

"You know, it occurs to me that we've all been so careful not to add more to Erin's plate lately, but she's a tough woman. Talk to her about it now, before you decide to buy the business, so she can get it on her radar for after the wedding."

"That's a good idea," Millie says with a nod. "Do you really think Rem or Ryan would back the loan? I mean, I can go to the bank, but I'd rather keep it in the family if I can."

"Absolutely. Hell, we'll all back you."

"You can't afford that on a cop's salary."

I narrow my eyes at her. "I do just fine, thank you very much."

"Hey, no offense. I'll go see Rem and Erin tomorrow. Hell, I'll have Ryan meet with us, too," she says with a sigh. "I should have just come to see you the other day, after Marion brought it up, rather than being a nervous wreck about it the last few days. It's been exhausting. And then Holden showed up at the coffee shop today, and he always makes my brain want to bleed out of my ears."

"What did you just say?"

That makes her blink and swallow hard, then she shrugs a shoulder. "Nothing. I'm obviously so tired, I'm delirious."

"You're talking about Holden Lexington, right?"

She sighs and rubs her fingers over her forehead. "I can't believe I freaking said that. I'm such an idiot."

"Answer the question, Mill."

"Yeah, Holden Lexington. And you can forget I said anything because it doesn't matter. So what if he's hot? So what if he's good in bed? I don't care."

"You think Holden Lexington, the son of the arch

nemesis of our family, the one who's at least ten years older than you, is *hot*? And, as if that's not bad enough, he's had his motherfucking hands on you?" I run my tongue over my teeth and try to decide if I should hunt the man down and kick his ass tonight or wait for morning. Just out of principle.

"Jesus Christ, I have to leave," Millie says, sitting up. "My mouth won't shut the hell up."

"Millie, you slept with Holden Lexington?"

"Forget I said that, Chase." She shakes her head, blowing out a gust of breath. "Seriously, wipe it from your memory banks. It was a long time ago, and it won't happen again. He didn't hurt me. It was consensual—"

"For fuck's sake." I drag my hand down my face.

"And it's done. When he's around, he scrambles my brain a bit, but it's nothing I can't handle. Now, let's get back to the topic at hand."

"Millie, Dad would never be okay with you being with him."

"I'm not *with* him!" she yells back and stands to pace the room. "I can't believe I even said anything. I guess I was just dumping all my secrets out, and that came tumbling with them. And trust me, I regret it. I am not now, nor will I ever be, with Holden. Trust me on that."

But I see the look in her eyes, and I know that she wishes things were different.

Personally? I don't have an issue with the man. But I'm not lying when I say that Dad would never be okay with any of us marrying into that family.

Hell, Remington would blow a gasket if he knew.

"You can't tell anyone," she says, as if she's reading my mind. "Promise me, Chase."

"I won't speak of it," I reply evenly.

"And you won't go talk to Holden or rough him up."

I take a deep breath. "I don't want to promise that."

She just lifts an eyebrow, and I let out the breath.

"Fine. I won't say anything to him, either."

"Okay. Thank you." Her shoulders fall in relief. "So, Summer Quinn, huh?"

"You're changing the subject."

"You bet your ass I am."

"CHASE, YOU'RE SERIOUSLY SO TALENTED." Erin runs her hand lovingly over the top of the bar that I've just finished for her. "If the police thing doesn't work out, you can make a good living making things like this."

"It's always good to have something to fall back on," I reply with a grin. "I'm glad you like it. Send me a list of the other things you need to have done before the wedding."

"It's in two weeks," she reminds me, and just saying that out loud has worry filling her eyes. "And I need something big."

"How big?"

"Well, I'd like a stage."

I stare at her, shuffling my feet. "You want a *stage*? How big?"

"Big enough for a band?" She bites her lip. "We've

hired a band for the reception, and I know that my uncle Leo and Sidney will want to sing. I can't have all of that in the grass."

"Hold on." I shake my head and let out a laugh. "You're telling me that *Leo fucking Nash* is going to sing at your reception?"

"He's my uncle."

"He's a freaking superstar."

"He's my *uncle*," she stresses. "And he and my mom usually sing something together. Now we have Sidney in the family, too, so she'll want in on the action. You don't understand. This is what we do at family gatherings."

"Leo performs at your family gatherings?"

"Yes."

I shake my head in disbelief. "Okay, well, that actually sounds awesome, but I can't build something like that in two weeks, sweetheart. You're going to have to rent it."

"I was afraid of that," she says. "Okay, I can rent it. I just thought it would be nice to have something permanent out here that we can use for future events."

"We can discuss that later." I grin at her. "I know that my brothers geeked out about who your dad is, and don't get me wrong, I loved watching him play ball when I was a kid, but the fact that Leo Nash is going to sing at my brother's wedding is kind of mind-blowing."

"He's a lot of fun," she says with a grin. "And he takes requests."

"He and your mom sing together?"

"Sure. They used to be in a band together, long before

Nash was famous, but then Mom went to nursing school, and Leo went off to be rich and famous. They grew up as siblings. They were in foster homes together."

I tip my head, listening raptly. "That's fascinating."

"We have all kinds of interesting stories in our family." She laughs and pushes her hand through her hair. "Okay, I'll get that list to you, but there isn't much left to do. Oh, and I went ahead and hired Charlie Lexington."

I quirk a brow at that. "Really? How did you manage that?"

"I told Remington and your father to get over themselves and to let me have this so I didn't go insane, and they stopped grumbling about it."

I laugh and reach over to pat her on the shoulder. "You're good for this family."

"Damn right, I am. Now, tell me, how are things with Summer? It's all over town that you two went on a date."

"Yeah, two weeks ago." I rub the back of my neck as I scowl. I haven't seen in her two fucking weeks, and it's driving me nuts. "We've been too busy to see each other since. I've been working a lot of night shifts and helping out here at the ranch, and *life* is crazy, you know?"

"Did the date not go well?" Erin frowns at me.

"It was great. I'm crazy about her. I've been sending her lunch every day. All the delivery kids in town are going to college on what I tip them."

"You send her lunch?" Her face goes all gooey. "That's so romantic."

"It would be more romantic if I could just see her myself."

"I'm sorry. I know part of that is because you've been doing so much work for the wedding. What time is she done at the shop today?"

I check the time. "In about an hour, I'd say, give or take."

"You need to get out of here and go spoil her tonight. If she's been as slammed as you say, then she's likely exhausted and could use some pampering."

With a frown, I push my hands into my pockets. "How, exactly, do I go about that?"

"Cook her dinner, or order in, and put her in a hot bath. Rub her feet. Snuggle with her. Be *nice* to her, Chase. You're good at that."

"I don't have anything—"

"I swear, I have to do everything around here." Erin rolls her eyes and takes my hand and drags me into the house behind her. She grabs a basket out of the mudroom and then scurries through the house, filling it up. A jar of sauce and noodles go in the basket. "Make her spaghetti. It's easy and delicious. I even have some French bread you can take."

After the kitchen, we climb the stairs to the main suite and through to the bathroom.

"Here are Epsom salts for a hot bath. Bubbles are romantic, but these salts will help with sore muscles. It'll feel better, and they don't cause...girl trouble."

"Girl trouble?"

"Trust me on this," she says, shaking her head. "I'm tossing in some really nice lotion for her feet and hands.

You can rub her back, too, but don't do that just to lead to sex."

"I—"

"Men do that all the time and think we don't know what they're up to. Trust me, we know. Rub her feet and hands, put on her favorite movie to watch, and snuggle with her or talk with her. Or, if she doesn't want to talk, just relax. You know, *pamper the woman*."

"I really like this idea." I grin at Erin as she passes me the basket.

"So will she."

On my way back to town, I call Summer at the flower shop.

"This is Summer," she says when she picks up.

"Hey, it's Chase. Remember me?"

"Are you the tall, dark, and handsome guy that I went out to dinner with a few weeks ago?"

"That's me."

"It's coming back to me." I can hear the smile in her voice. "What are you up to?"

"Well, I'm wondering when you're getting off work."

"I'm just finishing up here, actually. Why? What's up?"

"Would you and Lily like to meet me at my house for the evening? As you pointed out, I haven't seen you in *way* too long, and we need to rectify that. Lily's welcome at my place."

"We'd like that. When should we get there?"

"You can come straight over after work."

"Great, we'll see you soon."

More than satisfied with the way this evening is shaping up, I get home, run upstairs for a quick shower to clean off the sawdust, and then pull on some jeans and a Fall Out Boy T-shirt. The doorbell rings as I'm walking downstairs.

She has perfect timing.

"Hey," I say with a grin when I open the door and see Summer, along with Lily on a pink leash, standing on the porch. She's holding a tote bag full of Lily's things. "You are a sight for sore eyes."

She smiles back at me, but I can see the fatigue in her beautiful blue eyes, and I know without a doubt that Erin hit it right on the head with this idea.

"Come on in." I hold the door for them, take the bag from Summer, and then close the door behind them. Summer takes Lily off of the leash and collar, letting her loose in the house.

"She's good about not chewing or peeing on things," she assures me. "And I brought her bed from the shop. It's in the car."

"I'm not worried about any of that." Unable to resist, I tug her into my arms and hug her for a solid ten seconds. Just like the last time, it takes her a moment to wrap her arms around me, but when she does, she hugs me tightly. "How are you, Blondie?"

"I'm good. I have no complaints."

"We're going to keep the no-complaint trend going through the night," I inform her. "I'm going to cook us some dinner, and while I do that, I'm going to draw you a bath upstairs."

She pulls back and stares at me with wide, blue eyes. "Really?"

"Really. I have a huge tub up there that I've never used, but don't worry, it's clean."

Her lips tip up in a grin. "I'm game for that. Do you want me to take Lily home?"

"No way. She's going to hang with me. Do you prefer white or red wine?"

"White," she decides. "Wow, this is a fun surprise. Thank you."

"I've missed you," I admit, not embarrassed in the least to admit it. "Two weeks is a long damn time."

"I missed you, too." She reaches up and cups my cheek in her hand, surprising us both. "But thank you for having lunch delivered *every single day*. That was uncalled for and appreciated."

"You're welcome."

"I have to admit, though, this is better." She grins down at Lily, who has decided to lie across both of our feet. "Someone's jealous."

"Well, she'll have to get over it." I press my lips to her forehead, breathing her in, and then lead her to the stairs, disrupting Lily, who follows us. "Come on, I'm putting you into a hot bath."

"I won't disagree. I know that I said the last time I saw you that I wasn't going to complain about my job anymore, and I'm *not* complaining because I love it, but my feet are *killing me*. I always forget how exhausting the summers are until I'm smack dab in the middle of it."

"Let's see if we can help with that a little."

With Lily watching, and sniffing out every inch of the bathroom, I start the hot water running in the bathtub and pour in the amount of Epsom salts that Erin told me to.

"I have a robe on the back of the door," I say as I gesture behind me. "And I have a T-shirt and some shorts there, that will absolutely be too big for you, but they're clean."

"And red is my color," she says as she picks up the T-shirt and buries her nose in it. "Thank you for all of this."

"We haven't even done anything yet." I grin at her and reach out to rub the pad of my thumb over her cheek, needing to feel her skin. "I'll be right back with your wine."

Not to be left behind, Lily follows me downstairs and watches with her head tilted as I pour a glass. She's right on my heels, as if we're playing a game, as I climb the stairs once more.

"I've got a new shadow," I inform Summer as I pass her the glass. "I think she likes me."

"She definitely does, because if she didn't, she would be stuck to my side." Summer sips her wine and nods with approval as I light the candle on the vanity. "This is great."

"Good. You get cozy, and I'll be downstairs in the kitchen if you need anything."

"You never mentioned before that you can cook," she says before I can walk out.

"Oh, I suspect there are all kinds of things we'll learn about each other." I wink at her, gesture for Lily to follow me, and close the door behind us. "We're going to give your mom some alone time."

Lily smiles up at me, and we head back downstairs.

As I brown the ground beef for the sauce, I hear music come on upstairs and grin. Glad that she's comfortable up there, I add the beef to the sauce and set the stove on low so it can simmer.

I won't boil the pasta or put the bread in the oven until she's done with the bath so everything is fresh, so, for now, it looks like things are on autopilot. Just when I've loaded the last dirty dish into the dishwasher, I hear a crash from above and take off at a sprint through the house and up the stairs. I push through the bathroom door without even thinking about it and stop dead in my tracks as I take in the scene before me.

"Holy shit."

CHAPTER SEVEN
SUMMER

This bath is exactly what I didn't know I needed. After remembering how miserable I was in Missoula, I've made a conscious effort to be grateful for my little flower shop in my sweet town, because I *am* thankful to be here. I've never been happier in my life, so it seems silly to complain about being successful while doing something I love. I enjoy the weddings and the hustle and bustle of the summer, working with brides on their visions. I only get one or two bridezillas a year, and that's not so bad at all.

But man, it's tough on the body. I'm on the go from before dawn until sundown, and I'm starting to feel it. But we only have a couple more months to go of the crazy season.

This hot bath, with the salts that Chase added, soothes my sore joints and muscles, and I lean back against the end of the giant claw-foot tub and close my eyes.

I could conceivably fall asleep in here.

"Music." My eyes pop open, and I reach for my phone. I had set it on the floor next to me in case I needed it. After finding my favorite playlist and turning up the volume, I put it back on the floor before I resume lounging in what I've decided to call the deep end of this magnificent pool. Chase's house is big, and from what I've seen of it, it's pretty. Well kept.

And totally *not* Chase. I don't know why I know that, I just do.

I'm lying here, totally zoned out, when all of a sudden, there's a loud *crash*, and glass shatters everywhere.

My heart's in my throat as I rear up and discover that a mirror fell off the wall and broke, scattering glass all over the place.

I'm just reaching down for my phone when the door bursts open, and Chase rushes in, then stops short, taking in the scene with frantic eyes.

"Holy shit."

I squeak and plunge back into the water. "Keep Lily out of here."

He turns and speaks to the dog. "No, girl, you stay in the hall. You stay." Chase steps inside and closes the door behind him. "Are you okay?"

"I think so. Gave me a heart attack, but I'm okay. You're barefoot, Chase. Don't walk in here."

With his face set in grim lines, he surveys the scene, and then his gaze finds mine. Those eyes flicker down to my nakedness that is not at all concealed by the water, and there's not much I can do to cover myself.

"You're staying in there," he informs me, "while I clean this up. Give me just ten minutes."

He doesn't wait for an answer before he hurries out again, and I can hear him talking to Lily as he rushes down the hallway.

I'm not thrilled that *this* is how he saw me naked for the first time. Talk about not being the least bit romantic or sexy, but at least I'm clean. I smirk and shake my head. Is that the best I can come up with? I'm *clean*?

The door opens once more, and Chase returns with shoes on and a broom, dustpan, and vacuum in tow.

"I barricaded Lily in the mudroom with a cushion from the couch to lie on and a bowl of water," he informs me. "She's not thrilled about it, but I wanted to make sure that she doesn't hurt her feet."

"Thank you, that's perfect. I'm sorry your mirror broke."

"It's not your fault," he says with a frown as he gets to work sweeping the glass. "It looks like the landlord hung that thing in the drywall, not a stud. It was only a matter of time before it came down. I'm just sorry that it happened when you were in the tub. I guess my plan for making you relax just landed all over my floor."

He glances my way again and then drops the broom.

"What? What's wrong?" I cover my breasts with my arm, but he's not looking down there. His eyebrows are drawn together in a frown as he gently takes my chin in his fingers and examines my face.

"You have a cut on your cheek," he murmurs, looking closely. He grabs a tissue and dabs at it, pulling back with only a little blood. "It's not bleeding anymore. Does it hurt?"

"I didn't even know it was there."

"I don't want you sitting in glass-filled water. Stand up, sugar."

"Uh, Chase? I'm not the most modest person on Earth, but I'm naked. I don't think there's much glass in here. I can wait."

"Oh, trust me, I noticed that you're naked." He smiles tenderly and wipes his thumb over my cheek. "I won't look if you don't want me to."

I bite my lip. It's not that I don't want him to look; it's just...

"Summer, there is glass in that water, and I don't want you sitting in it anymore," he says, his voice still calm. "I'm going to carry you to my bedroom so you can dry off and pull on some clothes, and I'll finish this up in here."

It makes perfect sense. Trusting him, I nod and move to stand, but he catches my hand in his and helps me to my feet. Then he reaches for a towel and wraps me in it before simply looping his arms under me and lifting me easily against him.

"I'm getting you all wet," I say with a laugh, and without even thinking about it, lean in to press my face to his neck.

"Don't care." His voice is a little rougher now, and when we're back in his bedroom, he lowers me to my feet. Goose bumps break out on my body. "I'll get you fresh clothes, too."

"Chase." He turns back to me, his face set in strained lines. He's obviously making an effort to be a gentleman and keep his eyes *up*. Not that it matters now because I'm covered, and he's already seen me. "Come here, please."

His brow lifts, but he doesn't argue. With his shirt and jeans wet, he returns to me and stands just two feet away.

I want him. I've wanted this man for what seems like forever, but especially over the past few weeks. He's sexy and kind, and I feel safe with him, which is the biggest thing for me.

I can *trust* him.

"Summer," he murmurs, his eyes dropping to my lips, "I need you to tell me what you want me to do right now because keeping my hands to myself is getting harder and harder, but if you tell me to leave the room, I will."

He would. I know he would, and that's why I absolutely do *not* want him to go.

Without a word, and with my eyes on his, I let the towel fall to the floor, and his eyes don't move from mine as his jaw clenches and his hands fist at his sides.

"I'm not sending you mixed signals," I inform him and raise my chin. "The bath was nice, and now I want...*you*."

He steps to me and frames my face in his hands, those long fingers pushing into my hair.

"You're sure?"

"Never been so damn sure." My eyes lower to his lips. "Please, for the love of all that's holy, tell me you'll kiss me now."

His lips tip up in a grin, and then they're on mine, all soft and smooth and hot. It's the heat that hits first, like a fist slamming into a wall. I tug his wet shirt out of his jeans, and he quickly pulls it over his head and tosses it aside.

And I need a minute to take him in.

"Muscles for days," I mutter, making his hazel eyes warm. My fingers graze down his chest, over the ripples of his abs. "Okay, maybe I'm a little self-conscious now."

He laughs and takes my mouth again, and my hands dive into his jeans. I want him as naked as I am. I want to *feel* him, all of him, pressed against me.

And he doesn't disappoint.

When his shoes and jeans are finally shed, Chase nudges me back to the bed, and when my knees hit the side of the mattress, he guides me down and climbs over me. He's leaving open-mouthed kisses down my neck while his hand skims down my chest to my breast and pauses there.

"Damn, you're amazing." God, I love his voice. It's smooth as silk one minute, and the next, rough with need. "Every fucking inch of you is *amazing*."

I sigh and let my hands take a journey of their own, exploring him. His cock is hard and heavy against my hip, and I admit, it's a little intimidating.

But I don't have time to think about whether or not

I'll accommodate him when that magical hand of his journeys farther south and covers my center, making me gasp.

"So hot," he mutters. "So fucking wet for me."

I moan, and my hips lift when he presses a finger inside of me, but I feel myself holding back, as though the thought of letting go with him means that I'm surrendering everything, and that scares me.

Chase, and what he makes me feel, scares me.

And yet, I've never wanted anything so badly in all of my life.

"Go over," he growls and nips at my jaw.

"I can't." My breath is lodged in my lungs as I strain for control.

"Go the fuck over, Summer."

My head moves from side to side, and I bite my lip. "I can't."

"You can." His touch gentles, his fingers slow. "Eyes on me, babe."

I shake my head again, and suddenly, his hand is gone from my core, and he's tipped my face to him.

"Open your eyes."

I do as he asks and feel myself melt at the look on his face. He's not impatient or demanding. He's *smiling* down at me.

"I'm right here," he says softly and nips at my lips. "And we have all night for you to trust me enough to let go."

"I don't." I take a breath and frown. "I don't do that."

His eyes narrow for just a heartbeat, and he tips his head to the side. "What do you mean?"

"Nothing, go ahead. Just do it." Could I humiliate myself any more than this?

"Whoa." Now he seems frustrated as he takes my chin in his hand again and frowns down at me. "Back up, Blondie. I'm not going to just *do* anything here. Don't you shut down on me. You have a *partner* now, so let's figure this out."

And just like that, I've ruined this amazing moment. "I should have just faked it."

He chuckles at that and brushes his nose over mine. "No way. No need to fake it. Let's try this."

He doesn't run away. To my surprise, he's all patient humor as he kisses me again, and I turn into him, as if he's a magnetic force that I just can't resist.

His hands resume roaming over my skin, but not to my center, not yet. His thumb brushes over my nipple, and his mouth moves down my neck, reigniting the heat that had cooled to embers.

"Your skin is like gold silk," he mutters and kisses my collarbone. "So soft and warm. And when you blush like that, it makes me throb for you."

Oh, I like his dirty mouth. I like that a lot.

"You make the sweetest noises," he continues. "Tell me what you're feeling, Summer."

"Hot."

He grins against my breast. "And?"

"I don't know."

"Yes, you do." His fingers drift up the inside of my

thigh as his nose traces a circle around my navel. "Does this tickle?"

"No." My legs scissor. I want him inside of me. "It feels...sexy."

"Good girl. How does this feel?" He brushes the edge of my folds, and I inhale sharply. "Use your words."

"Sweet. It's like a sweet hurt that feels good."

"Oh, I like that." He presses a kiss there, and I bite my lip again, fighting for control. "What if I do this?"

He traces my clit with his finger, and I moan as he settles in and laps at me, feasting on me.

"Holy shit."

"What does it feel like?"

"Like I'm going to...Oh, God, like I'm going to explode."

"And you don't want that?"

"No. Yes." I grip onto the sheets, and he lifts my legs onto his shoulders. "Chase."

"Look at me." I thrash my head from side to side, and his voice firms. "Open your eyes, Summer."

I do and look down to find his gaze on mine, hovering over me, and I know, down in my gut, that this is *not* how I want to come for the first time. "Not like that."

He quirks a brow. "Okay. How?"

"Up here." He moves over me and brushes my nose with his. "Like this."

"Any way you want it, sugar." He kisses me once more, and I can taste myself on him. My body calms, putting me right back into my comfort zone, but this time, it's a comfort zone that's on fire.

I hear Chase open a packet, and I lift my legs higher on his hips, ready for him.

"You need," he kisses my chin, "to open," my cheek, "your gorgeous eyes for me."

He likes it when I look at him, and it makes me feel vulnerable.

Just like succumbing to an orgasm does. And that's my hangup. I don't want to be vulnerable with anyone.

"You're overthinking again," he murmurs and presses the tip of his cock against me. "I'm going to take this slow."

"Just—"

"Say *just do it*, and I'll spank your ass." I blink at the words said so calmly yet so firmly as his hazel eyes are bright with lust and are pinned to my own. "*We're* doing this, babe. You and me, together."

I take a deep breath and hold his gaze as he presses into me, and when he's seated fully, I grin at him.

"I didn't know if you'd fit."

"Jesus, saying shit like that makes it hard for me to go slow." He rests his forehead on mine.

I laugh now, squeezing him, and he groans. He laces our fingers and presses my hand to the bed above my head as he starts to move, and all of the sensation from a moment ago comes back, pushing me higher and further than I've ever been before.

"I see you shutting down," he says. "Don't do that, Summer. We've come too far for that."

I don't want to. It's an automatic reaction to intimacy.

"Ah, babe," he moans. "So fucking good. You're so fucking beautiful."

His words, most of all, are what's driving me up further. And then he releases my hand and cups my face, kissing me long and slow as his hips move. I grip onto him, feeling myself slide closer and closer to a place that I've never allowed myself to go to before.

"That's it," he croons to me as he keeps the rhythm slow, with long, deep strokes. "Ah, your pussy is a fucking vise around me. Jesus Christ, Summer, go over."

"Yes." The climax rips through me like claws, the heat, the absolute *need* pushing through me in waves. "Chase!"

He moans as he follows me, pushing against me with small, intense pulses. Every muscle in his impressive body is tight, and when he opens his eyes and pins me in that intense hazel gaze, I realize that *this* is what intimacy is.

Body, mind, and soul.

I press my hand to his cheek, and he turns to kiss my palm before he shifts onto his side and rolls me to face him. He brushes my hair behind my ear and kisses my nose.

He's the most affectionate man I've ever been with.

He's the most *everything* man I've ever been with.

"I'm hungry," he decides and continues to brush my hair in his fingers. "We should eat. We worked up an appetite, and I need you to be fueled up so we can do it again."

That surprises a laugh out of me, and he grins at me in return before kissing me sweetly and then with more heat.

He groans and pulls away. "If we don't get out of this bed now, we won't until morning."

"I have to feed Lily and check on her." I brush my fingertips down his arm, enjoying the way the muscles ripple under my touch. "And I'm hungry, too."

"It's settled, then." He rolls out of the bed and pads down to the hall to the guest bathroom to clean himself up, and I wander into his closet to find a clean shirt. Just as I'm buttoning the denim shirt, Chase finds me and grins. "I like that."

"I need underwear."

His eyes heat now. "I'd be okay if you went without it."

"No." I can't help but laugh. "That's not comfortable. But if you pull a pair of women's panties out of a drawer, I'll punch you in the gut."

"Violent after sex, huh? I'll remember that. No, I don't have any women's underwear lying around from previous conquests, but I do have some boxers you can borrow."

"That'll do."

He passes me a green pair, and as I climb into them, he throws on a pair himself, along with a T-shirt, and then glances over at me, and a slow smile spreads over his face. "Oh, yeah, that'll do nicely."

Has anyone ever made me feel as sexy as Chase does? As comfortable?

No.

Which honestly explains a lot.

"Should we finish cleaning up the bathroom?" I ask as he takes my hand to lead me out of the bedroom.

"Later," he replies. "It'll be there much later."

"We didn't even drain the tub."

He shrugs and gestures for me to precede him down the stairs. I can already hear Lily's nails tippy tapping on the tile as we walk into the kitchen, and I see her staring out at us from behind her gate.

"Hi, good girl," I croon as I let her out. "I'm going to take her into the backyard. Is that okay?"

"Make yourself, and her, at home," he assures me as he kisses me on the head. "I'll start the pasta and bread."

"Mm, pasta. It's my love language." I wink at him and then take Lily out the back door so she can sniff around and do her business. It takes her longer than usual because she has to check out *every* square inch of the yard, but I don't mind. It's a quiet summer night, and with the sun finally dipping into the horizon, the hottest part of the day is over, and there's a light breeze in the air that feels nice.

Finally, when she's finished, we walk back into the house, and I see that Chase is just taking the bread out of the oven.

"Good timing," he says with a grin. "I hope you're hungry because there's a lot of food here."

"So hungry," I assure him. "I'll feed Lily really quick,

too, but she'll still beg for scraps. Food is also her love language."

With Lily's food bowl full, I help Chase plate up our meal, and we take our plates, along with fresh glasses of red wine, into the dining room. He sits at the head of the table, and I sit to his right, curling a leg under me as I lower myself to the chair.

"This looks delicious," I comment as I take a bite of bread and then moan in pleasure. "There are few things better than warm bread from the oven. Especially when garlic is involved."

"I love watching you eat," he says and just rests his chin in his hand. "It's sexy as hell."

"Eating?" I smirk at that. "That's a new compliment I haven't heard before."

"Why do you think I feed you so much? Because it's sexy." He frowns and reaches up to graze his fingertip over where the glass scraped me. "I'm so sorry about that mirror, sugar."

"It seemed to work out in the end." I tilt my head, and that satisfied smile spreads over his lips once more.

"That it did. Speaking of that, are you going to tell me that you'd never had an orgasm before tonight?"

I choke on my pasta and reach for my wine, washing it down.

"I haven't had enough wine for this conversation."

"You don't need alcohol to be honest with me." He takes a bite of his food and watches me. "We're past that."

"Okay, fair enough. No, I hadn't."

"Why?" He takes another bite, and it's as if we're talking about what subjects we took in college.

"Because I didn't, *don't*, do well with intimacy," I reply before taking a bite of my bread, pausing to chew and think it over. "Trust issues, I guess. I told you about Dennis. Turns out my instincts were right on that one. We had a lot of sex, and it was fine, but it was just that. Fine."

He pauses with his hand halfway to his mouth. "Are you telling me that Dennis was your only partner before me?"

"I haven't dated since then." I shrug. "I don't sleep around. So, yeah."

"Okay." He nods and continues to eat, not making a big deal about anything that we're talking about, and I love that about this conversation. He makes me feel completely at ease.

"Are you so calm and collected about everything because you need to be for your job?" I slip Lily a noodle before I reach for another slice of bread.

"I've always been pretty mellow. Until it's time *not* to be."

"And when does that happen?"

"If things get heated at work, or when I have a gorgeous woman in my bed who won't give in and come when she knows she wants to."

That makes me squirm in my seat, and he grins.

"You were pretty calm about that."

"Didn't feel like it," he replies. "I wanted to pound

into you and *make* you let go. But that wasn't the way to handle it."

"No." I shake my head slowly. "It wasn't. Although, now, it doesn't sound too bad."

He laughs and tucks my hair behind my ear. "I plan to take you in every way there is, Blondie. Hard and fast and slow and soft, and every way in between. And trust me, you'll come. You'll come a lot."

I swallow hard and stare down at my plate. "Well, then."

CHAPTER EIGHT
CHASE

Lily's snoring on the mat in front of the kitchen sink, after having just come in from her last go-around the yard for the evening, so I have to lean over her to finish rinsing the dishes and set them in the dishwasher. This dog is hilarious.

"It would be convenient if you moved out of the way," I inform the canine, but she just opens one eye for a brief second and then goes back to snoring peacefully.

"She's spoiled and lies where she wants," Summer informs me as she joins me in the kitchen. "But I can move her for you."

"I'm done here." I set the dishwasher to run and then turn and pull this gorgeous woman into my arms, where she fits perfectly. "How are you, sugar?"

"I'm great. I just cleaned the bathroom upstairs."

I scowl and nudge her back. "You didn't have to do that. I told you to go relax."

"It was driving me crazy," she admits with a grin and

cups my face. "And it didn't take long. I wouldn't have been able to relax until it was cleaned up. Don't worry, I put my shoes on first. I think I got all the glass up, and the tub is drained and clean."

Framing her face, I lean down to press my lips to hers, and when she sighs sweetly, I deepen the kiss.

She's addictive. I knew she would be, and that once I started kissing her, getting my hands on her, I wouldn't want to stop.

I was right.

But I pull away and kiss the back of her hand, then lead her through to the living room. Lily wakes up and follows us, hops up onto the couch, and curls up in the corner, immediately snoring once more.

"I'm glad she's made herself at home." I grin and take the other end of the sofa and pull Summer down next to me. The lotion Erin gave me sits on the end table, but before I rub Summer's feet, I pass her the remote to the TV. "Pick something to watch."

"Me?" She shrugs a shoulder. "Okay."

As she turns on the television and starts to look around for something to watch, I pull her feet into my lap and reach for the lotion. Summer sighs as I start to rub the sole of her foot and lands on *Ted Lasso* on Apple TV.

"Have you seen this?" she asks.

"No, but I've heard good things."

"Me, too. Let's start it." She sighs and looks over at me. "You're *really* good at that. Did you take lessons on foot massage or something?"

"I have to admit that I have no idea what I'm doing, but if you like it, I'll keep it up."

She grins and sighs once more when I switch to the other foot.

"They've been sore," she admits softly. "I'm just on them a lot, so this is a treat. I probably should invest in some new sneakers, but who has time?"

"Maybe you should hire more help, just for the summer season," I suggest. I don't like that she's exhausting herself. Even if she loves what she does, she can't work herself into exhaustion.

"I definitely will next year. Our town is becoming more and more popular as a destination wedding location, and I could take on double the events that I do now, if I wanted to. To do that, I'd need to double the workforce. I'm not afraid to do that, but it can't happen this season."

She clears her throat, ignoring the television altogether, and watches my fingers dig into her arch.

"What made you decide to be a cop?"

"I don't know, I just always knew that's what I would do. It wasn't a question. When I was a teenager, I was convinced that I'd move to a big city and be on a force there, where the action is."

"High-speed chases and murder and all the exciting stuff?" she says, waggling her eyebrows.

"That's right." I finish with the second foot and then take her hand, squeeze some lotion into her palm, and keep rubbing. The moan that comes out of her delicious little throat makes me want to lay her down and fuck her into next week. Instead, I clear my throat. "And I tried it."

"You did?" That has her opening her eyes in surprise. "Where did you go?"

"I was in Seattle for about a year, and it *was* exciting. But it was also kind of sad, and I didn't like being so far away from the ranch. Montana is my home. It's where I'm supposed to be, and it didn't take me long to remember that and move back. I was hired on here, and I'll retire from here someday."

"Well, I'm glad you came back. I would have missed out on this really great hand massage if you hadn't." Her smile is soft and sweet. "You do a good job here, Chase, and I'm not just talking about the massage. I *enjoyed* working with you when everything went down with Erin a few months ago. You're smart, and even though it was a stressful situation, you were excellent at calming me down and communicating clearly what you needed me to do."

I reach for her other hand, kiss the palm, and then begin to massage it.

"I don't have a lot of experience in dealing with the police," she continues with a rueful smile, "since I've never been arrested and haven't needed to work on an investigation before."

"No speeding tickets?"

"Not even one. My point is, you make people feel safe here, and that's a gift. I don't think just anyone could do that."

"Thank you." I don't know what else to say. "I'm glad

you feel safe. That's always the goal. Any more issues at
your house, with noises or slashed tires?"

"No." Her smile is sleepy now, and she yawns.
"Nothing going on there, thankfully. Everything's been
quiet."

Her voice softens, her eyes slide shut, and within just
a few minutes, her breathing evens out with sleep.

I reach for the remote, turn off the TV, and sit in the
quiet, watching Summer and Lily snooze away. Having
them both here feels *right*. I've wanted Summer in my
house, and in my bed, for a long while, and now I finally
have her here. Lily is cute and not any trouble at all. I'll
have to get a couple of beds and some bowls for her
because now that I have them here, I plan for them to be
here often.

Finally, I stand and lift Summer into my arms. She
curls into me and presses her face into my neck the way
she did earlier after the bath, and I feel the same zing
shoot down my spine. Lily's head comes up off of the
couch, and I nod, gesturing for her to follow us, which
she happily does, hot on my heels as I carry Summer up
to the bedroom and gently lay her on the bed.

Lily jumps up with her and curls into Summer's side.

"Leave some room for me," I whisper to her and rub
her head before I go back downstairs to turn off the
lights, make sure the doors are all locked up tight, and
then return to my girl.

I climb in behind her and pull her to me, tucking my
arm around her middle.

Yeah, this feels right. Having her warm against my

body and listening to Lily's little snores as my eyes droop is the most contented that I've felt in years.

Maybe ever.

I'm going to do whatever it takes to make her mine for good.

———

"I HAVE TO GO." Summer sips the mug of coffee I just passed to her. "I have to change and get ready for work."

I sip my own brew. "It's barely six."

"Yeah, well, I'm usually at the shop by now, but I admit, I slept well, and a handsome man did some delicious things to me when I woke up, so I'm not complaining."

I grin and reach out to brush my thumb under her eye. "You're sweet. Maybe we should both call in sick and stay here, naked and rumpled, all day."

"Don't tempt me." She chuckles and looks down at Lily, who's been watching us with sleepy eyes. "Are you ready to go home?"

Lily turns in a circle.

"Here." I take the mug out of her hands and watch as she scowls at me. "Don't punch me; I'm putting this in a disposable cup."

"I thought I was going to have to maim you there for a second."

I snap the lid on and pass it back to her. "No need for that. I'll help you out to the car. And, in case you ever need to get in here, the code to the door is 5391."

"Is this the equivalent of you giving me a key to the house?" she asks.

"Pretty much."

Carrying Lily's bag of goodies, I follow Summer down to her vehicle, and once she has it loaded, and Lily in the front seat, I pull her in and hug her close.

"I'll bring you lunch."

She chuckles against my chest. "I won't even attempt to tell you that it's not necessary. I'd like to see you later today."

"And tonight?"

She tips her head back so she can smile up at me. "What are you thinking?"

"I think it's time I made good on my promise to take you to Ciao for dinner."

"Oh, yeah, I'm down for that."

"Good." I kiss her nose, and she pulls away to walk around and get into her car. "I'll see you later."

She blows me a kiss, and then she's gone. Rubbing the back of my neck and wishing for the rest of my coffee, I walk back inside and lock the door behind me. The house already feels empty without them, which is a little ridiculous to me, given that they were only here for *one night*.

But that's all it took.

It doesn't take me long to shower, drink two cups of coffee, and dress for work. I'll change into my uniform at the station, so I always try to get there twenty minutes before my shift starts.

It's quiet in Bitterroot Valley this morning as I drive

through town. And that's just the way I like it. The station is quiet as I walk through to the locker room, and I go through the motions of changing into my uniform and checking everything on my belt. Then, I move to the weapons vault to choose the weapons that I'll have on me and in my vehicle.

And once I'm in the car, ready for my shift, I get a call first thing.

"Mrs. Wilburn is holding up traffic again," I'm told. "She's ten miles outside of town, doing twenty-five in a seventy, with at least a dozen cars behind her."

"I'm on my way."

Mrs. Wilburn has to be at least eighty, and she likely shouldn't have her license anymore. She refuses to drive over twenty-five miles per hour, regardless of where she is, and she's become a pain in my ass.

With my lights flashing, it doesn't take too long to find her, and when the other drivers pull over to make room for me, I turn around on the highway and get behind the old woman, turning on my siren.

Like a good citizen, she pulls over onto the shoulder, and the drivers that she was holding up pick up speed, waving at me with gratitude as they pass by.

I walk on the inside of the shoulder and knock on her passenger window.

"Hello, dear," she says when she rolls it down. "What's wrong? Are you looking for a fugitive? I don't think I saw anyone out here, but I'll keep my eyes open."

"No, ma'am, we had another complaint about your speed."

"Oh." She frowns. "I'm sorry. Sometimes my foot just gets away from me, and I go too fast."

"No." I laugh now and shake my head. "You go too *slow*, Mrs. Wilburn. You can't go twenty-five in a seventy. It's not safe."

"I've never heard of anyone complaining about someone going too slow. Why, I'm just being safe."

"No, actually, like I said, it's *not* safe. I have to give you a ticket this time, ma'am."

"For going *slower* than the speed limit? That's ridiculous. I'll call your mother, Chase Wild."

"And I'm sure she'd love to speak with you, but that doesn't change the fact that I have to write you a ticket for reckless driving. You're considered a hazard on the road."

"Well, I *have* to get into town for my hair appointment, don't I? How else do you suggest I get there? Fly?"

"Maybe someone could drive you."

"I'm perfectly capable of driving myself."

Right. As we've established. She needs to be moved into town so she doesn't have to drive on the highway at all anymore, but that's none of my business.

"I need your driver's license and registration, please."

"This is ridiculous."

Rather than giving me what I need, she rolls up the window and simply pulls back out into traffic. It's not a high-speed chase. I hit my lights and siren, but she ignores me all the way into town, and when I pull in behind her in the parking lot of her beauty salon, she ignores me when I try to speak to her.

She just hobbles right inside, moving surprisingly fast for a woman with a walker.

"Mrs. Wilburn, you're under arrest."

Gasps sound through the place, and everything goes quiet. You could hear a pin drop.

"I am not."

"Yes, ma'am." My face is grim as I rest my hand on my weapon. "I do *not* want to cuff you, ma'am, but I need you to come with me."

"I can't. I have an appointment."

"You left the scene, and you ignored me, so you're absolutely being arrested today. You'll be able to call one of your kids to come bail you out in a little while."

"How *exciting*," someone whispers as they hold up their phone, clearly videoing this whole thing. "Martha Wilburn is being arrested."

"I'm staying right here."

And with that, she simply sits on the floor. I've never seen an old woman, who has to walk with a walker, be suddenly so...limber.

"I need backup," I say into the radio on my shoulder. "Resisting arrest."

Mrs. Wilburn, the sweet old lady, leans over and bites my fucking leg.

"And assaulting an officer. Holy shit."

IT's BEEN A SHITTY DAY. One call after another, all petty crap, but it's keeping me busy, and the time is going fast. I have just enough time carved out to deliver a sandwich to Summer, and I'm headed there now, when I get another call.

"Shoplifting," I hear through the radio, "at Pocket Full of Polly. Three underage males are inside the business."

"Copy," I reply with a sigh. "ETA two minutes."

It ends up being thirty seconds, since I'm almost to the flower shop, which is just a block down from Summer's place. Polly owns a dress shop, full of frilly, girly things.

What are three *boys* doing shoplifting in there?

"Hello, Chase," Polly says when I walk through the door. "Thanks for coming. I caught this young man shoving a bracelet into his pocket."

"It's a present for my mom. I was gonna pay," the kid says with a scowl.

"Uh-huh," Polly says, rolling her eyes.

I shift my gaze between the three boys. I've seen them all in town plenty, and they've been in trouble before. If Bitterroot Valley had a gang, this would be it.

"What the hell, guys?"

"She's overreacting," the middle one says with a sneer.

"Steal from my store, and I'll have your ass," Polly counters. "I want to press charges."

"Shit," the middle one whispers mournfully.

"That's your right." I nod, eyeing Jake Hunter, the one who isn't saying anything. "What did *you* do?"

"He's the only one who didn't do anything," Polly says. "I'm not pressing charges against him."

"Great, I'll just go," Jake says and moves to make his escape, but I catch him by the shirt.

"Stop. You'll stay, or I'll *find* something to arrest you for."

It takes me fifteen minutes to take Polly's statement, and I call to have another officer come take the two boys to jail so I can give Jake my undivided attention.

"Thanks, Chase," Polly says with a wave as I escort Jake outside.

"Come on, let's have a seat."

"She said I didn't do anything," he insists. "I just want to go home. Or away from here, anyway."

"Humor me." I point to the park bench, and Jake drops down onto it, looking at me with dark eyes full of attitude. "What the hell are you doing hanging out with those kids?"

"They're my friends."

"Your parents would smack you on the head if they saw you hanging out with them."

"Yeah, well, they're dead, so it don't really matter." His chin is firm and defiant, and I blow out a breath, nodding slowly.

"I see." Jake's parents died in a car accident last year, leaving him without any family. I know he's been in a foster situation since then. "Let's get you out of that crowd, man. I'm sure I could get you a job working with horses. You're good with them."

"Stupid," he mutters, staring at the ground, but I see the way his eyes light up at the mention of the animals, and an idea begins to form in my head.

"It's not stupid. You have talent, and you're wasting it on shit that's going to get you into big trouble. What if I could get you a job working for my brother?"

"I don't want to work for Rem," he says, shaking his head.

I don't blame him. Jake's dad worked out at the Wild River Ranch for many years, so being out there would likely be hard on the kid.

"Not Rem," I counter. "Ryan."

"The rich dude?" He smirks. "What could I do for him? He don't even live here."

"First of all, we need to work on your grammar. Second, Ryan *does* live here, and he recently rescued some horses that were in a really bad situation. They're healing."

Just like you.

"And I know he's been looking for some help with them."

"I'm just a kid, dude."

"You may call me Chase or Mr. Wild, but you won't address me as *dude* again, got it?"

He sulks down on the bench, and I wipe my hand down my face.

"If you want the chance to work for Ryan, I'll talk to him."

He's quiet for a long minute, scowling at the grass in front of us. Finally, he says, "I guess it would be okay."

And that's as good as I'm going to get out of this kid.

"Do you have a cell phone?"

"Duh."

I narrow my eyes at him, and he swallows hard.

"Yes, sir."

"What's the number?" I pull my own phone out, and as he rattles off the number, I put it into my contacts and shoot him a text. His phone pings with it, and I nod, satisfied that he didn't give me a bogus number. "Now I can call you after I talk to Ryan."

"Why? Why would you do this?"

I sigh, tucking my phone away. "Because you're a good kid, Jake, and I liked your parents. They'd want someone to look out for you."

"I don't need no one."

"Don't be an asshole." That makes his eyes go wide. "We *all* need someone, even when you're a know-it-all teenager. Especially then. Ryan's a good guy, and it's honest work. You like horses. Why *not* do it?"

He lifts a shoulder, but I see a smile tugging at the corners of his lips.

"Stop hanging out with those kids. Nothing good can come of that."

"Making friends isn't easy when you're the orphan in school."

Surprised by the admission, I narrow my eyes at him. "Kids suck."

"Yeah. Big time."

"Don't settle for jerks as friends, Jake. Just don't. And call me if you need something. I'll be in touch about Ryan."

He turns his face to look at me. "I can go?"

"Yeah, you can go. Stay out of trouble."

He gets up to leave and then turns back to me. "I guess you're not so bad."

"That's high praise coming from you."

He does grin now, and then he jogs away, and I pull my phone out once more to call my brother.

"I hear you're arresting old ladies today," he says by way of answering.

"Yep, that's why I'm calling you. I'm hauling you in."

CHAPTER NINE
SUMMER

I frown as I check my watch and realize that it's past the usual time that Chase has lunch brought in. Not that he's under any obligation at all to do so, but I know he mentioned bringing it himself today, and I'd love to see him, even if it's for a few minutes.

It seems that after one night of amazing sex and snuggles, I'm addicted to the man.

"Why do you keep checking your watch, darling?" Aunt Paula passes me the daisies I asked for. "Are you late for an appointment?"

"No." I shake my head and smile over at her. "I'm glad you came in today. It's always fun having you in the shop."

"And I love being here," she assures me just as Sharla rushes in to gather more deliveries. "I'll help you load these."

"I won't turn that down," Sharla says. "I'd like to get back out there ASAP."

Ida and I, along with Margie, continue to build bouquets while Lily snores in her bed in the corner, and suddenly, the bell over the door rings, and Chase walks in.

He's so freaking handsome in his uniform, I immediately begin to salivate.

"Ladies," he says with a nod, carrying a paper bag. "I brought you all lunch."

"All of us?" Ida asks in surprise. "You didn't have to do that, Chase."

"My treat today," he says with a wink. I can see that something's on his mind. He's smiling and acting normal, but I can see the tension around his eyes.

"Rough day?" I ask him.

"It's been a *shit* day," he replies easily. "And I have to cancel our date tonight."

"Okay, that's not a problem. Do you need anything?"

His eyes soften now, and he reaches out to tuck a stray piece of my hair behind my ear.

"No, sugar, I'm okay." Lily wakes up and sees Chase, comes jogging over to greet him, and Chase bends over to pet her. "It's just one of those busy days, and we had a guy call off for his evening shift, so I'm covering the first half of it. I won't be home until later this evening."

"I'm sorry." I wrinkle my nose. "I'll be happy to take a rain check."

"You'd better take a rain check." His eyes light up when Aunt Paula walks in. "Well, hello, Miss Paula."

"Chase. Well, aren't you handsome in your uniform? How are you?"

"Now that your niece has agreed to finally put me out of my misery and date me? I'm great, thanks." He smiles over at me, and I feel heat spread through me. I'm not embarrassed. I'm *pleased.* "I'd better get back to work. There should be enough sandwiches in there for everyone."

"Thank you." I walk around the counter to join him as he walks to the door. "I'm sorry your day turned into a bit of a mess, especially after we had so much fun last night."

"It's part of the job," he replies easily. "And it's not *that* bad, just...unusual. Maybe there's a full moon or something."

"I'll have to check on that." I boost up onto my toes and offer him my lips, not caring in the least that my entire staff, plus Aunt Paula, are watching us raptly. And Chase doesn't disappoint. He wraps his arms around my waist, dips me back, and plants his lips on mine in a kiss that belongs in a sexy movie.

And when we pull apart, the other ladies applaud.

"Bravo," Ida calls out. "Bravo."

"That'll have to hold me over," he murmurs, staring down at my lips. "I'll call you later."

"I can't wait."

He plants one more on me, and then he pulls away and walks right out the door, and when I turn back to the others, they're grinning widely. Sharla, who hasn't left yet, pumps her fist into the air.

"Girl, that was a *kiss*," Sharla says.

"He's really good at it," I admit and press my lips

together, still tasting him there. "And yes, as you heard, we're dating. It's new, and it's fun."

"Good for you," Aunt Paula says and frames my face in her hands. "It's about time you had some fun, my darling."

"Well, I am having a good time." I chuckle and open the brown bag, surprised at the stack of sandwiches nestled inside. "There's definitely enough in here for everyone. Maybe two for everyone. I hope you're hungry."

"He brings—or sends—lunch for Summer every day," Ida informs my aunt and waggles her eyebrows. "He's discovered what her favorites are, and he makes sure she eats."

"Oh, that's lovely," Aunt Paula says, her hands crossed over her chest. "I just love a man who pays attention to his girl."

We've just dug into the bag, with a couple of the sandwiches to spare, when Polly hurries in.

"Why aren't you in your shop?" I ask her.

"I'm taking a break," she says and leans on the counter, breathless. "I locked up for a hot second because I had to run over here and talk to you."

"Okay, what's wrong?"

"Nothing." She shakes her head and then reconsiders. "Well, that's not true. I caught some kids shoplifting and called the cops. Chase showed up and took care of it and left with the one boy that I didn't press charges against, Jake Hunter."

"Poor Jake," Aunt Paula says. "That poor boy has been through so much."

"I know," Polly says with a nod. "Well, Chase escorted him out, and I figured he'd lecture him, of course, which he *should*. But then, I had a question for Chase, and I hurried out after him to see if I could catch him, and I overheard him talking to the kid, and I just have to say..."

She pauses for dramatic effect, and I'm on the edge of my proverbial seat.

"*Holy shitballs*. Jake called Chase *dude*, and Chase said, 'You may address me as Chase or Mr. Wild, but you will not call me *dude* again.' And it was hot as fuck, Summer. I'm telling you right now, you need to give that man a chance because he made *me* tingle, and I'm not even into him like that."

"Oh, you haven't caught Polly up," Ida says with a laugh. "She's giving him a chance, honey."

"*WHAT*?" Polly stares at me, stunned. "Drinks, The Wolf Den, tonight. I won't take no for an answer."

I haven't even had a chance to get a word in edge-wise. "My evening just conveniently freed up, so I can do that. I'll have to take Lily home first, and then I can meet up with you."

"I'll take that sweet baby home with me," Aunt Paula says with a smile. "I'd love the company. Besides, it's almost the weekend, and you'll be too busy for her anyway. She can hang out at the cottage with me for a few days and chase butterflies while I work in the garden."

I started taking Lily to Aunt Paula's house on the weekends during wedding season because it's not fair to leave Lily alone all day. They both enjoy the company, and I think Lily considers the cottage her weekend vacation.

"You know what? That works for us. Lily will love it." I nod and grin at my best friend. "The Wolf Den it is. Here, take a sandwich."

"I can't wait to hear all about this." Polly grabs a sandwich, then turns and hurries back to the door. "See you later!"

THE WOLF DEN is hopping for a Thursday night, and when Polly and I arrive, the only table available is a round six-top.

"If you'll seat us there, we'll take it," Polly says.

"Works for me." The hostess winks and, with menus in her hands, leads us through the full room to the only empty table. Polly and I sit next to each other, and to our delight, Pete magically appears with waters and huckleberry margaritas.

"I took a chance," he says with a wink. "If you don't want them, they're on me."

"Oh, we want them," I assure him. "We absolutely want them."

"Good. Do you need time with the menu?"

"I do," Polly says. "I know Summer always gets the same thing, but I'm an adventurous woman."

"No problem," Pete says with a laugh. "I'll be back."

I glance up and see that Millie just walked in, so I wave her over.

"Hey, ladies," Millie says, looking cute as can be in her cut-off shorts and red tank. "Fancy meeting you here."

"You should join us," I invite her. "These are the only available seats in the house anyway."

I gesture to the hostess, who nods agreeably, and Millie slides into a seat.

"You know what? I'd love to. Thanks, guys. How are you?"

"Summer's going to fill me in on the love affair she's having with your brother," Polly informs Millie, who raises an eyebrow and turns to me.

"I'm just in time, then."

The door opens again, and I glance over in time to see Erin, along with a woman I don't know well but have seen around town, walk in, and I wave for them to join us, as well.

"Did we not get invited to a party?" Erin wants to know.

"It's an impromptu party," Polly says with a laugh. "You two join us."

Erin turns to her friend and then back to us. "This is my friend, Abbi. Her daughter and Holly are besties, and it turns out that Abbi and I enjoy hanging out together, too, so it's a win-win."

"Sit, sit," Millie says, pointing to the chairs. "Summer's going to spill all the tea, or huck margaritas, about her and Chase."

"Oh, I need to hear this," Erin says as she sits. I wave Pete back over, and he takes everyone's drink orders. When he's gone, Erin leans her chin on her fist and gives me her undivided attention. "Go. Talk. Tell us everything."

I look at Abbi, the gorgeous, curvy blonde, and wince. "Are you sure you want to hear this?"

"Are you kidding me?" She nods, sending that blonde hair waving, and I need to ask her what kind of shampoo she uses. "Hell yes. I want to know everything. Don't leave out any of the details. Use the dirty words."

"I already like you," Polly decides, and Abbi smiles happily.

"Well, I don't know where to start. I guess, a little backstory, Chase asked me out a few years ago, but I declined."

"Why?" Millie asks, frowning. "I mean, he's my brother, but I feel confident in saying that he's easy on the eyes, and he's not an asshole."

"You're right. I just wasn't ready to date *anyone* yet. I had recently left a bad relationship, and I was building a business, and you know how it is. I didn't want to date."

"Fair enough," Abbi says with a nod.

"Well, when all the scary stuff happened with Erin earlier this year, I ended up working with Chase a little because the asshole used my shop to try to get to her." I offer Erin a sympathetic smile, and she simply shrugs. "And then, this summer, it seems that I've run into Chase a lot. Finally, he asked me out, and we went to dinner a couple of weeks ago."

"So far, I'm liking this," Polly says, but Pete arrives and takes our food orders, delivers the other girls' drinks, and then he's off again. "Okay, continue."

"Well, *then*, we didn't see each other for a couple of weeks because we were both busy with work and stuff, but yesterday, he surprised me with a really sweet evening at his place, and...we went to pound town."

Erin chokes on her drink, and Polly starts laughing so hard that she snorts.

"You *what*?" Millie asks, laughing.

"I had sex with him. You know...*pound town*."

"Oh, my God, that's hilarious," Abbi says, also giggling. "And how was it? Is pound town a fun place to visit with Chase?"

"You have no fucking idea."

"Hell to the *yes*," Polly says and offers me her hand in a high-five. "That's my girl. Okay, does he have a big penis? Because his uniform pants are kind of tight, and it looks like he probably does."

"Ew." Millie wrinkles her nose. "I don't want to know about my brother's dick."

"It's...yeah," I reply and sip my drink. "I was kind of scared that it wouldn't fit."

"You bitch," Polly says, shaking her head. "You lucky *bitch*."

"Must run in the family," Erin says with a satisfied grin, and I lean over the table to give *her* a high-five as

Millie makes gagging noises behind her hand, making me laugh.

"That's what I'm talking about." I smile over at Erin and then sit back, and Pete arrives with a heaping tray full of our meals.

"I need all the food in the land," Abbi announces. "I'm starving."

"Me, too. Okay, enough about me being the newest citizen of pound town," I say as I pop a chip into my mouth. "What do you do, Abbi? I know I've seen you around town, but I don't think you've been here long."

"Just a few months," she says with a nod. "I'm a single mom, and we came here not long after the first of the year. I own a housekeeping business."

"Hey, that's cool," Millie says. "Do you do rentals or businesses or what?"

"A little of everything, but I admit, the short-term rentals have been *insane* this summer. I had to hire four new girls and one husband/wife team."

I blink over at her. "So, you're not a one-woman show."

"No, ma'am. Bitterroot Valley Housekeeping Services at your service." She winks at me. "I've been in the cleaning business for a *long* time. My mom did it, and I'd help her out. I couldn't afford college, and honestly, I like to clean. So, why not do what you like?"

"Hear, hear." I hold my glass up in cheers. "I couldn't agree more, and that's how I ended up with a flower shop. Welcome to town, Abbi."

"Thank you. I think Erin and I also bonded because we're both new to town, but she and I agree that everyone here has been super kind and welcoming. Especially to Daisy, and that means a lot. I want my girl to thrive here."

"She's the *cutest*," Erin says. "Well, maybe she and Holly are equally as cute."

"I can agree with that," Abbi says.

"I also have something to talk about," Millie announces, and then takes a big bite of her cheeseburger. "And it's kind of a big deal."

"I love this night," Polly says and grins. "We need to do this all the damn time."

"I'm in," Erin says. "My cousins and I used to do this all the time, and it's really good for the soul. It's the one thing I miss the most about being in Seattle, so let's plan on it. Now, Millie, tell us. What's going on?"

"I'm buying Bitterroot Valley Coffee Co."

We're all stunned speechless for about three seconds, and then we're hooting and clapping, and I lean over to hug her tightly.

"Congratulations." I pat her back and then gesture for Pete to bring us another round. "We're celebrating, Pete."

"I've got you," he says with a wink before hurrying off to the bar.

"How did this happen?" Erin wants to know. "Marion hasn't said anything to me."

"We don't want to announce it officially until it's all done," Millie says, and frowns over at Erin. "And I'm sorry for holding out on you. You're my best friend."

"It's fine." Erin waves that off. "Is Marion leaving?"

"No, she's starting a catering company and doesn't want to handle both businesses, and, since I've been there for so long, she offered it to me first. I had a meeting with Ryan, and he's going to front me the money, and my next meeting was going to be with you, Erin, because I'm going to need a bookkeeper. But we're here now, and I couldn't keep my mouth shut anymore."

"Of *course,* I'll help you," Erin says and shimmies in her seat. "Oh, this is so fun."

"Look at us," Polly says, her gaze moving over all of us. "A table full of badass business owners."

Erin frowns at that. "I love the sentiment, but I don't own a business."

"Bullshit," Millie says before I can. "You do book-keeping, you're building that gorgeous event space at the ranch *you're* in charge of, *and* you're marrying my brother, which makes you the new co-owner of the ranch. You're one badass business owner, Erin Montgomery."

Erin blinks at her, and then she smiles and does another shimmy in her seat. "Holy fucking shit, you're right. I *own* shit. Damn, the taxes are going to be a pain in the ass."

"You're not wrong," I reply with a grin, and Millie scowls.

"I don't want to deal with taxes," Millie grumbles. "That's why I need you, Erin."

"I'll help," Erin promises. "Okay, you guys, we need

to keep doing this. And we should start a group for other women in business, to help each other."

"Oh, I like that," Polly says, nodding. "That has a lot of promise. I can't tell you how many times I wish I'd been able to ask questions from other business owners."

"I mean, you can call *me*," I remind her.

"Of course, but wouldn't it be fun to be able to network? There are so many amazing businesses in this town, and we could all grow so much by learning from each other. I'm all about lifting my friends up. Let's do this. We need a name."

"Will we need a handshake, too?" I ask, making the others laugh.

"What about *We're the Shit*," Millie suggests.

"Here she goes," Erin says, rolling her eyes. "She tried to help me with my social media handle. I didn't use her suggestions."

"I know," Millie continues, rubbing her hands together. "*Girl Gang*."

"That feels a little aggressive," I reply, and then we all goggle when Pete comes out carrying another huge tray full of every dessert on their menu. "Holy shit, Pete."

"You're celebrating," he says simply. "You need some dessert. We have a huckleberry cheesecake, chocolate cake, fried ice cream, apple pie, strawberry shortcake, and my personal favorite, salted caramel sundae."

"I think I just died and went to heaven," Abbi mutters as we all eyeball the treats before us.

"Dig in, ladies."

"I'm in love with Pete," Millie decides as the waiter walks away. "I'm going to marry him."

"He's already married," Polly reminds her and takes a bite of the apple pie, dissolving into a puddle of happiness. "Damn it, because I'd marry him, too."

"Back to names," I remind the table.

"*She Works Hard for the Money*," Millie suggests, and I shake my head at her. "What? You guys are no fun. Oh, how about—"

"I have it," Polly announces, holding her hand up before Millie can continue. "*Iconic Women's Collective.*"

"Now *that*," Abbi says, pointing her fork at Polly, "is one hell of a good name."

With all of us in agreement, we make it official by clinking our glasses together and smiling with excitement.

"This is the *best*." I smile at the others. "And I absolutely can*not* drive home tonight."

"I don't think any of us should," Erin says and reaches for her phone, tapping the screen. "Hey, babe. I need a ride home. Great, we're dropping Abbi off, too." She holds the phone against her shoulder and looks at us. "Want a ride, ladies?"

"I'll take one," Millie says.

"Me, too," Polly echoes.

"Not me." I reach for my own phone. "I've got a ride."

Erin fills Remington in on the rest of their plans while I dial Chase's number.

"Hey, Blondie." I can hear the smile in his voice, and it makes me melt. "It's loud where you are."

"I had an impromptu girls' night at The Wolf Den, and I've had some liquor. Are you up for giving me a ride?"

"Loaded question," Polly says, making us laugh.

"I can come get you. Does anyone else need a lift?"

"Nope, Rem's coming to get the others. I'd rather see *you*."

"I won't complain about that. Be there soon."

We pay our tab and make our way out into the warm summer evening.

"It's a nice night," I say, taking a deep breath. "I could probably walk home, but then I wouldn't get to see Chase, and that would be sad."

The door opens, and Evan comes strolling out. I didn't even see him in there.

"Ladies," he says with a charming smile and a nod. "Does anyone need a ride home?"

"Nah, we've got it covered," Millie says. "Thanks, though."

"You sure?" he asks me, frowning with concern.

"I'm great, thanks." Just then, Chase pulls in, and I hurry over to his truck. He climbs out and catches me up in a big hug, plants a kiss right on me, here in front of *everyone*, and then smiles down at me.

"You go, girl," Polly calls out. "Go get yourself some. Wrap it before you tap it."

"You guys *have* had some drinks," Chase says with a laugh as he escorts me around to the passenger side.

I toss a grin over my shoulder at the others, give them a thumbs-up, and then climb into the truck.

"I'm not really drunk," I inform him and reach for his hand. "But I shouldn't drive. Besides, I wanted to see you. How was the rest of your day?"

"It's brightened up considerably in the past fifteen minutes." He kisses the back of my hand. "Come on, sugar, let's go home."

CHAPTER TEN
CHASE

"Do we need to get Lily from anywhere?" I ask as we pull away from the bar.

"No, she's with Aunt Paula through the weekend," Summer replies and settles into the seat of the truck sleepily. "I have three weddings, and I won't have much time for her, so she's at the cottage."

"You know, I could take her sometimes, too. She's not a problem."

She squeezes my hand. "Thank you. She'd probably like that a lot. So, your place or mine?"

I have no intention of dropping her off and leaving her alone for the night, so I'm happy to see that we're on the same page there.

"As long as I'm with you, and I have you naked and writhing, I'm happy to go wherever you want."

"That's so *sweet*." I glance over and see her grinning at me. "Especially the naked part. Well, I will have to be up and out early tomorrow, so do you mind if we go to my place?"

"Your place it is."

The truth is, I'm glad she called. I had just gotten home, showered, and changed, and I was brooding because the day had gone off the rails from the start, and I didn't get to see Summer this evening.

And just as I'd opened my fridge for a beer, she'd called, as if I'd conjured her out of my thoughts.

"Did your day get any better at work?" she asks as I pull into her driveway.

"It calmed down, yeah. I'm just glad I didn't lose the whole night with you."

"It worked out," she agrees. "Come on, let's go in, and I'll tell you all about my girls' night."

But, once inside, I don't let her settle in so we can have a nice chat. Not yet, anyway. I turn her and pin her against the back of the door, cup that gorgeous face in my hands, and sink into her, running my lips over hers, nibbling at the corner of her delectable little mouth.

She moans, and my dick strains against my jeans. She pushes her hand into my hair, and I reach down to unfasten her pants.

I'm a man possessed, with only one mission in mind: get inside of her.

I plant my hands on her ass and easily lift her against me and carry her to her bedroom, and she chuckles against my lips.

"I don't think any of this is funny," I whisper, and she grins wider.

"It's not," she says. "But the blinds are open, and I'm not an exhibitionist, so it made me giggle."

Setting her on her feet, I cross to the window and close the blinds, and when I turn around, my mouth goes fucking dry.

She's already stripped out of her shirt and bra, and she's pushing her jeans down her hips, swaying side to side as the denim slides down those spectacular legs, her pink panties along for the ride.

"You promised me naked," she reminds me with hot blue eyes. "So, let's get naked."

With three strides, I cross back to her, but she presses her hand against my chest, stopping me.

"I want to see you."

With a grin, I gently take that hand in mine and lift it to my lips, nibbling on her fingertips.

"You're going to see me, sugar. Trust me on that. But first..." I lift her onto the bed, hook my hands behind her knees, and drag her to the side of the mattress, before falling to my knees beside it and opening her wide. "I have something to do."

"Oh, Jesus," she moans as I drag my finger down her slick entrance.

"Look at that," I murmur lazily. "All wet and hot and ready for me."

"I'm perma-wet," she informs me. "I need to start packing extra panties with me whenever I go somewhere because holy shit, Chase, you turn me *on*."

Satisfied pride fills my chest, and I can't resist lowering my face to her, lapping up that glistening wetness. I love how pink and swollen she is, and I haven't even really begun.

I fuck her with my tongue, and then I move up to her clit and push my finger inside of her, and her back arches on the bed as she fists the bedsheets, writhing as an orgasm consumes her.

One down, several to go.

I tug my shirt over my head and discard it, then drop my jeans and nudge Summer back further on the bed. Gripping onto her ankles, I pull her legs straight up into the air and hug them to my chest as I slip right inside of her, unable to go slow or hold back from pounding into her, reveling at how perfectly her pussy grips me like a fucking fist.

Her arms are over her head, pushing against the headboard, and those amazing eyes practically glow with primal lust.

"Thought of this all fucking day." My voice is a rough growl. "Tell me you thought of me."

"All." She licks her lips. "Fucking day. Jesus, Chase, where did you learn that move? You know what? I don't wanna know."

I laugh and spread those legs now so I can lean down and cover her mouth with my own as my dick slides in and out of her. Her nails rake down my back, those legs hitch up higher on my hips, and she plants her lips against my neck, just below my ear.

"So good," she whispers. "God, Chase, it's so goddamn good."

I moan as she bites my shoulder.

"Go over again." Now that I've given her orgasms, I can't get enough of it. That *anyone* would leave her wanting is beyond me. I want her to do nothing *but* come every time I get my hands on her. "Come for me, baby."

Her eyes glass over, and she bites her lip, and, with her eyes on mine, I feel her climax move through her, and it pulls me with her.

"So…" I pass Summer a bottle of water and climb into the bed, sitting next to her. "You had fun with your friends tonight?"

"I can honestly say that tonight was one of the best nights of my life." She stretches her legs out and sips her water. "We had the *best* time, Chase. We laughed so hard, and we ate good food, and Pete spoiled us with complimentary desserts because I told him that we were celebrating."

"What were you celebrating?" I brush her blonde hair behind her ear.

"Millie's buying the coffee shop. Did you know?"

I smile, stupidly proud of my baby sister. "Yeah, she told me. Wanted my advice about it. I think it's a great idea."

"It's an *amazing* idea, and she's so relieved that Ryan agreed to help her. I love that your family is so tight and that you help each other out."

Her phone rings, and she scowls and checks the display.

"Speaking of families, why in the hell is my mom calling me so late on a Thursday night?" She shakes her head, declines the call, and sets the phone aside.

"You can answer it. It might be important."

"No." She shakes her head and sips her water. "We don't have that kind of relationship. I'd be the last person she'd call in an emergency. Anyway, as you can see, I don't have the kind of family you do, so it's refreshing to see it. And Millie is just over the moon. Nervous, sure, but also really proud of herself and excited. And it occurred to us that all five of us sitting there are businesswomen. We now all own businesses."

"Because you're all badasses."

She grins and leans over to kiss me. "We sure are. And, we decided to start a...well, a club, I guess, for all women business owners in town. It's a great way to network and lift each other up. We're calling it the *Iconic Women's Collective*."

"That's pretty badass, too."

"I know. We got pretty tipsy by the end, so we'll come up with how we want to execute this later, but it felt so good to be with other women close to my age, who own businesses and thrive doing it, you know? Take Abbi, for example. She just moved here this year, and she started her own cleaning company. She has five employees. Or is it six? Anyway, she's kicking ass in her business. I'm really proud of all of us."

"You should be." This side of Summer, the passionate businesswoman, is almost as sexy as the one who was calling my name earlier.

Almost.

"It started out as just Polly and me catching up, and then the others arrived, and it snowballed into a fun evening. And *then*"—she reaches for my hand, lifts it to her lips—"I still got to see you, and that was the delicious icing on an already tasty cake."

"I'm glad you had a good day, sugar." I trace her finger with mine. "I arrested Mrs. Wilburn today."

Summer's eyes widen, and she gasps. "*What*? Why?"

I tell her the story of the old woman going so slowly and pulling her over, then her fleeing the scene, and ignoring me all the way to the beauty shop, before finally resisting arrest and biting my leg.

"Holy shit, Chase! Did she break the skin?"

"No, but it freaking hurt. I almost tazed her, but it would have killed the old bat."

Summer is laughing now, covering her mouth as she laughs so hard that tears form.

"How long will she be in jail?" she finally asks.

"Her kids busted her out on a three-hundred-dollar bond, but I have a feeling the judge will revoke her license. She shouldn't be driving."

Summer takes a deep breath to help calm the laughter and then wipes the tears away. "Man, I'm sure that's frustrating for her. But it sounds like she shouldn't be driving anymore."

"No." I grin down at her. "She shouldn't. I suppose you're slammed this weekend. You mentioned you have some weddings?"

"Three," she confirms. "We'll be running all over

town, starting early tomorrow. What do you have going on this weekend? Are you working?"

"No, actually, I have the weekend off. The surveyor had a cancellation, and he's coming out to the property tomorrow to look at my place by the lake."

"That's *awesome*." Her eyes light up.

"Then I was informed that we're having a bachelor party for Remington."

Her eyebrow wings up. "With strippers?"

I smirk and swipe my thumb under her eye where the cut from last night is almost completely gone. "No. Rem didn't want one, but Brady insisted that we have to do *something*, so all of us brothers and our dad are going camping for one night on the ranch. The hands are coming, too, and I think Brooks and a few other friends are coming along."

"That's going to be so fun," she says and leans her cheek on my shoulder. "Chase?"

"Yes, sugar."

"I don't ever want you to take me camping."

I tip her chin up so I can look into her eyes. They're full of humor. "And why is that?"

"Because it's *camping*. I'll hike, I'll go on picnics, I'll go out on a boat, canoe, paddleboard, and I'll fish. But I will not, under any circumstances, sleep outside."

"What if it's in a tent? Or a camper?"

"Nope. Absolutely not."

"So noted. No camping."

"THANKS, MARK." I shake the other man's hand. He's already packed up his equipment and helped me rope off where the house and shop are going to sit, and it made things really real for me.

I can't wait to get started.

"My pleasure, Chase. If you need anything else, just call me. I'll work you in."

I nod after him, and he climbs into his truck, starts the engine, and pulls away from the property.

Before he's out of sight, I see another truck coming this way, and Ryan waves at Mark as they pass each other.

It looks like all three of my brothers, along with my dad, are here.

"Are you about ready for this party?" Brady wants to know as he hops out, and then he notices the rope. "Well, look at that."

I watch my dad, as the brothers walk to the ropes, taking it all in. And Dad's eyes find mine.

"I hope this is okay with you," I say as he joins me, and we stand shoulder-to-shoulder, watching the others.

"Why wouldn't it be?" he asks. "Just look at that view. Why don't you tell me what you're thinking?"

I grin at him and go over my plans, the way I did with Remington just a couple of weeks ago.

And when I've finished, he's nodding, and we walk over to where the others are standing.

"That shop's going to be a honey," Ryan says with a grin. "You need it."

"I'm building that first," I agree. "I'm doing as much as I can by myself, so the whole project will take me a while."

"Why don't you just let me make some calls?" Ryan offers. "I can have this built for you by next summer, at the latest. My gift to you, man."

I shake my head. Leave it to my brother, the richest man in the state, to want to swoop in and handle things.

"I appreciate the offer more than you know, but I actually *want* to build it myself. It'll be an adventure. In the meantime, I'm not exactly homeless."

"If you change your mind, the offer stands," he replies. "Man, that view."

"I know." The five of us stand, hands in pockets, looking out over the small lake. "It's fucking awesome."

"Let's go." Remington claps me on the shoulder. "The others are already at the barn, loading up to head out."

"Let's go."

THERE ARE MORE people here than I expected there to be.

I didn't realize that Erin's dad, Will Montgomery, already flew out to help this week leading up to the wedding. Including Will, we have all the men in our family, the hands, Brooks and all three of his brothers, and a few other guys from town.

It doesn't surprise me. Rem is well-liked in our community, and I know that everyone loves seeing him happy with Erin, especially since his first wife passed away when Holly was born. He hasn't had it easy, but things sure have turned around for him.

He deserves every minute of happiness, and Erin makes him damn happy.

We're deep into the property, in a clearing that's surrounded by trees. We've come out here to camp since I was a kid. There's a circle of rocks and dirt that make up the campfire, and there are stumps placed around for us all to sit on. Some of us brought folding camping chairs. Tents are scattered further out, already set up and ready for later.

We have a table off to the side that's loaded down with coolers full of food and drinks.

No one will leave here hungry.

I'm staring into the fire, listening to Brady tell the group a story about Remington when Rem was in his early 20s and got caught with his hands down Mary Beth Anderson's pants in the back seat of his car.

Ryan passes me a fresh beer and sits next to me.

"I don't have any tales to tell," I inform my brother, who just smiles.

"Well, we *do*, but we'll keep them to ourselves." He clinks the neck of his bottle against mine, taking a swig. "Jake starts at my place Monday morning."

I lift an eyebrow and nod, still staring into the flames. "Good. He's got a way with horses, and I know he'll handle yours with care."

"He'd better. When did his parents die?"

"Last year." Grimly, I pull my hand down my face. "Fucking mess of a car accident, just outside of town. It was icy, and his dad was going too fast. I don't know why, or what he thought he was late for. Anyway, they skidded into a tree, and both died on impact."

"Jake wasn't with them?"

"He was at school," I reply, remembering that day clearly. I worked the scene all fucking day in below-zero temps.

"He doesn't have any other family?"

"None that we've found. He's in a foster placement."

Ryan nods slowly and sips his beer. "Okay, well, we'll see how this goes, then. The kid has a hell of an attitude on him."

"Yeah, well, I think I would, too, if I were in his shoes. Thanks for taking him on, man. He's not a bad kid; he's just been dealt a shitty hand."

Ryan nods again, and then there's loud laughter, and we look over in time to see Will stand, holding his hands up like he's holding an imaginary football and he's going to make a pass.

"I *knew* he was open," Will says loudly. "And I was going to land that pass, but suddenly, a fucking elephant plowed me down, and I saw stars."

"You lost me fifty bucks on that game," someone yells out, and Will laughs. "Yeah, well, I'm sure you're not alone there."

"Is it fucking crazy that Rem's father-in-law is a goddamn Hall of Fame football player?" Ryan asks me.

"A little bit. But it's also fucking crazy that you've managed to make a billion dollars before you're thirty-five."

"I'm telling you, let me help you with your investments, and I'll make you a rich man."

"I don't need to be rich." I shrug, and Ryan snorts.

"Come on, man."

"I don't. I do just fine."

"If you change your mind..."

"I'll let you know. Yeah, I get it. I'm not trying to be an asshole when I turn you down. I love you, and I'm damn proud of what you've built. I just don't need the same things."

He nods, thinking it over. "Yeah, I get it. I don't think you're trying to be an ass, Chase. It's not really about the money for me."

I lift my eyebrow at him and take a sip of my beer.

"Okay, the money is part of it. I *like* the wealth. I also give a shit ton of money away."

"I know." Ryan donates more money than any of us will ever know.

"It's the game of it. The puzzle. It's exhilarating, and I do really well at it. I know it's a far cry from this life here on the ranch, but that doesn't mean that it was wrong of me to go after it."

I glance over at Remington, who's chatting with Brooks and smiling.

"Rem doesn't think it was wrong."

"Yeah, he does." Ryan swallows the last of his beer and shakes his head. "I worked fucking hard to make a name for myself in the world of business, and now that I have, I can be *here* in Bitterroot Valley. I can work from home, and I do, sometimes eighteen hours a day."

"Technology is a beautiful thing."

"You said it."

"But are you happy here, Ry?"

"Yeah. I am." He looks over at me, his gaze serious. "Happier than anywhere else in the world, and I've been just about everywhere."

"Then that's all that matters." I slap him on the shoulder and stand. "Now, let's go tell some of our stories after all and embarrass the fuck out of Rem."

Ryan smiles slyly. "Fuck yeah, let's do it."

———

"I CAN STILL OUTSHOOT YOU," Remington says with a satisfied grin as we both take off our ear and eye protection. All the guys stayed out on the ranch today to hike, have target practice, or just hang, taking in the fresh air.

"Maybe I'm drunk." I smirk at him.

"You haven't had a drink all day," he reminds me.

"Maybe I let you win since it's your party."

"Whatever helps you sleep at night." Rem pats me on the shoulder as we walk away, making room for some of the others to take their turn shooting their rifles at the targets.

"Come on, little brother," Brooks says to his brother, Beckett. "I'll show you how it's done."

"Whatever, old man."

Rem and I grin at each other and wander over to the food table, where we both grab a bottle of water out of the ice.

"It's nice to be able to trust the people we invite out here," Rem says with a contented sigh. "Everyone knows and understands that this is an active shooting range, and they respect it. I don't have to worry about anyone being stupid or showboating and getting anyone hurt or killed."

"If it were any other way, we wouldn't have offered this up to everyone today," I reply with a nod, and we watch silently as both Brooks and Beckett shoot their rifles at the targets. Their family has also been around for a long while, although they're still considered *move-ins* because they've only lived in the valley for roughly thirty years or so. Their family owns the Double B Ranch.

"What's Summer up to this weekend?" Rem asks.

"Working. She has weddings back-to-back, pretty much through the middle of September."

He nods thoughtfully. "Where do you think that'll go?"

I eye him and sip my water. "I think she'll continue designing flowers for weddings, I suppose."

Rem rolls his eyes. "You're a smartass. Come on, I'm your big brother. You're supposed to talk to me about this stuff."

"I'm... I could see myself falling for her. She's fucking amazing, and I've been attracted to her for years. The chemistry is crazy. She's driven and smart."

"You like her."

I eye him again and nod. "Yeah, I *like* her. A lot."

"Good place to start," he says, clapping me on the

back. "I think she's great. She's been a good friend to Erin and Millie."

"I suspect she's a good friend to everyone."

"Except the part where she talked my soon-to-be wife into hiring Charlie Lexington."

"Dude, get over yourself. Charlie's the best there is, and you want Erin to have the best."

"But why does she have to be a *Lexington*?"

I laugh and shake my head. "Because the universe has a sense of humor, that's why. I'm going to take the horse and go for a ride. I'll probably be out of cell range for a while."

"Want me to go with you?"

"You can't bail on your party."

He glances around, shrugging again. "Half the guys are off doing other things anyway. I think Brady took a few guys fishing. I'm surprised that you didn't want in on that."

"I plan to go next week." And take a certain someone with me. "Come on, let's go."

"Where are you going?" Ryan calls out.

"Just for a ride," Rem replies. "Wanna join us?"

"Hell yes."

IT'S LATE when I decide to leave the ranch and head home. We spent all weekend on the land, enjoying time with friends, and it was a good time. I have no complaints at all.

But I miss Summer, and I plan to call her as soon as I get home.

First, I stop at the police station real quick to grab my duty belt and clean my weapon before my shift tomorrow.

I've just walked inside when Sergeant Prescott waves me over.

"How's Summer?" he asks.

"As far as I know, she's fine. Why do you ask?"

He narrows his eyes. "She didn't call you?"

My gut tightens, and the hair on the back of my neck stands up. "Why would she need to call me, Sarg?"

"She had an incident last night," he begins.

"Is she in the hospital?"

"No, no. Nothing like that—"

Before he can say more, I take off and run back to my truck, putting it in gear and racing toward Summer's house before I even have the door closed.

But when I get there, her house is locked up tight, and she doesn't answer. I call her, but it goes to voicemail.

"Summer, it's me. I just spoke to my sergeant, and he said something happened last night. I need you to answer the phone, sugar."

Running back to the truck, I toss the phone onto the seat and drive over to my own place, trying to figure out how to get a hold of her.

I can call her aunt. She'll know where she is.

But when I get home, I see Summer's car parked in

my driveway, and for just a moment, my heart calms in relief.

She's safe.

That's all that matters.

But then I run to the front door, and when I find it locked, I key in the code and push the door open. Lily lifts her head from where she's sleeping in a little dog bed and then pads over to greet me.

"Hey, baby. Where's your mama? Summer!" I rush back to the kitchen, but I don't see her, so I take the stairs two at a time.

I can see that she slept in my bed last night because the covers are messy on her side, and when I push into the bathroom, I find her in the bathtub, with head-phones on. Her eyes are closed, and she's bopping her head back and forth in time with the music in her ears.

"Summer."

Obviously, she has the volume up, and I'm going to startle her, but I need to know what in the ever-loving *fuck* is going on.

"Summer!"

She jumps, gasps, and slams her hand over her mouth, those baby blues wide, and then sighs.

"You *scared me!*"

She takes off the headphones and sets them on the floor beside the tub.

"What the hell is going on, Summer?"

"First of all, please let me get out of this bath, and I will tell you everything."

"Are you okay?"

Her eyes soften. "Yes. I'm okay. And I'm sorry I came here without asking you, I just—"

"Get dressed." I turn to leave the room. "We'll talk downstairs."

Lily's waiting in the bedroom, sitting on the middle of the bed, watching with interest.

"Come on, girl."

She follows me down the stairs, and it's not even five minutes later when I hear Summer coming down the steps. She's in a white tank top, *no bra*, and a pair of pink sweat shorts. Her golden hair is piled on top of her head, and her face is clean of makeup.

I can't resist, I rush to her and pull her into my arms, holding on tight, and she clings to me almost desperately.

"Talk to me, babe."

"Okay." She pulls away and curls up on the end of the sofa, pulling those long legs up under her. "I worked late last night. Saturdays are always busy, you know? But I wanted Lily with me because I missed her, so on my way home, I stopped and picked her up from Aunt Paula. Then I took her home. At first, everything was normal at the house."

"At first?"

"Yeah." She swallows hard and pulls Lily into her lap and kisses the dog's head. "I got settled, took off my shoes, put some water on to boil for tea—you know...the usual stuff. Lily had to go outside, so I took her out in the yard, and she did her business, but when I turned to go back in—"

She pauses, swallows again, and tears spring to her eyes, so I reach over and take her hand in mine.

"Hey, I'm right here."

"Spray paint," she manages. "Someone spray-painted the back of my house. *Fucking Whore* was written all over it."

"What in the actual *fuck?*"

"The cameras didn't alert me on the app, so the police had me bring up the footage last night, and all that's there is a hand right before he painted over the lens."

"Jesus Christ." My heart is thudding, my mind racing. She was alone all night after that.

"Why didn't you call me?"

"Because you were out with the others, and I wanted you to have *fun*—"

"Whoa." I pull back and scowl at her. "You call me, no matter what, no matter where the fuck I am, Summer. Even if you just want to say hello, but *absolutely* when something like *this* happens."

"I was safe," she retorts. "I didn't want to stay at home, and the first place I thought to come was here, so I loaded Lily up, and we came over. You gave me the code to the door, and I know I should have asked, but—"

"You're always welcome here, and I'm *glad* that this is where you came, but damn it, you should have called me. My guys should have called me. For fuck's sake, I spent all day at the ranch, just dicking around, when I should have been here with you."

"No." She shakes her head and squeezes my hand. "I

wasn't here most of the day. I had another wedding to see to, and I took Lily with me. There was nothing to do, Chase."

"Nothing except make sure that you're okay. Be here for you. Investigate who decided to vandalize your home."

"The police are working on that," she says with a sigh. "And I'll be honest, I'm starting to think that it isn't just kids. It's not random."

"It's not random," I agree with her, and now I move to the couch and put both Summer and the dog in *my* lap. "Who have you pissed off, Blondie?"

"No one that I'm aware of." She sighs against me. "You're sure you're not mad that I invaded your house?"

"I gave you the code so you'd use it." I kiss her head and breathe her in. "I think, until we get this all figured out, you should just plan on staying here."

Her head comes up at that, and she stares up at me with grateful blue eyes. "I was kind of hoping you'd say that."

CHAPTER ELEVEN
SUMMER

God, it feels so *good* to be in his arms. I've been a nervous wreck for the last twenty-four hours. I'd been in the bath, trying to soothe my nerves with hot water and music, when he came in and scared the bejesus out of me.

"So much for being an independent woman," I mutter and sigh when he presses his lips to my forehead. I freaking *love it* when he does that.

"You *are* an independent woman, but when something like that happens, you *need* to call me. I was scared shitless when I went to the station and was hit with that bomb, and I didn't know if you were safe or what even happened."

"I'm sorry." I look up at him, and Lily climbs out of our laps to curl up on the other side of the couch. "You're right, that wasn't fair. I thought for sure you'd come here first, and I'd fill you in. It wasn't my intention to scare you."

"Okay." He takes a long, deep breath, kisses my head again, and then sets me aside so we can face each other and talk. "Let's think about this. I'm going to ask you again, who have you recently pissed off?"

I bite my lip and frown, thinking it over. "Honestly, I can't think of *anyone*. There haven't been any unhappy customers. I don't have any beef with any of the other shop owners in town. No arguments or hard feelings of any kind, Chase."

He sighs and narrows his eyes, staring over my shoulder as he thinks about it. "You don't think it could be your ex? The one you ghosted?"

"No. Definitely not. He moved on before he realized I'd left, and he's pursuing his own career in Helena. Trust me, he doesn't think about me. I was never that important to him."

And thinking about that doesn't even hurt my feelings. Because he wasn't very important to me, either.

"Someone pissed off at your parents?"

I frown, but I don't immediately deny it. "I don't know. I wouldn't think so. My dad's been retired for a couple of years now, so he doesn't have any influence as far as laws and such go. He kind of flies under the radar, mostly working as a consultant. Besides, most people didn't even realize that he *had* a daughter because I didn't like being in the spotlight with them. I pretty much just showed up when I couldn't get out of it."

"I'm not writing that off," he replies and reaches out to tuck my hair behind my ear. "You haven't received any correspondence from anyone that felt weird? Emails, messages on social media, random calls or texts?"

"No, nothing. Not even at the shop. Which is why I keep circling back around to it being kids or something random. Maybe it's some kids who started out choosing my house randomly, but then decided to continue targeting me for the fun of it."

Chase narrows his eyes at that thought and nods slowly. "That could be the case. I'll ask around tomorrow. What's your schedule like this week?"

"I'm gearing up for your brother's wedding. I still have to fulfill my weekly commitment to the resort—I do all of their flowers every week—but other than that, it's all hands on deck for the Wild wedding. I'm not even taking any more orders for deliveries and such." I grin at him, so freaking happy to see him, and take his hand, linking our fingers. "What about you?"

"I'm working the next three days, and then I'm off until the following Tuesday, so I can help out at the ranch. Looks like I'm one of the hands that's on deck."

I laugh and then sigh with contentment now that he's with me and I can enjoy a quiet moment with him. "I think this week is going to *fly* by."

I'M NOT WRONG. The week flies by, and now my team is gathered at Paula's Poseys, all bleary-eyed and yawning, but they've made it on time.

"We're all here," Ida says, blinking sleepily. I asked

my whole staff to arrive at the flower shop at six this morning because it's finally the weekend of the Wild wedding, and that's our only focus for the next two days.

"I appreciate you all coming in so early," I reply, passing out coffees from Bitterroot Valley Coffee Co. "I have breakfast sandwiches here, along with some donuts, because we might need a little bonus sugar energy today. Let's run down the plan."

As we all sip coffee, I pull up the notes on my iPad.

"Okay, all the bouquets for both today and tomorrow are done. Centerpieces, boutonnieres, petals, all ready. I also have all the flowers in the cooler for the arbor tomorrow."

"That arbor is going to *rock*," Sharla says around a bite of breakfast sandwich.

I grin at her and take a bite of my own. "I know. I rented a van for the weekend so we don't have to drive back and forth from the ranch as much. Today is the rehearsal dinner. We have ten centerpieces, a bouquet for the bar, and all the vines to hang around the edges of the tent. Erin wants it to look like we're walking into a faerie garden."

"You know," Vickie says with a frown, "I was originally under the impression that this was going to be a small-ish family wedding out at the ranch."

"There's nothing small about those two families," I remind her. "And they're wealthy. They want *beautiful*, and that's what it'll be. I want you all to stay hydrated today. It's going to be hot, so be sure to drink lots of water. And I have snacks in the van, as well. I'll keep you fed and watered because it's going to be a long, hard day, and then we're going to tear it all down tonight after the party and start from scratch again tomorrow."

"I might venture to say," Ida says, "that this could be the poshest wedding to ever be held in this town."

"And aren't we lucky that it's *our* flower shop they hired?" I wink at the older woman, who grins back at me. "We can do this, you guys. I've closed the shop down through Sunday, so all hands are on deck with me out at the ranch."

"Of course, we have this," Sharla agrees. "Are we going to wake everyone up when we get there?"

"Probably not. They know we're coming early. I want to see how the setup actually works out, with the tents and tables and everything. Charlie Lexington should be out there as we speak, ready to greet vendors and make sure everything runs smoothly. We're going to make sure that she has no need to even think about our side of things."

"How are we going to keep the flowers from wilting?" Vickie wants to know. "If we set up too early, they'll die in the heat."

"We're starting with the vines," I inform her. "That'll take us half the day, and they're heartier. Then we'll work on the more delicate flowers. We'll bring the van back here to load up the flowers mid-day."

"I like it," Ida says, nodding.

"Now, before anything else, I want to remind us all that we signed contracts that include nondisclosure agreements earlier this week, and it's imperative that we remember ourselves at all times. No photos of the guests, no asking for autographs, no posting to social media. I have permission to take photos of our work when we're finished, but that's it. No selfies with Erin's family."

"We understand," Vickie says with a nod. "And we won't do anything to embarrass you."

"Or get me sued," I remind her. "If you breach those contracts, you'll be fired on the spot. I have to be a hardass on this one, guys. My business is on the line."

"We've got your back," Ida agrees, nodding.

"Let's do this."

I load up the last of the sandwiches and donuts because I know we'll need the fuel later, and we head out to the vehicles. Sharla gets into the van with me, and the others pile into Ida's car, and we're off, headed out of town to the ranch.

"I've never seen the ranch," Sharla says. She's excited, barely able to sit still in her seat. "I've heard it's gorgeous, and of course, I've seen the photos that Millie posts on social media. I admit, I'm *so* excited to get a glimpse of some of Erin's famous family."

I spare her a glance. "Sharla, like I said at the shop, I need you to be professional this weekend. I get that the people at this wedding are celebrities, but we have a job to do, and I want to make sure that Erin and Remington are comfortable."

"I won't embarrass you," Sharla promises me. "I won't ask for autographs or photos or *anything*."

"Good, because you know what's on the line if you

do." Sharla's the youngest of us, and I know that she's already starstruck, and we haven't even seen anyone yet.

"I know," she says. "I'll be a wallflower and get my work done, but man, it's so *cool*."

"I can agree with you there. It *is* cool. It'll be something we never forget, that's for sure."

As I pull in ahead of Ida, there are two armed security officers at the gates of the Wild River Ranch.

"Hi, I'm Summer Quinn, the florist. This is my employee, Sharla, and I have three more in the vehicle behind me."

The man checks his list and nods. "Thank you. Just a reminder, there is to be no photographing the guests today."

"I understand. I did have it added to my contract that I can take photos of the flower arrangements for my website."

"I see that here. That's not a problem."

"Thank you."

He nods and gestures to someone else, and then the gate opens, and we drive through.

"He was sexy," Sharla says, dancing in her seat. "And I'm glad he's not mad at *me* because, with those muscles, he looks like he could do some damage."

"I think that's the point."

I drive us past the farmhouse and barn, out to the field where the event center will be. There's already a massive tent in place, with another, smaller tent to the side. A row of mobile toilets and wash stations sits about twenty yards away behind a temporary, discreet wood fence.

"Wow," Sharla whispers as I come to a stop. She's staring up at the mountains. "Holy shit, Summer."

"I know. It's so freaking beautiful."

The sun is rising over the peaks before us, sending a soft, golden glow over everything, and it's enough to steal your breath away.

"New life goal unlocked," she whispers.

"What's that?"

"To get married out here someday."

"That's a damn good goal to have. Come on, let's get going."

Just after we arrive, other vendors come pouring in behind us. Sound equipment, tables, chairs, food and drinks, and a team of five photographers.

"Okay, since the tent is up, let's start with the vine borders around it, just like I sketched out."

"We've got it," Ida says with a nod, and we get to work, all of us with specific tasks that I outlined well before today.

I enjoy the hive of activity bustling around us, and as the morning progresses, more and more bodies appear, as if from thin air. The air practically hums with energy and excitement, all of us excited to be pulling together to make something magical.

Before long, I realize that it's not just vendors roaming around, but family members, as well.

"This is Summer, my extraordinary florist and friend," Erin says, gesturing to me. I'm embarrassed as hell because I'm sweaty, with my hair pulled up, no makeup, and in just a T-shirt with my logo and denim shorts, but I smile. "Summer, this is my mom, Megan, and some of my aunts, Alecia, Natalie, Nic, and Stacy."

"Hello." I nod to them all. Jesus, every single one of them is absolutely gorgeous. "I take it everyone arrived safely, then?"

"We did, the entire brood," Natalie confirms. "It took four planes, but we did it. We've also taken over the entire town, I'm afraid."

"I don't think anyone is complaining," I reply with a laugh. "Your family might single-handedly boost Bitter-root Valley's economy this weekend."

"Is there anything I can do to help?" Alecia asks, her eyes roaming over everything with interest. "I used to be an event planner, and I can do just about anything."

"You're a *guest*," I remind her kindly. "Not that I don't appreciate it, but I promise you, we have it all handled. It's going to be an amazing couple of days."

"I had no idea how absolutely gorgeous it is here," Nic says, turning in a circle. "I mean, we've seen photos, and I know you've told us, Erin, but nothing does it justice."

"I know," Erin says with a little happy dance. "And I get to *live* here."

"Mom!" We all turn as a little girl, Holly, comes running our way. "You forgot me, Mom!"

"No way," Erin says as she scoops Holly into her arms and kisses her cheek. "You were still asleep when we left. How did you get out here?"

"I brought her." A devastatingly handsome man joins us. He has a quick, charming smile, bright blue eyes, and shaggy dark-blond hair that just begs for a woman's fingers. He turns that smile onto me. "Hey, I'm Hudson, Erin's favorite cousin."

"Don't let the others hear you say that," Natalie says with a laugh. "Come on, I want to see *everything*."

"It's going to look completely different tomorrow," Erin informs them as they walk toward the tents.

"You know," Hudson says, smiling after his family, "Erin insisted that she wanted a simple, small wedding. I think it's blown up a bit beyond that."

"It's the biggest project I've ever taken on," I agree, nodding as I resume sorting some vines. "But it's going to be gorgeous. What do you think of Bitterroot Valley, Hudson?"

"I think it's amazing. Views everywhere you look, nice people, good food."

"Where did you eat?"

"We hit up a BBQ place last night."

"Oh, sure, Rocky Mountain Smokehouse, right?"

"That's it. Freaking *amazing* ribs." He reaches down to help me straighten out a vine that's decided to fight me.

"Is this your first visit here?"

"Nah, we came skiing last winter. That's when Erin decided to stay, and I can't say that I blame her. How long have you lived here?"

"About five years." I stand and find Hudson smiling down at me. "What?"

"You sure are pretty, Summer Quinn."

Just then, strong arms circle my shoulders from behind, and a face nuzzles my neck.

"Good morning, sugar," Chase says. There's a little... edge to his voice, and I look up at him and find him glaring at Hudson.

He's jealous.

"Chase, this is—"

"Hudson," Chase says with a nod. "We've met."

Hudson rocks back on his heels, that charming smile still in place, and nods slowly. "I get it. It was nice to meet you, Pretty Summer."

And with that, he winks and then sets off to catch up with the women.

"Was that necessary?" I ask as I turn in Chase's arms and give him a hug.

"Fuck yes, it was. I didn't like the way he was smiling at you."

"And how was that?"

"Like he wanted to eat you for fucking breakfast." He lowers his lips to mine, and I'm immediately swept up in him, the way I always seem to be whenever he's near me. "And only I get to do that."

"Hmm." I pat his chest and grin up at him. "If he had suggested any such thing, I would have turned him down. Probably."

Chase growls in his throat, making me laugh.

"Okay, caveman, I have to get back to work. I'm on a schedule here."

I wasn't wrong this morning when I told my staff that it would be a long, grueling day. It was just that, and I was like a mother hen, hovering over everyone to make sure they were hydrated, had food, and weren't overworking themselves.

To my absolute shock, Chase has asked me to be his date tonight. At first, I decline because I'm working, but it seems the man can talk me into just about anything. However, I don't have time to run all the way home to get ready and then come back, so thankfully, Erin lets me use her guest suite in the farmhouse so I can get ready for the party.

My staff leaves when I do. They are going out to dinner and then home to rest for a few hours, but they'll be back around midnight to help me tear everything down so we have a clean slate for tomorrow morning.

I hurry through my shower and do my hair and makeup in record time before donning my red, off-the-shoulder dress, just in time for Chase to pick me up and bring me out for the party.

I have to admit, everything out here looks *spectacular*. We pulled off the faerie garden look, complete with twinkle lights and a waterfall in the far corner of the tent. Chase's bar is in another corner, with my flowers draped across the front. Two bartenders bustle behind it, filling orders.

To my surprise, there's a full stage set up on the opposite end of the tent, complete with instruments and microphones, and I'll be interested to see what they use that for, given how many musicians are here tonight.

"Have I mentioned that you're fucking gorgeous?" Chase whispers into my ear. We're sitting across from his parents, who I really like. Joy, Chase's mom, keeps grinning over at me. But it's disconcerting to have her son whisper sweet nothings in my ear while she watches us dreamily.

"You have," I murmur and take a sip of my wine. His jaw just about came unhinged when he saw me in my red dress.

"Summer," Joy says from across the table, "I just have to say, these flowers are absolutely beautiful. You did a wonderful job."

"Thank you. My team and I worked hard to make sure Erin got exactly what she had in mind."

"I love it," Joy continues and winks at me, then moves her gaze to Chase, and I can see the wheels spinning in her head. "Is this your first date with Summer, Chase?"

"No, ma'am," Chase says with a shake of the head. "And it won't be the last."

"How nice," she says, and if I'm not mistaken, her already wide smile grows. "How is your aunt Paula, Summer? She didn't make it to our last book club meeting."

"She's great. I'm sorry she missed the meeting. She was probably helping me at the shop. She spends more time there in the summer, which I really appreciate."

"Did I overhear that you're the florist?"

I turn to the woman sitting next to me and nod, butterflies suddenly filling my stomach. Somehow, I was seated next to Sidney Sterling. *The* Sidney Sterling. My favorite country singer of all time. The woman whose every song I know by heart, and even got to go see in concert last summer in Seattle. I've been tongue-tied since she introduced herself to me and shook my hand.

A hand that I might never wash again.

"I am," I reply with a nod.

"Wow, you do great work. This entire setup looks like it came out of a magazine."

"Thanks. I didn't do it alone. I have a talented staff."

"She's being modest," Chase informs Sidney. "She's fucking brilliant."

Sidney grins and winks at me. "You have an admirer. And he's a hot one."

"Don't make me kill Chase," Sidney's husband, Keaton, says from the other side of her. His voice is totally mellow, his face bland, but his eyes are sharp. "I *like* him."

"No one's hotter than you, babe," Sidney replies with a laugh. "I'm so glad that Erin didn't have us all sitting in bunches. You know, in family groups? I like meeting new people, and this ranch is absolutely to *die for*."

"It was smart of her to have us mingle," Joy agrees from across the table. "I suspect that some of us might have been a little...intimidated to approach some of you otherwise."

"Don't be," Keaton insists. "We're all just a bunch of normal people. Some of them are idiots."

"Our families have that in common," Chase says with a laugh, and the two men high-five over the table.

"I heard that," Brady calls out from the next table over. "I know you're not calling *me* an idiot."

"Or me," a man I recognize as Vaughn freaking Barrymore, the hottest actor of our generation, says with a laugh.

"I am talking about him," Keaton says with a whisper. "He married my sister, so I can give him a hard time."

Before we can continue the conversation, there's a commotion on the stage, and we all quiet down, turning to see what's happening.

"That's our cue," Sidney mutters to her husband, who reaches out and rubs her cheek with the back of his finger.

"Hello," Meg, Erin's mom, says into the microphone with a little smile. "First of all, be kind, okay? I don't sing in public much anymore these days. Is anyone going to come up here with me, or what?"

To my shock, I watch as Leo motherfucking Nash stands at a table across the room, and with a cocky grin on his crazy handsome face, he struts up to meet her. Other members of the family join them, including Sidney and Keaton.

"They make up an entire band," I whisper to Chase, who just nods, his gaze pinned to what's happening before us, but he reaches for my hand and holds on tightly.

"For those who aren't part of the crazy Montgomery

clan," Leo says into the mic, "I'll give you a little backstory. Meg and I grew up together as foster siblings, and way back when the Earth was cooling, we were in a band together. *Then* we went our separate ways for a while, and, well, blah blah blah..."

"He got famous," Meg says into the mic. "I became a nurse. We both married into the Montgomery family."

"What are the odds, right?" Leo asks, making us chuckle. "We still like to jam together, and I'd say that music is a big part of our entire, big, loud family. We do monthly dinners as a family, and we usually jam at those."

"So, why break tradition, right?" Sidney asks, speaking for the first time.

"If it's okay with you," Leo continues after smiling at Sidney, "we'd like to play a few songs. Meg's going to join us on the first one, but then she's going to be a party pooper and ditch us."

"Trust me, you'll thank me," Meg says with a grin.

"Let me introduce the band," Leo says, turning to look at the others. "We have Sidney Sterling on vocals and guitar."

"Holy shit," I whisper, making Chase smile.

"Keaton Williams on the keys," Meg adds, over the applause.

"Hudson Williams on the sticks," Leo says, and Hudson does a quick drum solo.

"Then we have Brax Adler on the guitar and vocals," Sidney puts in, pointing to the man across the stage.

"I think I've died and gone to heaven." This comes

from Ryan, who's sitting behind me. "Is this even *real* right now?"

"What, like you couldn't afford to hire them for a house party?" Brady points out with a snicker, earning the bird from his brother.

"Boys," Joy warns them with a sigh.

"Just wait," Erin says, her face bright with pride and excitement. She and Rem are sitting at our table, closest to the stage. "Just wait for it."

"So, this song that we're going to sing is a sentimental one," Meg says and smiles down at Erin. "Leo and I have sung this song a hundred times together, usually at weddings. We sang it at Jules and Nate's wedding, and maybe every other wedding in the family, now that I think about it."

There are nods and applause throughout the room, and then Brax starts to pluck the strings on his guitar in a sweet intro that already has tears springing to my eyes, and they haven't even started singing yet.

"It's called 'Marry Me,'" Meg says, and then she starts to sing the romantic lyrics. When the verse changes, Leo takes over, and his gritty voice sounds natural singing the ballad. When they join together in the chorus, I have to take a long, deep breath as emotion slams into me so unexpectedly.

The song is just so *pretty*, and here in this beautiful space, it feels like a fairytale.

Chase squeezes my hand in his and brings it to his lips, but I can't take my eyes off Meg and Leo, who both look down at Erin and Remington, their voices melting together so effortlessly.

And when the last notes drift away, Erin jumps up and runs onstage, pulling them both in for a big hug as she wipes at tears of her own.

In fact, as I look around the room, taking in super-stars and athletes, it occurs to me that there aren't many dry eyes in the whole place.

"Thank you," Erin says. "Thank you for that."

"I love you, my baby," Meg says, holding her daughter's face in her hands. "Now, these guys are going to play for a while, unless there are any objections."

There's laughter all around, and then Meg leaves the stage, returning to her husband, and Sidney says into the mic, "Who wants to hear some more music?"

The applause erupts, and the band starts playing a Nash song that I've listened to my whole life. And *then*, still to my utter astonishment, because I'm quite sure I'm dreaming, Leo Nash himself starts to sing.

"I love this song," I mutter, dancing in my seat.

"He wrote it for my aunt Sam," Erin says. "The song 'Sunshine' is for her."

"You have a swoony family, Erin."

"Don't I know it."

CHAPTER TWELVE
CHASE

"Oh, my." We all turn and find Mom standing on the threshold of the big family room in my parents' house. This is where all the guys are getting ready for the wedding. All of my brothers and my dad are here. Erin's dad decided to get ready with his family up at the resort, which was probably for the best, given how many of them there are and how small Mom and Dad's house is.

"What do you think?" Remington asks, adjusting his bowtie. I know that he doesn't love wearing the monkey suit—hell, none of us likes it, but I have to admit, we all clean up nicely.

"I think," Mom says, tears in her eyes, as she walks over to smooth down his lapel, "that I have the handsomest men in the world, right here in my house."

"That's a given," Brady says with a smug grin.

Mom takes a turn with each of us, kissing our cheeks and brushing imaginary lint off our shoulders, and then finally makes her way to our dad, who scoops her into his arms and plants a big kiss on her.

"You're damn beautiful," he mutters in her ear.

"I'm ready!" Johnny, Remington's son, comes running out of the bathroom. His tie is crooked, his jacket bunched up at the shoulders, and he forgot to zip his fly, but he's all smiles. "I look dang good."

"Yes, you look very handsome," Mom says with a laugh and bends over to kiss his head. "But let's straighten you out a bit, shall we?"

"I lost another tooth," Johnny says proudly. "It's gonna look awesome in the pictures, and I got another five dollars."

"How much do you have now?" Ryan asks.

"Forty dollars!"

The kid's been losing teeth all summer, and the tooth fairy has been damn busy and is likely now broke.

"What will you do with all your riches?" Mom asks him.

"I wanna buy a bike."

"How's Erin, Mom?" Rem asks. "Is she nervous? Is she okay?"

"She's having a great time," Mom assures him. "This morning, they started with mimosas and a nice, big breakfast. Then the glam squad arrived, and they've been laughing and playing music and enjoying each other all day. She's not worried at all, my boy. Erin loves you, and this is her home."

"I know," he says, and seems to almost be in awe of

the idea. "I'm afraid she's going to come to her senses and run back to Seattle."

"Not a chance," Johnny says. "She loves me too much."

"You're right about that," Rem says and leans down to kiss his son's hair. "Did you use shampoo in the shower?"

"Yeah."

"Are you sure?"

"Dad, it's our wedding day. I'm not going to show up smelling bad."

"I'm headed out," I announce, and earn scowls from the other members of my family.

"Where are you going?" Brady asks.

"I have to go collect my sexy date, and then I'm going to meet all you bozos—not you, Mom—at the ceremony. Summer's getting ready at the farmhouse so she didn't have to run home to change after she was done setting up flowers."

"That girl has to be exhausted," Dad says. "She didn't leave here until almost one in the morning last night, and she was back here by six this morning."

"Yeah, *setting up the flowers* is way too simple for what she and her team did today," Ryan adds as Remington nods. "Yesterday, she turned that tent into something out of *The Secret Garden*, and today? Today belongs in a Disney movie."

"It's really pretty," Johnny agrees.

"It's important to her that everything is perfect for Erin," I reply, stupidly proud of my girl. I've seen it. Erin's going to be *so happy* with everything, which is all any of us want. "Now, I'm going to go get her. I know she wanted to double-check a few things before everyone else starts arriving."

"Chase, before you go," Mom says, and I'm sure she's going to ask me what my intentions are with Summer, but instead, she simply smiles at me. "I like her."

"Yeah. Me, too. I'll see you all in a bit."

I want to make sure that Summer has eaten today and that she's feeling all right. Yeah, she's worked her ass off, and I need to make sure she remembered to take care of herself.

I can hear the music from inside the house as soon as I step out of my truck. Country music is blaring, and when I walk inside, there's maniacal giggling to go along with it coming from the kitchen.

But just stepping out of Erin and Rem's guest suite is Summer, and my heart stutters to a stop.

Her golden hair is swept up in wavy strands, pinned back from her face, and spilling around her shoulders. Her dress, a long, lavender thing that sits high on her neckline, is sleeveless and has a cut-out that shows off her impressive cleavage and hugs her every curve perfectly.

"Are you going to speak, or am I imagining you standing there?" she asks with a grin as she walks toward me.

I move my head from side to side, still soaking her in, as she continues to move so gracefully, so fucking *elegantly*, that I'm sure I've swallowed my tongue.

"You look handsome," she says and reaches up to straighten my tie.

"You're the most beautiful woman I've ever seen in my fucking life."

I hear the growl in my voice, but I can't help it. I feel...*primal*. I want to keep her just for me and not share her with any of the idiots that will be at this wedding today.

Her eyes jump up to mine, and she takes a quick breath before I loop my arms around her waist and pull her to me, lower my lips to hers, and kiss her the way she *should* be kissed when she looks like this.

Like I never want to let her go.

"Wow," she whispers when I pull back.

"You know that it's rude to be more beautiful than the bride, right?"

She laughs now and smooths her hand down my chest. "That's such a cliché thing to say, but it's also very sweet. Just wait until you *do* see the bride. You'll swallow your tongue."

"Too late," I mutter. "Already did. Come on, let's head over. Are you sure you want to wear heels?"

"The floor in the tent is concrete," she reminds me. "The ceremony might be grass, but that won't take long. I want to wear pretty shoes."

"Then wear them. I'll carry them for you when you decide your feet can't take any more torture."

"That's chivalrous." She grins up at me as I escort her to the passenger side of the truck. "Is it true that the guests are being taken over to the event on wagons?"

"Yep. There isn't space for parking over there yet, so everyone's going to park by the barn. Rem found some wagons to borrow, and the hands are going to drive people back and forth."

"That's *super* cowboy."

"Erin's marrying a cowboy," I remind her.

"You're a cowboy, too," she says, glancing up at my black hat. "And I like it."

I grin and close her door and then drive her over to the event site, let her out by the tent so she doesn't have to walk far in those heels, and then drive the truck over to where the family is allowed to park. When I join her in the tent, Summer's bent over a table, fussing with a centerpiece.

I can't help myself. I walk up behind her, slide my hand down her ass, and lean into her.

"Someone is likely watching," she says, but I can hear the smile in her voice.

"But photos aren't allowed," I remind her and lean in further to kiss the back of her neck. "I can't wait to get you home, see how this dress looks on my floor, and sink inside of you."

I turn her around so I can drag my fingers down her cheek.

"You're gorgeous, Blondie. I love it when you're all dolled up. I can't get enough of you when you've got your hair up in a bun and you're working at the shop, but my favorite Summer? The one that stars in every fantasy I've ever had in my life?"

She swallows hard as I lean in to whisper in her ear.

"My favorite is when you're naked and sweaty, with no makeup, and tangled up in the sheets of my bed. I can't get enough of *that*."

We can hear the wagon rolling up with the first wave of guests, so I kiss her cheek and start to pull back, but she stops me.

"And my favorite," she says, breathing just a little harder now, "changes daily because I *love* it when you're in your uniform. It's hot, and I don't care if that's a cliché. And you're certainly sexy today. But Chase? When you're in cowboy mode, with your jeans and boots and hat? It does things to me that I didn't know were possible. The cowboy cop vibe is *epic*."

Shit, I wish that I could bunch that dress up around her waist and take her right here, right now. But that's not possible.

So, I smile down at her and nuzzle her nose with mine.

"Later," I promise her, "I'm going to fuck you until you can't remember your name."

"I can't wait."

"THIS IS A *PARTY*," Polly says with a big grin and sips her signature cocktail, which Erin had the bartender make just for this event.

A huckleberry mojito.

"You look *amazing*," Summer says to Polly. "You know I'm jealous that you can wear green like that."

"It's just because I'm a redhead," Polly replies, and then smiles over at Erin's cousin, Drew, and his wife, London. "It's so good to see you again, London."

"Oh, you, too. Tell me you sell that dress in your shop because I'll be stopping in to buy it."

"I do, actually," Polly says with a laugh. "And I'd love it if you came in before you leave town. I want to pick your brain, actually."

"Pick away," London replies.

I like that friends and family are sprinkled together so there aren't any cliques. Similar to how last night went, the seating arrangement at this reception is perfect. At our table, we have Summer and me, Polly, Ryan, Drew and London, and Brady next to Zoey, who is Erin's younger sister and didn't come with a date.

London owns Seattle's professional football team and has other investment businesses, as well, including ones in fashion. And from what Erin has mentioned in the past, London loves Polly's shop.

Also, it's not lost on me that we have two billionaires under the age of thirty-five at this table.

"Well, not that I carry it in *my* shop, but I was wondering what you think of this season's ready-to-wear line from Dior?"

"Oh, it's *divine*," London replies and thumps her hand over her heart. "And if this is the direction that the house is going in, I can't wait to see what they unveil at fashion week in Paris. Are you going?"

Polly laughs, sipping her drink. "No."

"Why not?" Ryan asks her, speaking for the first time.

"Why am I not going to fashion week in *Paris*?" Polly asks him. "Oh, I don't know, probably because it's Paris, and while I love that some people can afford to do that, I'm not one of them. However, London, you *have* to take a million pictures and send them to me."

"Polly, come with me," London invites, and it stuns Polly speechless. Under the table, Summer reaches for my hand and squeezes it. "Be my guest for the week. I always get a two-bedroom suite at The Ritz, and I'd be happy to share it with you."

Polly blinks and frowns down into her drink and then shakes her head and smiles up at London. She *wants* to go. Anyone can see it written all over her pretty face.

"Thank you so much for the offer, but I can't get away for a whole week."

"Why not?" Ryan demands again.

"Because I have a business to run." Polly sips her drink again and then sets it down. "Actually, since I have both of you here, I have a couple of investment questions."

"Shoot," Ryan invites her, London nods, and Drew turns to Brady to discuss football.

Summer leans into me and whispers in my ear, "I don't know why she turned London down. Fashion week in Paris is Polly's dream."

"You'll have to ask her about it later." I kiss Summer's cheek, and suddenly two little girls come whizzing by the table. One I recognize as my niece, Holly, and the other is her friend, Daisy.

Daisy's shoe catches on a chair, and she pitches

forward, planting her hands and knees on the concrete next to Brady.

He immediately springs into action, pulling Daisy onto his lap, and the little girl begins to cry.

"Hey now," Brady says, checking out her hands. "Look here, you don't even have a scratch."

"M-m-my knees," she says as big alligator tears track down her cheeks, and Brady pulls the skirt back far enough to expose her little knees.

"Well, those have a little scrape," he concedes. "But it's not too bad."

"But my pretty dress is dirty."

"Hey, you're beautiful, Daisy, and your dress is just fine, I promise. I wouldn't lie about that."

Daisy hiccups twice and then wipes at her tears as Holly stands close by her friend, watching.

"It's okay, Dais," Holly says, patting Daisy's shoulder. "You didn't even rip it or anything. And your bow stayed in your hair."

"It did?" Daisy reaches up, and sure enough, the bow is still there, which makes her smile. "Okay."

"What's going on?" Abbi, Daisy's mom, appears at Brady's side and frowns down at her daughter. "Are you okay, baby?"

"Yeah." Daisy smiles up at Brady. "Thanks, uh... which one are you again?"

"Brady," he replies with a grin. "And you're welcome."

Abbi smiles at Brady, and I can see the interest in her pretty brown eyes, but then she notices Zoey sitting to

Brady's left, and she nods politely before following after her daughter.

Brady watches her go.

"You'll sprain your neck," I say quietly, and smirk when my brother scowls at me. "She's pretty."

"She's a mom."

"So?"

Brady shrugs. "I'm just saying."

The band that's been playing up on the small stage slows it down to an oldie from the eighties, and I take a second to just look around the room and take it all in.

My parents are dancing, of course, because this music is from their era. I see Rem and Erin chatting with Brooks and several of Erin's aunts and uncles.

Roger Sherman, Erin's former landlord, is all smiles as he dances with one of Erin's cousins, and I notice that Charlie Lexington is speaking to the photographer and pointing to the cake.

Looks like that might be next on the agenda.

My dad hasn't said a word today about a *Lexington* being present at a Wild wedding, and I think that's something to celebrate all by itself. Not that he would have made a scene or embarrassed Rem and Erin, but I'm surprised that he hasn't at least sent a glare Charlie's way.

But he hasn't, not even once, and I'm glad.

"You're deep in thought," Summer murmurs next to me.

"Just taking it all in."

"I have to say it, Chase. That arbor you built is absolutely *stunning*. It was perfect for the ceremony."

"I made the bones, but you worked some serious artistic magic with the flowers. I hope that goes on your résumé."

"It'll be front and center on the homepage of my website," she agrees with a nod. "Because yeah, it's something. But working with what you built was a dream. It went smoothly, and that's because you built it to be strong and stable."

"I'm glad it was good to work with because you'll be doing it often once this place is up and running."

"You know, this is going to be an amazing venue." She turns to me, her eyes bright with excitement. "Chase, it's *already* stunning, and it's literally just a tent. I love that Erin wanted to keep that side free from any flowers or coverings so we can all watch the mountains as the sun sets, and from inside, with a wall of windows?"

She kisses her fingertips.

"Chef's kiss. This is going to be a wedding destination venue that will be in magazines and on TV shows. Once social media gets wind of it, it'll be booked up years in advance."

"I hope so."

"I know so. I do this for a living. Charlie and I were talking about it this morning, and we know that it's going to be a big deal. Hell, Sharla's already decided she wants to snag a husband, just so she can get married out here."

"Wow." I raise an eyebrow and can't help but laugh.

"And what happens after the wedding day?"

"I don't think she cares, honestly."

We laugh, and I tug Summer over into my lap, wrap my arms around her for all to see, and don't give a shit if anyone looks at us sideways.

She isn't a secret. She's *mine*.

"How long do we have to stay?" I whisper in her ear.

"It's your *brother's* wedding," she reminds me with a wry smile. "So, I'm going to say at least until after they cut the cake."

"What's taking so long with that?" I grumble.

"Oh, there was a huge cake issue," Summer informs me. "But Charlie got it managed, and it should be here soon."

I scowl over to where a cake sits on a table. "It's right *there*."

"It's fake." Summer's voice is light as she smiles down at me. "It's just for show. The *real* cake is on the way."

"I didn't even realize."

"Exactly. That's what you have Charlie for."

"Well, it better get here soon."

"What's your hurry, cowboy?"

I run my fingertips up and down the smooth skin of her back. "I just discovered that you're not wearing a bra under this dress."

"There's no place to *put* a bra under this dress."

I groan, and she laughs and wraps her arms around my neck, kissing me sweetly.

"Don't worry, you'll live."

CHAPTER THIRTEEN
SUMMER

Holy shit, I'm going to die.

I bolt up in the bed, yanked out of a dead sleep, my right calf cramping and seizing so bad, I'm sure that this is it.

This is how I go out.

"Shit. Shit. Shit," I moan as I try to rub the cramp out of the tight muscle. When that doesn't work, I stand up and try to walk it off, stretching it out. At first, it's absolute agony, but after a few minutes, the muscle starts to relax, and I'm left with an ache and I'm pretty sure a little PTSD.

Suddenly, it occurs to me that Chase isn't in the bed. I frown at the clock and see that it's just past three in the morning, and when I run my hand over the sheets, they're cool to the touch.

He hasn't been here in a little while.

We got home from the wedding late. Not only did we stay for cake, but we danced and enjoyed everyone for *hours*, and we ended up being some of the last to leave. Despite being exhausted, we still managed to strip each other naked and make love.

One thing I've learned since I've been with Chase is that the man is almost insatiable, and he's *patient*. He's teaching me things about my body that I never would have known before.

Bless his cowboy heart.

Wrapping his white dress shirt around me, I go searching for him, frowning when I don't find him in the house at all.

Even my *dog* is gone.

"Did they go for a walk in the middle of the night?"

I prop my hands on my hips, and that's when I see the light on in the garage. Slipping my feet into some flip-flops, I make my way outside and spot the man, dressed in jeans and a plain, green T-shirt, bent over a piece of furniture, sanding it by hand.

The lights in the garage cast a soft yellow light, and it's quiet out here, with just the sound of crickets setting the tone of the soundtrack. Lily's head comes up from where she's curled up in a little bed that Chase must have carried out here for her, but at first, Chase doesn't notice me.

He's obviously deep in thought, running that sand-paper back and forth rhythmically. I wonder what's going on in his head. He even seemed lost in thought at the wedding reception tonight, and when he made love to me when we got home, it was *intense*. Almost broody.

And that's not like him. I'm not worried. It doesn't

feel like it's something bad, or about *me*, but just...something.

I step inside the doorway, and his gaze lifts to mine, but he doesn't smile.

"Did I wake you?" he asks, his voice soft.

"No." I take a deep breath, inhaling the scent of pine, and shake my head as I walk further into his workshop. "I had a leg cramp. Woke me up out of a dead sleep."

"You've worked your ass off for a few days now and probably haven't had enough water." He sets the sandpaper aside and crosses to me, cradles my face in his hands, and kisses me tenderly. "Which leg?"

"Right calf."

Taking my hand, he leads me over to a dresser and boosts me up onto it so I'm at eye level with him.

"Are you okay?" I ask him, taking *his* face in my hands now. He doesn't look troubled, but he does seem somber. "What's wrong?"

"I just couldn't sleep," he murmurs, and I lean in to kiss him. "Brain wouldn't turn off."

"Maybe you're *too* tired. That happens to me sometimes."

"Maybe." His lips tip up into a sweet smile, and he runs his big hands down my thigh and to the calf in question. "Is it sore?"

"Oh, yeah. Still a little pissed off."

He rubs gently, and I sigh. Yes, the muscle is tender, but it's loosening up even more under his touch.

"I'm sorry I wasn't there to help," he says.

"It's okay." I brace myself on his shoulder as he

continues to work on the muscles. "I see that you kidnapped my dog."

"She came willingly," he replies with a grin. "I like having her around. She's a sweet little thing."

"I'm glad she likes you. So, what was your busy mind thinking about so hard that you couldn't sleep after all that fun we had tonight?"

He keeps his eyes on my leg, and just when I think that he won't answer me, he says, "I didn't think Rem would ever get married again. Losing his first wife was hard on him. Add in being a single parent, and not wanting to get hurt again, I never thought I'd see the day that he'd fall in love, that he'd open his family up to someone new."

"I'm glad they found each other," I reply. "They're really good together, as if they should have been a family all along. And I don't mean that to sound disrespectful to his late wife."

"I know what you mean. I've never seen him so happy." His eyes find mine now. "*Never.* And that makes me happy for him, too. Rem and those kids deserve to have someone amazing like Erin in their lives."

"I agree." I sigh, feeling the loss of his touch as he lets my leg hang loose and wanders over to the table he was sanding. He leans on it, sighing. "Why does it make you sad, Chase?"

"I'm not sad." His voice is matter-of-fact, completely calm, as he shakes his head. "That's not it at all. I guess I was just thinking about them and how well they fit together. How sometimes, things just fit, like a puzzle. Even when you didn't realize that a piece was missing."

I tilt my head to the side, listening. I'd say that's how I feel about *him*. He's the missing piece in my life, and now that he's part of it, I can't imagine not having him in my world. The thought of going back to my life without him makes my heart ache.

"Sometimes, the trick is to stop fighting with the piece," I whisper, and his gorgeous hazel eyes find mine again.

"There's that." He inhales, lets it out, and his eyes travel down my torso. "What's under the shirt?"

With a grin tickling my lips, I let the fabric fall open, exposing about three inches of flesh down the middle. I'm completely naked beneath the cotton, and Chase's hands immediately fist when he realizes it.

He doesn't rush to me. He stays planted where he is, under the soft glow of the lights, watching me with those sober eyes. Chase is usually so fun-loving, so full of humor, but tonight, he's serious and wrapped up in his feelings, and it's a side to him that I haven't seen before. It's just as sexy as his fun-loving side.

As he watches, I slowly spread my legs on the top of the dresser, and his jaw tightens, that sexy muscle on the side of his face twitches, and it fills me with feminine satisfaction.

"Chase," I whisper, and that's the invitation he seemed to be waiting for because he pushes off the table and slowly walks over to me, his eyes pinned to mine. He stops about three feet away and lets those eyes travel down my body and back up again, and then he licks his lips.

"This," he says. "*Exactly* this, how you look right now, is my favorite."

He brushes his thumb across my bottom lip, and I poke my tongue out so I can lick him. His eyes narrow on me as he pushes his thumb further into my mouth so I can lick and suck him. No, I haven't seen this side of Chase before. This broody, intense side.

And I absolutely want him.

Once again, he drags his now-wet thumb over my lip, then down my chin and between my collarbones and cleavage. He still can't see my breasts because they're covered by the shirt, but my nipples are almost painfully hard from this intense, quiet foreplay.

I glance down, but his hand is on my chin in the blink of an eye, forcing my gaze back to his.

"Eyes. On. Me."

The intensity makes me swallow hard and the ache between my legs pulses. "Okay."

"It never fucking stops." His voice is rough but still calm as he holds my gaze and rubs his fingertips over my clit. "This yearning for you. This absolute *need* for you, it never goes away. When I'm not with you, I'm thinking about you. If you're in the room, it's like you're a fucking magnet. I *have* to be with you."

"I'm right here."

With my eyes still on his, I reach for the waistband of his jeans. His eyes narrow as I unfasten them, nudge them down over his hips, and feel him spring free. I take his thick, heavy cock into my hand and pump him twice before sweeping my thumb over the crown and feeling the wetness already there.

"I'm right *here*, Chase. I'm not going anywhere."

He fists his hand in the nape of my hair and crushes his mouth to mine, kissing me almost desperately as I guide him to me, and he slips inside of me, one agonizingly amazing inch at a time, until he's seated fully, and we're both breathing hard, staring at each other.

"Mine," he growls. "This is *mine*."

"Yours," I agree before he kisses me again and begins to move. The thrusts are slow but hard, as if he's hammering the point home that I belong to him, and just like always, he surprises me with not just how he can make my body feel, but the way he makes my *heart* feel. So full, so freaking *happy*, that I'm surprised light doesn't shoot out of my pores. Even when he's buried so deep inside of me, I can't get close enough to him.

He picks up the pace, and I lift my legs higher on his sides, feeling the orgasm moving through me. As I let go, he pumps into me twice more and follows me over the edge.

He leans his forehead against mine as we both work to catch our breath, and then he kisses my forehead sweetly. Tenderly.

Lovingly.

"Did I hurt you?" he asks.

"Never." I shake my head, and, with him still seated inside of me, I take his face in my hands and kiss him. "You could never hurt me, Chase Wild."

"I love you," he murmurs, those serious eyes so full of emotion. "I've been gone over you for *years*, Summer."

"I'm really glad I stopped fighting it," I reply as love and joy fills me to almost bursting. "Because I love you, too."

He sighs and closes his eyes, resting against me. I can see the lines of exhaustion on his face. Is *this* what he was out here agonizing over all night?

"We should go to bed."

He nods and pulls out of me, then moves over to his washbasin and takes some paper towels from the roll, hurrying back over to clean me up before helping me onto my feet.

"So, what's the story with this dresser?" I ask him, gesturing to the one I just hopped off of. "Did you make it?"

"Yeah, for Bridger Blackwell."

"Brooks's brother?"

"That's him. He's not getting it now, though."

I frown up at him. "Why not?"

"Sentimental reasons. That one stays here. I'll build him another one."

I laugh and then sigh a little when Chase lifts Lily into his arms to take her up to bed. I follow behind them, turning off the lights and locking the garage behind us, and then we're inside, walking up the stairs to the bedroom.

Lily, with a big yawn, curls up in her bed and goes right back to sleep, and Chase snuggles up behind me in the bed.

"Were you out there worried about telling me you love me all night?" I ask him and wiggle around in his arms so I can see his face.

"No." He kisses my hand and finally offers me a small smile. "No, I really was thinking about Rem and the wedding and all of that stuff. I guess big life events will do that to a person. Telling you I love you isn't something I struggle with because, like I said, I've had strong feelings for you for a while. A long while."

I grin and kiss his chin.

"I might have had a bad moment or two, wondering if you felt the same." He sighs with the admission, and I can see the vulnerability in his eyes, and it makes me love him even more.

"I'm catching up. And I'm going to be frank here for a minute."

"We're in the dark, in the middle of the night. There's no better time to be perfectly honest."

That makes me smile. "You're right. I'm actually glad that we came together when we did, and not several years ago when you first approached me because I wasn't ready for you yet, Chase. I was still bruised and determined and just not in the right place for this relationship. It never would have worked out between us if we'd dated back then."

"Well, then I'm glad that you turned me down, even if it was a blow to my ego."

With a chuckle, I move in to rest my cheek against his chest and snuggle in. "Your ego's just fine."

CHASE: *Hey, beautiful. Lunch should be delivered in about ten. I couldn't get away.*

I grin at his words and bite my lip as I type out a reply.

Me: I hope everything is okay. I missed waking up to you this morning!

By the time I woke up today, Chase had already gone to work. With wedding season wrapping up, I've had the luxury of coming into the shop a little later each morning, and it's been glorious. In the two weeks since the Wild wedding, things have slowed down considerably. And while my stress levels appreciate that, I know that in a couple of months, I'll be wishing for the additional income.

But, I've learned to make the busy months make up for the slow ones.

I'm just placing the last sunflower into a bouquet when my phone pings with a reply.

Chase: I got to see your gorgeous face this morning and kiss your lips before I left. Whose amazing life is this, anyway?

I laugh and shake my head. He's just so damn *sweet*.

"Oh, Lord, she's sexting again," Sharla says and makes a gagging noise from across the room.

"I am not."

"I can totally tell," she insists. "You get this goofy grin on your face while you tap away at your phone. It used to be really sweet, but now it's just...ew."

I laugh and set the phone aside, returning to the task at hand. "We do *not* sext. We just flirt a bit, that's all."

"I think it's great," Ida says, winking at me. "And you seem happier than ever."

"We are."

And it's true. The past few weeks have been...*bliss*. There haven't been any more scary issues at my place, but I still sleep at Chase's every night. In fact, things have been quiet and fun and *very* sexy.

I'm in love, truly in love, for the first time in my life, and I'm having a damn good time with it.

The bell over the door rings, and in comes Heather, the owner of Old Town Pizza, carrying two large boxes and one smaller box on top.

"Delivery," she announces with a happy grin. "Chase sent me in with two large pies and an order of bread sticks."

"I love that man," Ida says, "but my hips do *not*."

"I love that he sends you food so often," Heather says with a wink to me. "I mean, how romantic is that?"

"You know about it?"

"Honey, all of Bitterroot Valley knows about it. And let me just say, we're all rooting for you because that Chase Wild is just..." She fans her face with her hand, making us all laugh.

"I won't disagree with you there." I open a box and take a sniff at the pepperoni with olives that Chase knows I like. "This looks fabulous. Thanks, Heather."

"Anytime, sweetie. You all enjoy, and I'll see you later."

She offers us a wave, and then she's off, and Ida, Sharla, and Vickie join me to devour a pizza. Margie is out on some deliveries, but we'll be sure to save her some.

The afternoon moves by quickly, all of us taking turns with the phone, printing off online orders, and making bouquets.

It's approaching five when the bell above the door rings again, and I turn to see Evan walking in. I haven't seen much of him in several weeks.

"Well, hi there, Evan. How's it going?"

"Just fine. It occurred to me that I haven't seen much of you recently, and I was walking by, thought I'd stop in and see how you are."

"You know, I was just thinking the same. I'm doing well, thanks. What have you been up to?"

"Oh, you know, slaving away in the office by day and soaking up the last bit of summer when I finally manage to escape."

I grin and nod at him as I walk around the counter and set a plant that I just unboxed on a shelf for sale.

"I hear you. The days are getting shorter and shorter, and soon, it'll be winter."

"Don't say that word," he says with a frown. "Don't tempt the snow gods."

I chuckle and tuck my hair behind my ear. "You're right, I won't say it again. So, business is good?"

"Someone's always suing someone else," he says. "And I saw your father not long ago."

That has my back going straight, and I'm immediately reminded why I've always kept my distance from Evan.

"Oh?"

"I was in Helena last weekend for a political party thing, and he was there. He said to tell you hello."

"Interesting." That's about all I have to say about that. Evan has political aspirations, and that's why he wanted to date me in the first place.

It *reeked* of Dennis, and I wanted nothing at all to do with that.

"It was fun. You should go with me next time, see your folks, and spend some time with me."

His hand snakes out to move down my hip, just as the bell sounds over the door and Chase walks in. He takes in the scene before him, narrows his eyes when they land on Evan's hand on my hip, and he snarls, "Don't make me draw my weapon."

I laugh, but Chase doesn't move his gaze until Evan removes his hand.

"Oh, hey, Chase." Evan's all smiles. "Summer and I were just talking about getting away to Helena together."

"Whoa." I hold up a hand as Chase's jaw tightens. "We were absolutely *not* saying anything of the sort. I have no intention of going to Helena anytime soon, Evan."

His eyes turn cold as he looks between me and Chase, and I reach for Chase's hand, linking our fingers.

"I hadn't heard," Evan says stiffly.

"I find that *very* hard to believe," is all Chase says before Evan turns and walks out the door.

"Men," Ida says, rolling her eyes.

"He had his hands on you," Chase says.

"And in about two seconds, I was going to tell him to take his hand *off* me. What are you up to?"

"I'm here to collect my girl."

I frown up at him. "I'm sorry. I can't leave for a while yet."

"Well, yes, you *are* my girl, but I didn't mean you. I thought I'd pop in and get Lily and take her home with me."

And just like that, I get all gooey. "That's really sweet. She'd like that."

"I figured I'd fix her dinner, and she and I can stretch out on the couch together."

I laugh as I hook Lily up to her leash, and when Chase takes it from me, he leans in to kiss me.

"I'll see you in a few hours." I grin up at him.

"We'll be waiting."

CHAPTER FOURTEEN
CHASE

"So, you said you wouldn't camp," I say as I shift the truck into park and grin over at Summer, "but that you *would* hike."

"Sure, I'll hike." She frowns out the window. "Where are we, anyway? I know we're on the ranch property, but I don't think I've seen this spot."

"We're actually not too far from the lake, that way." I point to the right and get out of the truck, open the door behind the driver's side, and start gathering some gear. "I want to show you some of the property on foot today."

"Okay." She grins and hops out, opens the door opposite of me, and starts changing her footwear from flip-flops to the trail shoes she brought along.

We dropped Lily off at Paula's for the night, since it wouldn't be safe to take her with us today. Not only shouldn't she hike that far, given that she has a flat face and would overheat, but there's wildlife out here, and I don't want to take any chances with the little dog.

"I put on sunscreen before we left the house," Summer says as she sets a hat on her head. "You told me to bring the trail shoes, so I figured we'd be outside."

"Good idea." With the backpack full of water and snacks, along with some emergency supplies, on my back, I close the truck door and circle around to her. "You ready?"

"Ready."

We set off on a path into the woods that my family has used so often over the years that it's become a bona fide hiking trail. This is a great five-mile hike, with some pretty views, and my mom uses the path to find huckleberries in the summer. In fact, I have a couple of empty containers in my bag to hold the sweet purple berries because when Summer sees the motherlode, she'll want to pick some.

So will I.

She looks amazing today. She chose wisely, with long jeans—that way she won't get scraped up by the brush on the trail—and a T-shirt. Her hair is down under the Bitterroot Valley ball cap that she likely got from a gift shop in town.

She may not typically spend a ton of time in the woods, but she's quick, her footsteps sure on the path, and she looks like a pro.

"Did you mention before that you don't hike often?" I ask her.

"I don't *love* the great outdoors," she admits with a wince. "I know. I live in Montana, and I *should* love it, but it's dirty out here, and there are bugs, and it's just not my favorite. The view? Yes. That's my jam. But sometimes, getting outside in nature is good for you. It feels good today, and I'm excited to see where this trail leads."

"You won't be disappointed," I assure her, thinking of the view that I'm leading her to.

"Holy shit, Chase, there are huckleberry bushes!"

I grin as she pauses on the trail and starts picking berries. "Too many for us to eat."

"I wish I had containers," she says with a frown, and then smiles in delight when I produce two of them from my backpack. "Well, aren't you handy to have around?"

"Damn handy," I confirm, and we both get to work filling the containers.

"What about bears?" she asks.

"What about them?"

"They also like huckleberries. Should I be freaked out?"

"You should *never* be freaked out, babe. I won't let anything hurt you."

She smiles over at me. "That's one of the things I love about you. But seriously, there have to be bears out here."

"There are some. The ranch hands try to keep an eye on them as much as possible, but animals wander on and off the ranch every day. To our knowledge, there haven't been any grizzlies on the property in a couple of weeks."

That has her stopping with a berry halfway to her mouth, and her gaze whips over to mine, her baby blues wide.

"A couple of *weeks*?"

"That we know of. I won't lie to you. There *is* wildlife out here. Bears, mountain lions, wolves, along with the usual deer and elk. Sometimes we get moose. And all the smaller critters."

"And you want to *live* here?"

"Absolutely." I laugh and snap the lid closed on my container. It's only half-full, but picking these small berries takes time, and I'm done for now. I slip it into my bag and cross to her, wrapping my arms around her waist. "The animals don't want to hurt us, Blondie."

"Are you going to tell me that they're more afraid of me than I am of them?"

"It's a cliché, but it's true." I kiss her neck, and when she puts the lid on her container, I take it from her and slip it into my bag. "We can come out here just to pick berries whenever you want."

"The season's almost over," she says wistfully. "They'll be gone in another week."

"If you want to skip the hike, we can just do this and come back another time."

"No." She shakes her head and wipes her hands on her jeans. "We got quite a few—enough for a pie, anyway. I want to see what you want to show me. But I don't want to run into a bear."

"We'll keep talking," I assure her and take her hand in mine. "And I have bear spray if we need it."

"What about a gun?"

"I have that, too, but we won't need to shoot anyone."

She nods, and we keep going up the trail. It's an

uphill climb on the way to our destination, but that means that it's downhill on the way back.

"Wild forget-me-nots," she says, pointing to the little blue flowers with yellow centers along the path. "That's my favorite flower."

"Why?"

"Look how pretty and dainty they are," she says. "They're a happy flower. And they come back every year."

"I didn't know that. How did you come to know so much about flowers?"

"Well, working in the field for five years will teach you quickly." She grins over at me and then tips her face up to the sunshine when we come to a clearing. "I told you before that I spent many summers with Aunt Paula, and she taught me, whether we were in her garden or at the shop together. By the time I bought the business, I knew what was native to this area, when they grew, and I knew a lot about what and where to plant flowers, shrubs, trees... you name it. It's fun and makes people happy."

"My mom gardens," I say as I lift a branch out of her way.

"I know. She comes into the shop to ask questions a lot. Most people think that because I'm not a nursery, I don't know about planting flowers. I sell mostly already cut pieces, but I can help with just about anything."

"Have you thought about expanding to add a nursery side?" I ask her.

"No." She shakes her head definitively. "That's a lot

of work and takes expertise I don't have. We already have a nursery in town. But I love it when your mom pops in to ask questions. She's a wonderful woman, you know."

"I know." I nod, thinking about my mom. "She's proud of all of us, too. Now that Erin's taken over the bookkeeping for the ranch, Mom can finally retire, and she and my dad are planning some travel, but I think she'll want to stay close by most of the time."

"She's an important part of our community," Summer adds. "She's so active with volunteering and with clubs and groups. I see her in town all the time. I can't imagine Joy being gone most of the time and missing out on all the things happening in Bitterroot Valley."

"I can't either. But she's earned a vacation some-where tropical."

Summer grins over at me, and soon, we can hear the water.

"Is that a waterfall?"

I can't believe we've already made it this far on the trail, but I nod at Summer. "Yup."

"Oh, my God, I want to see it."

She practically skips farther down the path and turns a corner, and there it is. The top of the falls is at least thirty feet in the air, and the water rushes down into the creek below.

"I didn't even see the creek," she says as she sets her hands on her hips and watches the water.

"We were walking perpendicular to it. We'll walk along it on the way back."

She turns to me and then rushes over and jumps up into my arms. My hands land on her ass as she loops her arms around my neck and kisses me, pressing herself against me as we listen to the water, and the cool spray fills the air around us.

"I take it you like it," I murmur against her lips.

"Chase, it's *gorgeous.*"

"And you're not even looking at it."

She laughs, and I let her slide down my body, my hands still glued to her ass, and then she turns to take it all in again.

"I love water," she says, her eyes pinned to the rushing current before us. "I always have. Lakes, rivers, waterfalls. I *love* visiting the ocean. It's the sound of it, you know?"

I slip my hand in hers, linking our fingers, and stay quiet as she goes on.

"It's as if the sound of the water drowns out all the noise in my head, and I can just *be.* I don't have to worry or overthink anything because the water calms all those chaotic thoughts."

She turns to me again.

"How did you know that I needed this today?"

I shrug a shoulder. "The season's winding down, and I know that the summer was full of stress for you. Between the shop, the weddings, and the bullshit of someone trying to scare you, I figured it was time for a break. For some quiet. Even if it's just for one day."

She nods slowly, turning her gaze to the waterfall

once more. "I guess it really has been a pretty crazy summer, huh?"

"Pretty crazy," I agree. "But I'm glad that it has been. Because if those idiots, whoever they are, hadn't tried to scare you, we might not be here like this."

"Oh, I like to think that we would have found our way here eventually." She laughs and moves over to the small wooden bridge that my brothers and I made about ten years ago so we can keep moving on the path. "I would have figured it out. Speaking of figuring stuff out, are there any new leads on my case?"

"No." I refuse to sugarcoat it for her, and I hate that that one word has some of the light draining from her eyes. "I'm sorry, sugar, we're still investigating."

"It's not your fault."

"Feels like it is," I reply absently, but then she's in my arms once more, her hands framing my face.

"It's *not* your fault. You didn't do those things, Chase. Some asshole did. It's *their* fault. You're doing everything you can to keep me safe, to make me *feel* safe, and I appreciate it so much." She nuzzles my nose with hers. "So stop feeling guilty, okay?"

"Yeah, okay."

She smacks a playful kiss on me, wiggles out of my arms, and leads me down the trail.

Is it any wonder that I'm completely in love with her?

"Oh, look!" Summer points down the trail. "This path empties out down by the lake!"

"Yes, it does." I grin, excited about what I have to show her next. I haven't brought her out here since before Rem's wedding, and there have been some changes. Actually, a *lot* of changes.

"That view is just so great," she says. She's panting a little from the exertion of the hike, but her eyes are bright with happiness, and being with her today has been amazing.

Of course, every day with Summer is the best day of my life.

We come out of the woods near my property, and Summer props her hands on her hips while she tries to catch her breath.

"We're going to have to check for ticks later," she informs me.

"I can't wait." I laugh and take her hand, leading her toward my piece of the lake. "I have more to show you."

"Are those...is that a *foundation*?"

I'm all smiles as I guide her to the concrete foundation, and we stop, looking it over.

"This will be the shop," I inform her. "I'm hoping to have it framed in before the snow flies."

"You poured a *foundation*." She frowns up at me, blinking in surprise. "I didn't even know that it had been surveyed."

"That was right before the wedding," I confirm. "I forgot to tell you, with everything going on. I'm sorry about that. Then, this week, the concrete company had a break in their schedule, and I had them come out. It's just the shop, but—"

"But it's what you wanted," she says, finishing the sentence for me. "It's gonna be a *big* shop."

"Thank God," I reply with a grin. "I need a lot of space. But there's something even better to see."

"If you tell me that you already built the house, I'm going to be peeved because that's the fun part, and I want to know all the things. Mostly because I'm nosy."

If I have my say, she'll be making a lot of the decisions about the house because she'll be living there with me.

"It's not invisible, so no, not the house." With her hand in mine, I lead her down to the lake and point. "A dock."

She stops short and covers her mouth with her free hand. "You built a *dock*. I was too busy checking out the shop to notice this."

"To be fair, my brothers and my dad helped. Hell, even Brooks and his brother, Blake, helped a bit."

Brooks has a big family like mine, and there's always a brother to spare to jump in and help with a project.

"I can't believe you kept this a secret," she says as she takes the first step onto the wooden dock and then shivers in the cooler air, so I pull the flannel out of my bag and wrap it around her. "This is *gorgeous*."

"I wanted it to be a surprise, and it really didn't take that long."

Her eyes are pinned to the last of the surprise that's sitting on the end of the dock. It's a table set for two, with candles, flowers, and a cooler where the food for dinner is stored.

"Who was in on this with you?" she asks and reaches out to touch the forget-me-nots in the vase.

"My mom." I grin down at her. "I managed to get a couple of texts down to her so she'd know when we would be here."

"And so she'd know to pick these flowers. This is—" Summer swallows hard and then wraps her arms around me and holds on tight. "This is really great."

"Keep that in mind when we start getting bit by mosquitos."

"Too late. That's been happening all day." She laughs as I hold her chair for her, and then I sit across from her and pour us each a glass of wine. "What's the occasion, by the way? It's not my birthday."

"No occasion, other than it's a beautiful day, and I enjoy being with you."

Her smile softens, and she reaches out for my hand and then turns her face to the sun setting behind the mountains.

"We always manage to catch sunsets," she murmurs.

"It's our time of day." I pull her hand to my lips and kiss it. "There's no better way to end the day than with you."

"You're extra sappy today," she says. "But I like it. What's for dinner?"

"I don't know. Let's see what Mom made." I open the cooler and grin. "Fried chicken, mashed potatoes and gravy, salad, and it looks like some kind of cobbler for dessert."

"Wow. This feast with that view? Priceless."

And delicious.

There's not a morsel left when we've finished eating. We've just finished loading everything up into the truck, thanks to the flashlights on our phones, when we hear the call of some coyotes somewhere on the ranch.

"That's wildlife," Summer says with wide eyes and hurries to jump into the truck, making me laugh.

Before starting the truck to leave, I reach over and tuck her hair behind her ear.

"Thanks for today."

Her gaze whips over to mine in surprise. "You have it backward. Thank *you* for today. I had a great time, and I always love being out here on your property. Specifically, your spot on the lake. It's just so beautiful out here, Chase. When will you start building the shop?"

"Tomorrow morning, first thing."

That has her blinking in surprise. "You move fast."

"We're already into September, and the snow could decide to fall anytime. I figure I have six weeks, tops, of reliable weather, so I'd like to get it started right away. I'll be out here on most of my days off, but hopefully, you can join me sometimes, if you're up for it."

"I can't build anything."

"No, but you can help in other ways, and that's only if you want to. And if you don't want to, no problem." I just like having her close by, no matter what she's doing.

"I'm sure I can find ways to be of service." She takes a

deep breath and leans her head back on the seat. We're just sitting here, in the dark quiet, enjoying each other. I don't know why, but I'm not ready to head back to town quite yet. "It's so still out here. I bet there are no loud fireworks on the Fourth of July or New Year's Eve."

"No, we've never done that out here. Fire hazard. It would suck if we had a forest fire erupt, especially if it can be avoided."

"Has it ever happened before?"

"We've had lightning strikes that turned into fires," I confirm with a nod. "I was a kid, but I remember it was scary, only about three miles from our house, and we had most of Bitterroot Valley out here helping to keep the fire at bay. It took three weeks to put it out."

"Wow. That's intense."

"Hence, the no-fireworks rule. Honestly, we never missed it."

She sighs happily, and I can see that her eyes are getting droopy. After a long hike and a full stomach, she has to be exhausted.

"Let's head home." I start the truck and drive us through the property and out to the highway.

We're about halfway into town when I see a vehicle pulled to the side of the road with its hazards on. And when I slow down as we pass, I see that they're not simply pulled over.

They've hit a tree.

"Shit." I turn around in the middle of the highway and immediately reach for my phone to call the station. "This is Wild. I have an accident on Highway 98, approximately seven miles outside of town, eastbound. They've hit a tree. Red Ford Explorer, Montana license plate 48-92631."

"Copy that," the dispatcher says in my ear. "I have officers responding. Do you need an ambulance?"

"Yes. Two passengers, and I don't know the status of them. Definitely send the ambulance."

"Copy."

I turn to find Summer staring at me, her jaw dropped and eyes wide.

"You stay here, understand me?" I reach into the back and pull my weapon from its holster. "You wait here, and if I signal, you call 9-1-1."

"Jesus, Chase."

"Do you understand me?" I ask again, needing to be sure that she hears me.

"Of course. Should you wait here with me until help arrives?"

"I need to see if they're dead or how badly they're hurt." I reach over to cup her cheek, thinking back to last winter and the accident that took Jake's parents' lives. "I mean it, Summer. Stay here. If it's bad, I don't want you to see it."

"I'll stay," she assures me. "But please, be careful. It's dark out here."

"I'm going to keep the headlights trained on the vehicle," I reply and reach back for the yellow vest I keep in the truck for emergencies like this. "And I'll wear this so I'm visible. I'm also going to set out flares."

"Okay." She licks her lips. "I feel like I should do something."

"You're doing it. Stay put."

And with that, I get out of the truck and, shrugging into the vest, hurry over to the SUV. There's steam coming from the crumpled front end, and when I shine my flashlight into the cab, I see that both passengers are unconscious. One of them must have passed out after turning on the hazard lights.

Opening the driver's side door, I reach in and check for a pulse on the driver, relieved when there is one. He also reeks of beer.

"Fucker," I mutter and rush around to the other side of the SUV, open the door, and check the woman for a pulse.

It's thready, but it's there.

"Were you both drinking?" I wonder out loud as I hear the sound of sirens coming this way. Hurrying over to the road, I pick up a flare and wave it back and forth so they know where to go.

"Chase!" Jerry Coltrain, a fellow officer, hurries out of his vehicle toward me. "What's going on?"

CHAPTER FIFTEEN
SUMMER

Just when I thought that Chase couldn't get any sexier, *this* happens. Watching him go from my laid-back, sweet man to the hard, alert, assertive cop was maybe the hottest thing I've ever witnessed.

I'm so turned on right now, I'm throbbing between my legs. But I'm also a little scared and worried about whoever is in that SUV.

Chase sets out the flares, and with the headlights from his truck pointed at the vehicle, I can see him walk around the SUV to check on those inside. His face is hard and grim as he steps away from the passenger side, and then I see flashing lights and hear sirens. Chase rushes to the side of the highway, where he waves a flare in the air to flag the responders down.

From the darkness of the truck, I watch as Chase talks with an officer, gesturing to the SUV, and then back to me. I can't tell what he's saying, but every line in his impressive body is on full alert. It reminds me that when he's with me, Chase is pretty calm and patient, but at the core of it all, he's a cop. He's in control, and he's protective.

And it just makes me want to jump him.

After about fifteen more minutes of waiting as Chase speaks with the officers and other first responders, he returns to the truck and climbs in.

"What's happening?" I ask immediately as he fastens his seat belt and starts the engine.

"Well, it's their scene now, so we can go." He puts the truck in gear, checks his mirrors, and gives a two-fingered wave at the first officer as he pulls out and drives around them. "Both passengers are unconscious and smell like a brewery."

"Oh, shit."

"Yeah. They were still alive when the EMTs took over. I don't know what sent them into that tree, since there's no weather to speak of. Could have been an animal."

"Or alcohol," I mutter. "I guess it's a good thing they didn't hurt anyone else."

"That's the silver lining," he says with a sigh and glances my way. "Are you okay?"

"I'm totally fine." I'm turned on, that's what I am. I want to get my hands on him. I want to make him crazy, to feel the same things I feel. "How long until we're home?"

"Maybe fifteen minutes. Do you need a bathroom or something? Shit, I'm sorry, babe. It didn't occur to me—"

"I'm *fine*," I repeat and reach over to rest my hand on his hard thigh. "I just...I want to get you home. For stuff."

"For stuff." His eyes narrow on the road.

"Mm-hmm."

He goes just a little faster, and that makes me grin in the darkness. I *love* that Chase has a hard time keeping his hands off me. That he's not only affectionate, but our sex life is fun and *not* always missionary, in the dark, under the covers.

I have my knees pressed together on the seat by the time he pulls into his driveway, and I don't wait for him to walk around to open my door before I hop out, meet him at the front of the truck, and take his hand before almost pulling him into the house.

"I hate to say it out loud, but maybe we should come up on accidents more often. But just fender benders."

I spare him a grin, and as soon as the door is closed behind us, and we're safely inside, I squat down before him and go to work, opening his jeans. He's already rock-hard behind the zipper, and when I've pulled the tab down and tugged the button free, I nudge the denim and his boxers down his hips, and he springs free. He's heavy, warm, and smooth, and I wrap both hands around him, pulling up and down twice before I lick the crown.

"I don't know what the fuck got into you," he says as he pushes his fingers into my hair and fists them there, "but, Jesus, remind me to do it every goddamn day."

I chuckle and begin to lick and suck in earnest. I sink onto him and grip his tight, tender skin with my lips and pull up slowly, then my fingers journey over his balls to that sensitive spot underneath, where I rub firmly.

"Oh, God. I'm going to come, sweetheart."

I don't stop. There's no way in hell I'm going to stop. I hum around him, moving a little faster, a little firmer, and feel him tense as he growls low in his throat and coats the back of my throat.

I swallow and then kiss his hip, in that sexy dip of muscle that I didn't think was possible in real life and must have been photoshopped, but it's true. It exists.

On this man.

On *my* man.

"Talk to me," he says when he's caught his breath. "What brought that on?"

I push up his T-shirt to continue kissing his abs. "Outdoorsy Chase is sexy." Kiss his navel and he groans. "Family man Chase is hot." I climb to my feet and kiss his neck. "Cowboy Chase? Yeah, irresistible." I tug on his earlobe with my teeth. "But when you transformed into Cop Chase right before my very eyes and got all stern and bossy? Jesus, I was about to beg for you to fuck me."

"You like the bossy stuff?"

"I had no idea that was a thing for me, but I guess I do. You've taught me all kinds of sexy things about myself."

He hurries to pull his jeans up his hips, tosses me easily over his shoulder, and makes a beeline up the stairs for the bedroom, where he sets me on my feet and points to me.

"Get naked, but *do not* lie down."

I blink at him, and he cocks an eyebrow, as if he's asking, *Did I stutter?*

"No problem." I whip my T-shirt off, and then I

frown over at him. "Wait. We hiked all day and got a little sweaty, so maybe we should shower."

"I don't recall asking you to make any decisions."

And with that, he strides out of the bedroom, his shoulders so broad, his ass so fucking sexy in those jeans, and I bite my lip, *completely* turned the hell on. He's not being mean or abrasive, just bossy.

Like he was in the truck earlier, giving me orders because it was important. And I have a hunch that this is important, too.

So, I quickly shed my clothes, tossing them into the hamper, and I've just turned around when Chase returns. He takes my hand, kisses it, and leads me into the bathroom off of his bedroom.

"I'd already planned on a shower," he says with a grin. "And then I'm going to give you a massage. I don't want your leg cramping up again after today's hike."

"Oh, that sounds really nice."

He narrows his eyes just a little. "I don't think you'll describe it as *nice* when we're finished. Come on, get in."

The water is warm and feels great, washing away all the grime from being outside all day. We don't find any ticks on each other, but we do a great job of checking for them, and once we're clean, rinsed, and finished, Chase shuts off the water and leads me out of the shower.

He takes his time with a big, fluffy blue towel, paying close attention to make sure I'm dry, and when I'm about to walk to the bedroom, he stops me.

"Where are you going?"

"To the bedroom?"

"Nope. You're not dry."

"My hair can air dry."

But he lifts that brow again, and I feel a little thrill zip up my spine.

"Okay, what's next?"

He's mostly dry now, and still fully naked and half-aroused as he takes my shoulders in his hands and kisses my forehead tenderly. Then he kisses my nose and finally my lips.

"Don't worry about what's next, Blondie. I've got this. Okay?"

I nod, and he searches my eyes for a moment, and he must like what he sees there because he leads me to the vanity where he plugs in my blow dryer and treats me to having my hair blown out. He brushes and systematically moves the tool around my head, piece by piece, drying my hair, and when he's finished, he even reaches for my face moisturizer and dabs some onto his fingertips before working it into my skin.

I like the pampering. Having his hands on me, his *eyes* on me with gentle affection. And finally, he takes my hand in his, kisses it, and leads me out of the bathroom, shutting off the light as we go.

"Lie on the bed, face down," he says as he reaches for some lotion, and I do as I'm told. Happily. Willingly.

Joyfully.

And I sigh in delight when those big, strong hands of his start at my shoulders, and he begins kneading my muscles.

"You have the best hands," I say with a sigh. "Just the *best*."

"I'm glad you think so because I like having them on you."

I lose track of time, and likely my own name, as he works his way down my body, rubbing my muscles. When he gets to my leg, I let out a little moan.

"Does it still hurt?" he asks, pausing on my calf.

"A little, actually. And that was a long time ago, but I have had a few cramps since then."

"You didn't mention that to me."

I shrug and turn my head so I can see him. "They weren't as bad as that first time, and I can usually walk it out. I pissed off that muscle at some point. Oh, yeah, that feels good."

He finishes both legs and my feet, and then he sets the lotion aside and leans over to kiss my cheek.

"Roll onto your back, sweetheart."

Not feeling shy or hesitant in the least, I do as he requests, and I bite the tip of my finger as his gaze drifts up and down my body.

"You have a mark, right here." His finger drifts over a scar on my upper thigh. "What happened?"

"I walked into the corner of a desk when I was seventeen because I was reading a book and not watching where I was going."

"Jesus, you must have hit hard for it to scar."

"I was in a hurry to answer the door." I sigh when his fingers brush over the inside of my thighs.

"Why does it turn you on when I get stern?"

I think that over, frowning. "Because you're taking control of the situation, and I can trust that you have what's best for me in mind and that you can handle just about anything. *I* don't have to handle it, and I don't think I've ever had anyone in my life do that for me before. Not even my parents. So being with someone who can take the worry away from me? Yeah, that's amazing."

He doesn't respond right away, at least not with words. He covers me, kissing my shoulders and neck, and he takes my hands in his and presses them over my head on the mattress as he nestles between my legs and gently pushes inside of me.

"I'll never let anything happen to you," he whispers against my lips. We both sigh when he's seated fully, and then he starts to move, slowly at first, building us both up to a fervor that always seems to happen when we're together. "I'm happy to take care of you, especially like this."

I grin, but then my jaw drops open when he slips one hand between us and presses his thumb against my clit.

"I didn't know I could feel like this," I admit with a whisper.

"Goddamn, baby." He tips his forehead to mine, and we fall over the edge together.

It's raining harder than I've seen in *years*. I'm standing at the counter in the flower shop, watching through the window as it comes down in sheets, as if the gods are standing on the clouds, dumping buckets of water.

"It's angry out there," Ida says. "But it's supposed to be done by this afternoon and become sunny again."

"That doesn't seem possible," I murmur, shaking my head. "And we need the rain. It was a dry summer."

The bell over the door dings as Holden Lexington pushes inside, dripping wet.

"You don't own an umbrella?" Ida asks him.

"Hell no. I live in *Montana*. The weather changes on a dime." He strolls inside to the counter and grins at me. "I need a bouquet of flowers, please."

"Sure. Do you have anything specific in mind?" I ask him.

"Sunflowers, with red roses mixed in."

My eyebrows shoot up in surprise. "That's pretty specific."

"They're her favorite," he says with a shrug. "Do I need to come back for them?"

"I can deliver—" Holden's already shaking his head before I can finish the sentence. "Okay, no delivery. Give me five, and I'll have them ready for you."

"Excellent, thanks." He chats with the other ladies as I pull the bouquet together, and I have to admit, the bright yellow and deep red are stunning together.

"She has good taste." I pass him the wrapped bouquet with a smile.

"I'm the one with good taste," he says with a wink. "Thanks, ladies. Have a good day."

Just after Holden leaves, we see three people come

running down the sidewalk, huddled under umbrellas. They rush into my shop, bringing the rain with them, and when they lower the umbrellas, I realize that it's my *parents*.

"Mom?" I frown over at them, a little miffed that they're soaking my hardwood floor. "Dad? What are you doing here?"

"Surprise!" Evan, the third in their little trio, offers me a big smile as he spreads his arms out wide, as if he just jumped out of a cake or stuck a landing at the Olympics.

"Hello, doll," Dad says as they all walk over to me, and Dad leans in to buss my cheek. "We haven't seen you in a while, and Evan thought it would be fun for us to come for a visit, since you don't seem to make the time to come home."

"I *am* home," I say sweetly. My mom's looking around the shop with a wrinkled nose. She never could understand why I would lower myself to *retail*. "How are you guys?"

"Oh, we're just fine," Dad says. The whole time, Evan just stands there, preening as if he found the holy grail. "Let's head out and get some lunch."

"I'm sorry, I can't go. I'm working."

"Surely you can trust your employees to take over for the day," Mom says. "We're here to see *you*."

I notice that Ida doesn't jump in to shoo me out the door the way she would if Chase was doing the asking.

"I honestly can't, Mom. I'm sorry. We have a wedding tomorrow that we're getting ready for."

"Dinner, then," Evan says, rubbing his hands together. "The four of us will go out, on me. It'll be great."

My first instinct is to say no. To stand my ground. But I find myself nodding. "Okay, that sounds fine with me. I'll be done here at six, and I can meet you."

"Wearing *that*?" Mom demands, eyeing my simple T-shirt and jeans. "Evan will want to take us somewhere nice, Summer."

"You look great," Evan assures me. "Trust me, there's no place in town that requires formal attire. We'll see you soon, Summer."

And with that, they open their umbrellas, sending water spraying all over the place, and waltz back out the door.

It's as though a mini typhoon just came through the place.

"I'll grab a mop," Sharla says with a sigh. "Evan annoys me."

"Join the club," I murmur, just as the door opens again, but this time it's Jeannie, the manager of Mama's Deli, just down the street. She doesn't come inside but sends me an apologetic smile.

"I don't want to get your floor all wet, Summer. I have a lunch delivery for you from Chase."

At the mention of his name, joy rushes through me, washing away all the annoyance from just a few moments ago.

"Oh, thank you!" I hurry around the counter to

collect the brown paper bag. "I'm sorry you had to come in the rain."

"Oh, it's fine. It actually smells really good out there, but I can feel fall in the air. Okay, I'd better get back."

She waves, and then she's off once more, running through the rain.

"Where is Chase today?" Sharla asks. "And where's Lily?"

"They're together, out at the ranch," I reply as I unwrap a turkey on rye. I much prefer this to lunch with my parents. "He's working on his new shop."

"In the *rain*?" Ida asks.

"It's his day off, and he wants to get a start on it." I shrug and take a bite. "He said he'd keep Lily in the truck as long as it rained so she didn't get cold. I offered to bring her here, but he wanted to hang out with her today."

"Am I the only one who thinks it's the sweetest thing that he's kind of adopted you *and* your dog?" Sharla asks with a sigh. "It's super adorable."

"I agree. And Lily loves him. Half the time, she'd rather be with him anyway."

"You can trust a man who's good with animals," Ida says with a wise nod. "Animals know who the assholes are. Now, speaking of assholes, why are you going to dinner with *Evan*?"

"Because I'm going to shut this down, once and for all. Evan claims to understand that we're just friends, and then he pulls this? No. And my parents can't just show up here, act like complete snobs, and disrupt my life like that. It's rude, and it's disrespectful."

"So, you're going to put them all in their place," Ida says with a proud grin. "Good girl. I wish I could be a fly on the wall for that."

Surprisingly, the thought of the confrontation doesn't make me nervous at all. If anything, I'm anxious to get this over with.

"Hey there, beautiful," Chase says in my ear. I just closed up the shop, and now I'm headed over to Ciao, on foot, because it really did turn into a nice day after the monsoon earlier.

"Hi. How's it going out there today?"

"It was wet for a while, but the sun came out, and now we're plugging along. I'll head home if you're done."

"Actually, my parents surprised me today at the shop, and I agreed to meet them for dinner. I hope you don't mind."

"Of course not. They didn't tell you they were coming?"

"No, I had no idea, and I'm kind of pissed off at them, actually. They were rude when they stopped by, so I'm going to have a very frank conversation with them."

"Do you want me to meet you? For moral support?"

God, I love him.

"I don't want to subject you to that. You do your

thing, kiss Lily for me, and I'll let you know when we're done."

"Sounds good. I'll leave here before dark and head home. If you need a ride, just call me."

"I won't be drinking, but thanks. Oh, and we're going to Ciao, and that doesn't make me happy because *you and I* haven't had a chance to go there yet."

"It's just a restaurant, Blondie. It's fine. We'll go another time."

"Okay. Well, I'm here, so I'll let you go. See you later."

I hang up, pop my phone into my bag, and walk into the restaurant.

"How can I help you?" the hostess asks.

"I'm meeting three others here. The reservation was probably under Evan."

"Oh, yes, they're here. I'll show you." She smiles and gestures for me to follow her through the restaurant. It's cozy in here, with white tablecloths that have parchment paper over them, and it looks like people are drawing on them with crayons.

Then, I notice the artwork on the walls. Some are obviously by kids, but others are beautiful works of art done by adults.

That's kind of fun.

"Here you go," she says, after leading me out to the patio seating, and I nod my thanks and then take my seat next to Evan.

"You're finally here," he says and leans over to kiss my cheek, as if he's my *boyfriend.*

My parents smile at us, and I can just hear their internal dialogue.

"At last, she's met a nice boy who has political aspirations."

There's already garlic bread on the table and a glass of red wine waiting for me. I'm not a lover of red wine, but I take a nice, long sip, making my dad frown. Then I reach for the bread.

"That's a lot of carbs," my mom reminds me.

"Thank God." I eat half the piece in one bite, and my mom firms her jaw. She sent me to etiquette school when I was thirteen and is likely champing at the bit to tell me to behave myself. "So, please, tell me again why you're here."

"It's a surprise," Evan says and nudges me with his shoulder. "I thought it would be fun, and when your dad told me that they haven't been to Bitterroot Valley in so many years, I thought they'd like to see the life their daughter has made for herself here."

"And upon seeing it," Mom says, "I'm glad we came so we can talk you into moving back to Helena, where you belong."

I frown over at her. My father sighs, but he doesn't disagree with her.

And Evan just continues to smile, as if he's won the lottery.

"I *love* living here," I inform her. "I have a business."

"That you'll sell, of course," she says. "Certainly, once you and Evan are married, you won't continue to make flower bouquets."

"Wait." I hold up a hand and whip my gaze over to Evan, who's now squirming in his seat, but he flashes me that charming smile. "*Marry* you?"

"Not right away," he says, clearly grasping for words.

"Try not *ever*." I stare at my parents in disbelief. "I have a *boyfriend*. A man that I love very much, and it's not Evan. I have a business and a community that loves me. Why would you ever think that I'd give all of that up to move back to Helena where I have *nothing*?"

"You don't have *nothing*," Dad says sharply enough to garner looks from the next table. "You have your family. And you'll eventually see that marrying Evan is what's best for you. You've been groomed to be a politician's wife since you were a child, Summer. This is what your mother and I have always wanted for you."

"You'll be well taken care of," Evan assures me and covers my hand with his, making my stomach roll. I pull away from his touch and glare at all of them.

"You're crazy. First of all, I'm a grown woman, and arranged marriages are no longer a thing in this country."

"You'd be surprised," my father mutters, shaking his head.

"Second of all, I'm not moving anywhere. This is my home. Not Helena. I'm *happy* here, and as I've shown you over and over again, I don't want anything from you. Not your money or your political connections. Nothing."

"Keep going and *nothing* is exactly what you'll get," Mom says, her voice as cold as the Arctic.

"Fine by me. I don't need or want anything from

you." I turn to Evan now and see that he's frowning. His hands are in angry fists. "And you. You were supposed to be my *friend*. That's all you were. I never played games with you. I never lied to you. I don't have romantic feelings for you, Evan, and I don't want any kind of a life with you. You know that I'm in a committed relationship."

"This whole trip was a waste of time," Dad says, and I nod in agreement.

"It absolutely was. We'll go back to exchanging polite Christmas cards, and that's about it. And as for you," I turn back to Evan, "I want nothing more to do with you."

I slap my napkin onto the table and storm out of the restaurant. I'm not one for public displays, but there was just no choice in the matter. There was no other way to get my point across.

What am I to them, some sort of *whore*? Someone who can be bought and paid for?

You'll be well taken care of.

"Fuck that," I mutter as I stomp down the sidewalk. "I can take care of myself. I've been doing it for the better part of three decades."

Walking past the patio, I glance their way and find all three of them talking at once, frowning, clearly upset.

They can all go fuck themselves.

CHAPTER SIXTEEN
CHASE

"You know what?" I shove my phone into my pocket and gaze over at Lily, who's sitting up in the little pink dog bed I brought out to the job site for her to relax in. "I think we're done here for the day. Why don't we go ahead and head home?"

She tilts her head at my words, and I get to work, packing up the few tools I have out. I've always been good at cleaning up as I go, so there's not too much to do.

I had help out here earlier, but Brady and Remington went home about an hour ago, and after the call with Summer just now, I think I'm ready to go, as well.

"You're probably hungry," I murmur to the dog as I make sure that everything is locked and tucked away, out of the weather, not that anyone would steal anything out here, but it's better to be safe than sorry. I lift Lily and her bed into my arms and set them both in the cab of the truck.

I'm happy with today's progress. Two walls are up,

and with the promise of more help over the next few days, we should get the first floor framed in rather quickly. It's damn satisfying.

I feel bad that Summer's parents surprising her with a trip to town isn't a welcome one. If I lived far away from my family, and they rolled into town to surprise me, I'd be excited as hell. But one of the things I quickly learned about my girl is that we come from two very different backgrounds. Part of me wants to meet up with them at the restaurant to meet her folks and find out what the deal is there. But I could tell by her tone on the phone that this isn't a conversation that she's excited about, so I'll let her handle it without me.

Of course, at some point, I'll have to have a man-to-man conversation with her father, but there's no rush for that.

"It's not too busy in Bitterroot Valley for a Friday evening," I say to Lily as we drive into town. The heart of tourist season is definitely over, and there are fewer and fewer tourists in the area every weekend. It's a welcome change from the hustle and bustle of the heart of summer. I'm ready for the couple of months of relative quiet that we'll get before ski season kicks in around the holidays.

As I stop at a red light, I glance over to Ciao and notice that Summer and her parents are sitting out on the patio. I'd recognize her golden hair and the self-assured set of her shoulders anywhere.

But then it dawns on me that she's not only with her parents. She's sitting next to Evan Spencer.

I frown and lean forward and watch as that slimy son of a bitch wraps his arm around her fucking shoulders.

Someone honks behind me, and I realize that the light has turned green, so I drive ahead, scowling.

"What the fuck is going on?" My stomach fills with lead, and blood roars through my ears as anger sets in.

Why didn't she mention that Evan was going to dinner, as well? What kind of game is she playing?

"Maybe I didn't see that right." I take a right and drive around the block, intending to get another look at this cozy dinner. There can't be something going on between Summer and Evan. The thought is absolutely ludicrous. Besides, when would she have time? She's either at work, or she's with me.

Except when I'm working nights or swing shifts.

"Calm the fuck down," I mutter to myself. "There's a reasonable explanation, and you know it."

And if there isn't, I'll kill the slimy bastard.

As I turn the corner by Ciao and look at the patio, only Summer's parents and Evan remain at the table, deep in conversation. Summer's gone.

"Did she go to the bathroom?"

And then I see her. No, she didn't go to the ladies' room. She's striding—no, *marching*—down the street toward the flower shop, and I pull up to the curb and roll down the window.

"Summer?"

She doesn't acknowledge me, and she's muttering to herself. She looks pissed as hell.

"Summer!"

She jumps and looks my way, then walks to the door and sighs, pushing her hand through her hair. Lily jumps up to kiss Summer through the open window.

"Hey, sorry. I was going to get my car and then go to my place to get some things." She scratches Lily's head absently.

"Hop in."

"My car—"

"Will be there in the morning. Get in the truck, Summer." Her eyes narrow at the sharp tone of my voice, but she opens the door, scoops Lily onto her lap, and fastens her seat belt. "We'll go to your house first."

"I'm so mad I probably shouldn't drive anyway," she says and pushes her hands through her hair again. "I will tell you everything that happened, but right now, I need to seethe."

"Seethe away," I reply simply and drive into the neighborhood and park in Summer's driveway. Lily takes a second to squat in the front yard to relieve herself, and then the three of us go inside after Summer unlocks the door and disarms the alarm.

"Get what you need to get." I move to walk back to the kitchen for some water, but Summer rounds on me.

"Why am I getting attitude from you?"

I stop and, standing across from her, fold my arms over my chest, watching as she frowns at me. "I just rolled by Ciao on my way home and saw you on the patio with your parents and *Evan*, and the motherfucker had his hand on you—*again*. I'm doing my best to stay relatively calm and hear you out when you're ready to talk about it, Summer. This isn't attitude; this is barely restrained patience."

"I didn't do anything wrong." She points her thumb at her chest, and I nod.

"Okay."

"But you don't believe me."

"I didn't say that. I don't have any reason *not* to believe you, but I know what I saw, and I have questions."

She closes her eyes and turns her back to me, pulling her hand down her face. "I'm sorry. I'm so mad, and you're a handy target right now. You didn't deserve that."

"Apology accepted. So, wanna tell me what's going on so I don't go out, find Evan, and dispose of the goddamn body?"

She turns back to me and grins. "You'd do that for me?"

"No, sugar, I'd do that for *me*. What happened tonight?"

Lily kicks at her food container, indicating that she's hungry, so Summer scoops some food into the dog's bowl and then takes my hand and leads me into the living room where she sits on the couch.

"I don't want to sit," I tell her, and then she stands and paces to the window.

"Me neither, actually. I told you that they came to my shop. My parents. Well, Evan was with them. *Evan* is the reason they came to town in the first place. He said it was a surprise for me."

Her laugh holds no humor as she turns my way and shakes her head.

"They wanted me to leave work right then to join them for lunch, but I said no. I didn't want to go to dinner tonight either, but I decided to so I could shut them all down and remind them that I'm a freaking adult, and I'm not moving back to Helena, and I'm absolutely, unequivocally *not* marrying Evan, for fuck's sake."

"Whoa." I hold up a hand, and she stops talking. "He proposed to you?"

"No." She shakes her head and waves me off. "No, at dinner, my parents told me that I would sell the business and move back *home*—what a joke—and that once I married Evan, I wouldn't want to make flower arrangements anymore anyway."

My eyes narrow. My blood runs hot. The thought of Summer moving away is unimaginable, but marrying another man? Marrying fucking *Evan Spencer*? Not if I have anything to say about it.

"And then, I made it *very* clear that I have no intentions of doing any of that. *Bitterroot Valley* is home. And Evan is absolutely nothing to me. I'm *in* a happy, loving relationship. Why don't they respect that? Why can't they just let me live my own life?"

I cross to her and pull her against me, frame her face, and close my lips over hers, kissing her until neither of us can breathe, and I have to back away to take in air. She frowns as she stares up into my eyes and grips onto my biceps.

"Jesus, Chase, you have to know that I would *never*— Evan is—God, I would *never* betray you like that."

"You didn't tell me he would be there." I tip my forehead to hers and feel myself settle for the first time since I saw her sitting at that table. "It gave me a bad moment when I saw you."

"I was so focused on getting there, on telling them all off and standing up for myself, I guess it didn't occur to me to mention him, and I'm sorry for that. Earlier, at the shop, he didn't hurt my feelings. My *mom* did. She made my shop seem small and...*icky*. And I didn't really think of him. I *never* think of him, Chase."

"He had his hand on you."

"And I shrugged him off. You don't have to worry about him or anyone else, ever, because in case you've missed it, I'm so fucking in love with you, all I see is little puffy red hearts above my head all the time."

"Okay, then." I plant a kiss on her forehead and then realize that Lily is hitting the back door. "I'll go let her out, and you grab your things."

"I can do that," she replies, but her eyes don't leave mine. "Chase, are we okay?"

"Yeah." I wrap my arms around her and hug her close, breathe her in, relieved that the storm has passed. "Yeah, we're good, sugar."

Lily hits the back door again, and I grin.

"I'll take her out."

"Thank you."

Lily rushes out the back door ahead of me to sniff around the yard and do her business. It occurs to me that she hasn't been here in several weeks, so she has to take her time, checking out every nook and cranny. But that's okay because it gives *me* a chance to take a deep breath and settle my nerves.

I'm not typically a jealous man, but seeing Evan next to Summer in that restaurant tonight is something I don't want to relive any time soon.

Finally, once Lily has finished, we return to the back door and walk inside, and I hear voices.

Lily growls, and she *never* growls.

"Easy, baby," I murmur to her and instinctively push her behind me as I hurry out to the living room and find Evan standing on the porch, his face red with anger. Summer's blocking the doorway so he can't come inside, and I stay out of his sight but in Summer's peripheral vision so she knows I'm here.

"You have got to be *kidding* me," he demands, and Summer holds a hand up to me on the other side of the door where Evan can't see as if to say, *I've got this.*

So, with my hands fisted at my sides, I wait and watch. But if that fucker makes *one* wrong move, I'll have him on the ground.

"You're giving up a spectacular life for what, exactly? For a goddamn *flower* shop? For fucking *Chase Wild*? You're nuts, Summer. Do you even realize the opportunities that your parents can offer you? That *I* can offer? You don't have to work; you don't have to struggle. Jesus, you should be shopping and primping and volunteering. Having *fun*. I can send you shopping in all the best shops in the world. You won't have to slum it in Polly's place anymore."

"Number one, she's my best friend, and I love her shop, and number two, that sounds so incredibly boring and ridiculous." Her voice is calm, and she's not visibly reacting to him at all.

Good girl.

"Evan, I don't know what I can do that I haven't already done to make you understand that I'm not the woman meant for you. I'm not the girl you think you want."

"You're wrong."

Fucking asshole.

"No, I'm not." She gentles her voice, trying to make him see reason. "That life you described isn't for me. I'm sorry if that shatters some kind of dream or illusion of yours, but it's the truth. Like I told you and my parents at the restaurant, I *love* my life here."

"You don't know what you're talking about." I hear him turn to pace away from her. He's starting to lose control. I can sense it. "You're just confused."

"I'm not confused."

"YES, YOU ARE!" He pushes through the door now as Summer scurries backward, his hand raised to hit her, and instinct immediately kicks in, and I stand between the two of them, push my hand on the other man's chest, and glower at him.

"You fucking touch her, and it'll be the last thing you do."

Evan's eyes are wide as he stares up at me.

"This doesn't concern you, asshole."

"Agree to disagree." I drop my hand and back away just a bit to take Summer's hand in mine. "She said what she has to say. Now you can get fucked."

"Or what? You'll *arrest* me?" He sneers, and I slowly shake my head.

"No. I'll kick your ass. I can hurt you in ways that don't leave a mark. No one will believe that I'm the one who did it." He doesn't sneer now, and he swallows hard as he wipes his hand over his mouth, straightens his shirt, and squares his shoulders. His gaze turns to Summer.

"This isn't over."

"That's *exactly* what this is," she replies, her voice leaving no room for argument. "It's over, Evan. If it makes you feel better, you can keep my parents. I think you're all well-suited for each other."

Evan snarls as he turns and rushes out of the house, slamming the door behind him, and Summer steps into my arms and holds on tight.

"He was going to hit me."

"He was going to try," I reply and kiss the top of her head. "I have a feeling you would have fought back and beat the shit out of him."

"Oh, I would have fought back," she confirms. "Come on, let's get out of here, okay?"

"Fine by me."

With Summer tucked safely away at work, and Lily at Paula's for the rest of the weekend, I get into my truck and head over to the station. I have the next three days off, but I want to check in with my boss and fill him in on what went down at Summer's last night.

An hour later, with the knowledge that Evan was seen driving out of town this morning, following Summer's parents toward Helena, I get back into the truck.

Despite Evan being gone right now, Summer will have extra patrols driving past her house and her business for the time being. Technically, Evan didn't break any laws last night, but we all agree that it's a good idea to keep an eye on things for a while.

I'm ready to take some of my pent-up aggression out on my hammer, but first, I need to swing by Ryan's place to check in and see how things are going with Jake. Jake's two idiot friends, the ones he was with when they were caught shoplifting at Polly's place, were arrested again last night for minors in possession of alcohol.

Little idiots.

Ryan told me via text that he and the kid were down at the stables, so I drive straight there. Ryan's property is fucking gorgeous. He bought some acreage that had the stables and a house on it a few years ago. The old house was torn down, and he built himself a fucking mansion in its place.

Of course, my big brother can afford it.

The amazing thing is, although the house is big— way too big for just one person, in my opinion—and extra fancy with all the high-tech gadgets and doodads a man could want, it also fits into the landscape nicely. There's a lot of glass for looking out at the mountains, several outdoor living spaces that made me shake my head because, for at least six months out of the year, they're useless, and a pool.

My brother, one of the smartest men I know, put in a goddamn pool in Montana.

It takes all kinds, I guess.

Of course, Johnny and Holly, Rem's kids, had a lot of fun in that pool this past summer, so I guess it's worth it.

I pull up to a stop and grin when Ryan waves at me from where he and Jake stand with a couple of horses. This past spring, my brother rescued several horses from a neglectful situation, and they're still healing.

"Hey," I say as I walk to where the other two men are. I stand on the other side of the fence and grin when a pretty mare the color of chocolate walks over to me and nudges my shoulder, looking for some petting. "Hello, gorgeous. She's so damn friendly, Ry."

"She's a sweetheart," Ryan agrees with a nod. "I call her Ladybug. She seems to like it."

I pet the mare's nose and glance over at Jake, who's bridling a white mare.

"How's it going, Jake?"

"Fine."

Ryan rolls his eyes. "He's a kid of few words."

"I *am* doing fine," Jake says with a shrug. "I get to hang out with these girls all day. I have nothing to complain about."

"That's more like it." I grin and kiss the horse's cheek.

"Hey," Jake croons to the horse as he fastens the bridle. "That's a good girl. You're okay, sweetheart."

"Has a way with horses," Ryan says, and I see Jake smile, but he doesn't look this way. "And he's bunking here this weekend."

"You don't have a bunkhouse."

"No. Ryan set me up inside," Jake says, volunteering the information. "Janice and Wally took the kids to the hot springs this weekend."

"Why didn't they take you?" I ask him.

"Because I'm not their kid, no matter what the state says. They're just in it for the check every month anyway." He shakes his head and turns to get the blanket that goes on the horse's back under the saddle and then the saddle itself. "It's fine by me. I'm definitely *not* their kid, and I don't want to hang out with them any more than I have to."

I narrow my eyes at the boy. "Is everything okay in that house, Jake?"

"Fine." With the horse saddled, he hops up into the seat and looks down at Ryan. "I'll be back in a few."

Ryan nods, and as Jake rides away, we share a look.

"Something isn't right there," Ryan says. "He swears that they're not mean to him or anything, but they do shit like this all the damn time. Go do fun things with their *real* family and leave Jake behind. Sure, he's old enough to be home alone, but—"

"I don't like it either." I sigh, watching Jake ride the

horse gently in the field, speaking softly to her. "I'll make some calls and see what I can find out."

I glance back at my brother, and I can see the wheels turning in his head as he watches Jake.

"What are you thinking?" I ask him.

"I have a hunch, that's all. And if I'm right, I'm already fucking pissed."

I nod, understanding perfectly.

"I'll keep you posted."

CHAPTER SEVENTEEN
SUMMER

"I'm *so* excited." I practically bounce on my feet as Polly and I walk in the sunshine toward Bitterroot Valley Coffee Co. "I can't believe she actually did it."

"I can," Polly counters. "Millie's a smart girl, and this new business venture is going to be amazing for her."

Today is Millie's first official day as the owner of the coffee shop, and we're meeting over there with Erin, Abbi, and Millie herself so we can celebrate a bit and talk about our new *women in business* group.

I've been looking forward to it all week.

"You've been extra smiley the past month or so," I say to her. "In fact, since the Wild wedding, now that I think about it. Anything you'd like to share with the class?"

Polly bites her lower lip, and I stop cold, staring at her.

"Spill it, Polly Ann. Right now."

"I slept with Ryan," she hisses, looking around to see if anyone is in earshot as I goggle at her.

"What!"

"I'm not repeating that in public," she says with a short laugh. "It was just the one time. Well, about six times, but just the one night."

"*Six* times?" I demand. "Jesus, good for you."

"There's just something about those Wild men," she says, shaking her head. "It's like they're witches or some-thing, putting a girl under a spell. The *orgasms*, Summer. Jesus fucking Christ, I had no idea. There's some serious talent there."

I smile and waggle my eyebrows. "I get that, my friend. I totally get that. Are you still seeing him?"

"No." She shakes her head definitively, and I frown at her. "One-night thing, remember?"

"Why, though? If it was that hot and you like him, why just one night?"

"Hi, guys!" Erin and Abbi pull up in Erin's big white SUV, and Polly and I hurry over to meet them, putting an end to our sexy conversation, but I mentally bookmark the topic and plan to revisit it later.

"I have the flowers," I inform the others as I hold up the bouquet I'm carrying.

"I brought brownie cheesecake," Polly adds, and we all make *mmmm* noises.

"I don't even want to think about how many calories are in that," Abbi says, eyeing the covered plate that Polly holds. "But I'm going to eat the hell out of it."

"I have balloons," Erin announces. "This is the best party *ever*."

Before we can get inside the coffee shop, I frown at

Erin. "Is the rest of the family peeved that they don't get to be here to celebrate Millie's new business?"

"Nah, we're having family dinner on Sunday to celebrate," Erin assures me as she opens the door, and we all walk in, bright smiles on our faces.

Millie plans to close the coffee shop early today so we can have our party privately, and when we walk in, it's just Millie and...Holden Lexington. And sitting on the counter, in a vase, are sunflowers with red roses.

I think my heart just melted a bit.

"Ladies," Holden says with that charming grin of his. "I'd love to stay to help you celebrate Millie's new venture, but I've been told that men aren't allowed."

"Assholes aren't allowed," Millie mutters as she wipes the countertops.

Holden just grins at her. "The way she fawns over me is *so* embarrassing."

Millie rolls her eyes, and the four of us snicker as Holden turns his attention back to Millie. "Have a great day, Mill. You're going to *kill* it."

He nods at us, and then he's off, and I turn to stare at Polly in surprise.

She shrugs, Erin clears her throat, and Abbi pretends to be *really* interested in the menu.

Millie frowns and fiddles with the petals of one of the roses in the bouquet that Holden brought her, and then she bursts into tears.

"Oh, shit," I mutter as I set the flowers that I brought, and apparently didn't need, on the table. Everyone sets down their wares, and we hurry over to our friend. "What's wrong, honey?"

"Was Holden mean to you?" Polly demands. "'Cause I'll kick his ass into next week."

"She may be small," Abbi adds, "but she's mighty."

"No, he just came in to bring me these flowers and say congratulations. That's not it. It's mine." She gives us a watery laugh and wipes the tears from her cheeks. "It's just hitting me, you know? Over the past couple of months, it was just an idea, something to think about, but now, it's real. This is all mine. Well, Ryan's, technically, but I'll pay him back."

She sniffs and accepts a napkin from Erin, dabbing at her eyes.

"Sorry, guys, I'm so happy; it just all caught up to me."

"Well, of course, it did," Abbi says. "Owning your own business is a big deal. But this is going to be amazing for you."

"I have so many plans," Millie continues. "I can't wait to tell you guys everything that I want to do. The things I want to change and add."

"We want to hear everything," I tell her. "Let's eat and talk about all the things."

"We also have to discuss the Iconic Women's Collective," Erin reminds us. "And arrange our first iconic meeting."

Millie grins. "Anyone want some coffee?"

"Me!" we all yell in unison and then laugh as we grab a seat.

"How's married life?" I ask Erin as I slice the cheese-cake. "Is it boring yet?"

"I don't know if you saw the man I'm married to," Erin says with a smug grin, "but he's hot as fuck, and I can guarantee you that life with him is *never* going to be boring."

"She's so fucking smug," Abbi says, shaking her head. "If I wasn't so happy for her, I'd be disgusted."

"Holly has asked for a baby sister," Erin continues.

"Are you—"

"No," Erin says in response to my almost question. "Not yet. I want a little time with the family I already have before I start adding to it. Now, what about you, Summer? How are things with Chase?"

I grin and take a bite of my cheesecake, making everyone laugh. "Things are *damn fine*, thank you very much. Now, that's enough man talk. I have ideas for our Iconic Women's Collective group. Let's start things off with a cocktail party."

"Ooh, I'm always down for a cocktail party," Abbi says, dancing in her seat. "I love an excuse to dress up."

"Where will this cocktail party be held?" Erin wants to know.

"At the resort," I reply. "There's a gorgeous bar up there that I do the flowers for every week. The manager is a woman, and I'll bet I could talk her into shutting it down for us one evening. We'll have a keynote speaker, cocktails, and dinner."

"Can I suggest someone for the speaker?" Polly asks.

"I think it'll draw quite a crowd of entrepreneurs, especially if we get the word out on social media."

"Of course. Who do you have in mind?"

"London Ambrose."

We're all quiet for a moment, and then we grin, and Erin nods with confidence.

"London would do it in a heartbeat," Erin says. "This is right up her alley, *and* I sort of have an in with her husband. Since he's my cousin and all that."

"Lesson number one in business," Millie says. "It's not what you know, it's who you know."

"You've got that right." I clink my cup of coffee against hers. "This is going to be *the shit.*"

"We're looking at next Friday night." I sip my water and then pop a potato chip into my mouth. Chase and I are sitting on the park bench near my shop, sharing lunch, and I'm filling him in on the meeting with the girls earlier.

"And it's for women only?"

"Yep. And, of course, a woman doesn't have to own her own business already. Maybe she wants to start one up, or maybe she manages something. Really, it's about empowering others. And who better to start with than London Ambrose? The woman is *amazing.*"

"I agree. I think it's great. Good for you guys. I went into the coffee shop earlier. Millie is already doing great in there. She made me something called a Snickers mocha."

"She's going to do a signature drink of the day," I reply with a nod. "I think it's a good idea, but she might want to switch to changing the drink out weekly. Every day is a little ambitious."

"She's excited and has the energy for it now." He turns to me and slides the tip of his finger down my jawline, making my nipples pucker in anticipation.

Of course, I'm wearing a white T-shirt, and it hides *nothing*.

"God, you're fucking amazing," he whispers. He's sitting over there in his uniform, looking sexy as fuck, and I'm supposed to keep my hands to myself when he says things like *that*? "I want to take you home and slide right inside of you."

I swallow hard and lean into his touch. "Unfortunately, we both have to go back to work."

"That *is* unfortunate. Rain check?"

"Rain, sun, blizzard, you name it." He laughs, and I smile at him, enjoying the way he's looking at me, as if he could eat me whole.

"How's work?" He's likely smart to change the subject, but I really enjoy flirty Chase.

"It's good." I shrug a shoulder and glance over at my shop. "I've decided to start putting small bouquets of flowers outside in a bucket. They'll be wrapped in bunches with pretty paper, and I'll only charge five dollars for each bunch. I'll leave an envelope outside for the cash."

"The honor system?" He frowns, thinking it over.

"Yeah. It'll be flowers that I have a surplus of, and I think more people will pay for them than just take them."

"You have a lot of faith in people."

I shift in my seat and face him. "You see a lot of the bad in people, but the majority are not that way, you know."

"I know. You're right. I think it's a good idea."

I laugh at that and shove his shoulder. "You do *not*. You think I'll get ripped off."

"I think the theory behind the idea *is* great," he clarifies. "And yeah, you're gonna get ripped off. I'm going to have to stand outside in my uniform and give people the goddamn stink eye so they don't steal from you."

"You'd make a handsome flower guard," I say as I contemplate another chip. "I might hire you for it."

He smirks and tucks my hair behind my ear. "I'd like to stick around and discuss this further, but I have to get back to work, Blondie."

"Me, too." I sigh and look up at the sky. "I think it's going to rain later. Fall is definitely here."

"I'm ready for it," he says as we stand. "I think you're right about the rain. Let me know if you need anything."

"I'm fine. I'll see you tonight." He pulls me close and kisses the breath right out of me, before letting go so I can walk back to work. As always, I feel his eyes on my back, and I turn to blow him a kiss. "Love you, babe."

That devastating grin spreads over his face. "Love you back."

Just as I reach the door to Paula's Poseys, Evan walks out of his office and stops short when he sees me. In the past, he'd smile and maybe follow me inside to chat, but today, his jaw firms, he nods once, and then he marches away angrily.

At least he doesn't yell at me or try to talk me into going to Helena. Since that night last week at the restaurant, and then at my house, I haven't heard a thing from Evan *or* my parents, and that suits me just fine.

I glance over my shoulder and see that Chase hasn't moved. His arms are crossed over his chest, and his gaze is pinned to Evan as the man walks down the street.

I don't think that Evan will try to do anything to me, but I love knowing that Chase is nearby to have my back.

"What was for lunch?" Ida asks when I walk inside.

"Sandwiches." I reach for my apron and tie it on.

"Girl, you waste your lunch break with eating," Sharla says, shaking her head. "You need to take him home and give him a lunch break to *remember*."

I blink in surprise, but when I think about it, it's not a bad idea. Not bad at all. Maybe I'll suggest we have lunch at home tomorrow, and I'll surprise him.

I don't even have a chance to check my list for what's next when my phone makes the noise it makes when my house alarm goes off.

Scowling, I pull the phone out of my pocket and stare at the screen. Yep, the alarms are going off, and it says that someone was on my porch.

Immediately, I call Chase.

"Hi, sugar," he says in my ear. "What's that noise?"

"My phone. My house alarm is going off, Chase. And the app says someone was at my door."

"I'm headed there now." I hear him flip on the siren. "You stay at work, Summer."

"Like hell, something's happening at my *house.*"

"Please, stay where you are." His voice has that edge now, just like that night when we came upon the accident. "I'll call you as soon as I know anything."

He hangs up, and I blow out a breath. "I do not want to stay here."

"It's *your* house," Sharla points out and shrugs a shoulder. "You have the right to go."

"But you might be in Chase's way, especially if something nefarious is going on," Ida adds, shaking her head.

"*Nefarious?*" I laugh, shaking my head. "I doubt it. I'm going to go check it out. I never agreed to stay here."

"He's going to be *mad,*" Ida whispers, but I grab my keys and bag and head out to the car.

There are three squad cars in front of my house when I pull up, and Chase's eyes find mine when I jump out of my vehicle.

"I told you—"

"It's *my house,*" I remind him. "And I'm not in danger because you're here. What's going on?"

His mouth flattens in temper, and he looks away from me, shakes his head, and then props his hands on his hips.

"Chase? What the hell is going on?"

"Someone threw a rock through your living room window," he says. "It shattered the glass."

"*What*?" I move to walk to the house, but he stops me. "Chase, this is bullshit. Let me in there."

"It's a crime scene," he says, holding me where I am on the sidewalk. "You can't go in there, Summer, not until we investigate what happened."

"Chase." I stare up at him, feeling completely helpless as my hands start to shake. "Someone shattered my window. On *purpose*."

"It's definitely on purpose."

I search his hazel eyes. "What aren't you telling me?"

"There was a note attached to the rock." He rubs his hand over his mouth. "Summer, I don't think—"

"What did it say?"

"Summer."

"What did the fucking note say?"

He swears under his breath and shuffles his feet. "It just called you a fucking whore."

I take a step backward and feel like someone kicked me in the stomach. "Like the spray paint on the house. What the hell did I do to someone to deserve *this*?"

"You didn't do anything," he rushes to assure me, but I shake my head.

"Obviously, I did. If someone is doing all of this, I must have hurt them in some way, or I did something—"

"This isn't your fault," he assures me, taking my shoulders in his hands. "You didn't ask for this, babe. Let me take care of this. I'll handle it. If you don't want to go back to work, grab Lily and go to my place, and I'll meet you there later."

I nod and take a long, shaky breath. "You go back to

work. I think I *will* go back to the shop and keep my mind busy for a while."

"I'm sorry, Summer."

"Yeah, me, too."

When I get back to my store, I fill the others in on what's going on, and we spend at least an hour speculating on who could be behind this.

"It's not random kids," Ida says, shaking her head.

"I don't know anyone who has any kind of a grudge against me," I tell them, worrying my lower lip between my teeth.

"Except Evan," Sharla reminds me. I had to tell them all what happened last week because they asked what happened at dinner. "He was mad, and maybe he's the one doing it."

"I ran into him literally *minutes* before my phone went off," I remind her. "He can't be in two places at once. Besides, he was headed in the opposite direction, toward the courthouse."

"Yeah, and he's not the type to throw rocks through windows," Sharla concedes. "You're right. I don't know, but it's scary. I'm glad you're not staying there right now."

"Me, too." I don't know what I'd do without Chase. "I think the adrenaline is wearing off. It made me sweat."

"I'd be bawling my eyes out," Sharla says.

"I think I'm getting used to it. Isn't that horrible?"

"Yes, it *is* horrible," Ida says sternly. "And I plan to ask Chase what he's going to do about it. This has to stop."

"He's working on it," I assure her.

"We need to talk." It's several hours later, and Chase has just walked through his front door. I brought Lily here not long ago and have been waiting for him to get home.

"Yeah, we do." He kisses my forehead as he passes by to the kitchen and pulls a bottle of water out of the fridge, twists off the cap, and takes a long sip. "You go first."

"I'm selling my house."

That catches his attention. His eyes narrow on my face as he lowers the bottle.

"I have to, Chase. So much has happened that I just can't go back to living there. I'll buy something else or just rent somewhere for a while. If I need to, I can move in with Aunt Paula."

"You'll stay here," he says immediately.

"I don't want to put you out—"

"You've been living with me for months," he reminds me. "And if I have my way, you'll move in and live here permanently."

"Per—" I swallow hard and have to lower into the chair behind me. "Permanently?"

"Yes." He frames my face in his hands. "You'll stay *here*. It's where you belong, Blondie. Here with me."

CHAPTER EIGHTEEN
CHASE

The days are getting shorter. The sun hasn't even started to *think* about rising yet when I open my eyes and discover that my alarm will go off in just thirty minutes. Rolling over, I take in the sleepy Summer lying next to me. She's breathing softly, and she's so damn sweet it takes my breath away.

I understand why she wants to sell her place. There's been too much bad mojo there, and even when we find out who's been vandalizing her home, I wouldn't want to live there anymore either. Too much has happened for her to feel comfortable there.

But I don't want her to rent another place or go anywhere else. *This* is her home. I want her here every goddamn day. In *this* bed, in this house, or out at the ranch. I want to be wherever she is, always.

I drag a fingertip lightly down her nose, unable to resist her. She's so warm and...*mine*. I take a journey over her skin with just my fingertips, across her belly, and down over one hip, then back again, barely scraping my nails over her flesh.

"Mm." She turns into me and slides her leg against mine and then up onto my hip, opening herself to me. "Good morning."

"Morning." My lips claim hers gently, lazily, as we wake up with the world around us. With my hand wrapped around her throat and jaw, I explore her mouth and groan when she grips onto my already hard dick. Jesus, her touch always sends my whole system into hyperdrive.

But I want this morning to be slow. Easy. I'm making love to my girl, here in the early morning quiet, and nothing has ever felt so fucking right.

She guides me to her, and I easily slip inside of her, and we both sigh with pure, unadulterated pleasure.

"Never." My voice is hoarse, cutting through the quiet. "It's never been like this before, baby."

She moans as I start to move in long, slow strokes as the room shifts from dark to gray in the early morning light. She arches against me, clinging to my shoulder, as I feel her start to convulse around my cock.

"That's it, sweetheart." I kiss her cheek and then her nose. "Go over, baby."

That's all I have to say to have her calling out my name and coming hard around me. She's fucking spectacular.

"You, too," she whispers and digs her teeth into my shoulder, and I let go.

I'd like to stay here, inside of her, all damn day, but I can't. I have to get ready for work.

"Stay where you are." I kiss her once more and then roll away from her and head for the bathroom to clean myself up, and just when I grab a washcloth to wet for her, she appears in the mirror behind me. "You didn't stay."

"I have to use the facilities," she says with a grin as she wraps her arms around me from behind and presses a kiss to my back. "Sorry, I had to disobey."

"It's okay." I turn and catch her face in my hands. "I'll spank you later."

"Oh, no." Her eyes shine with humor as she does her best to sound disappointed. "Whatever shall I do?"

I laugh and kiss her hard. "Clean up, smartass. I'll be back in a minute with your coffee."

"Now, that, I won't complain about."

Leaving her in the bathroom, I make my way downstairs, and Lily is right on my heels. I let her outside to do her business while I get the coffee going, and by the time both mugs are full and ready, Lily's scratching at the door to come back in.

We have the morning routine down to a science.

Summer's yawning as she wraps herself in a robe and reaches for the coffee.

"Yes, please." She holds it in both of her hands and takes a sip, sighing with happiness. "So good. In fact, this whole morning is *so good*."

"It could be *every* morning," I remind her and brush her hair out of her eyes. "Just like this, sex and coffee."

"That's definitely something to consider." She smiles and offers her lips for another kiss. "Thanks for the coffee. And...everything."

"You're welcome." I take a sip and head for the shower. "I'd better get a move on, or I'll be late."

"That sex was totally worth it."

I grin back at her. "Absofuckinglutely."

"It's been a goddamn *week* since some fucker threw a rock through Summer's window, and you're telling me that no one knows *anything*?" I scowl at my commanding officer, feeling so fucking helpless. "No one heard or saw a damn thing on that whole block? This is a small town. People pay attention to shit."

"Maybe they weren't home," he suggests and leans back in his chair. "It was during the work day, and people have jobs, Wild. If they were being strategic, they chose the right time of day for that shit."

"It's infuriating." I pace his office and rub my hand over my mouth. "I *need* to figure this out, because she doesn't deserve to live her life constantly looking over her shoulder."

"From what I hear, she has *you* to protect her most of the time."

"She shouldn't have to have that, either. It's been months of harassment, and I'm pissed that we still don't have any leads."

"I don't like it any more than you do," he says with a

sigh. "Go back to the house, sweep for more prints, talk to more neighbors."

"The entire house has been swept, and I've spoken to every single person who lives on that street personally. But I'll ask around again. Thanks for listening."

"That's what I'm here for."

I leave his office and stride out to my car, climb inside, and head out on patrol. It's been a fucking *week*, and still, we have nothing. Either this bastard is smart, or he's damn lucky.

Maybe both.

Tonight is the party for Summer's women's group, so I won't see her until late. I'll take her lunch so I don't have to go the whole day without her.

And isn't that just ridiculous? I can't go one whole day without seeing her, without feeling like I'm going insane.

I sigh and push my hand through my hair.

"I'm so in love with her that I irritate myself." I let out a humorless laugh and turn right, just in time to see my brother, Ryan, walk out of an attorney's office.

I park at the curb and climb out of the car, approaching him.

"What are you up to?" I ask him.

"Oh, hey. I had a meeting."

I eye the door of the office and then turn back to him. "With an attorney?"

Ryan nods and shoves his hands into his pockets. "You know, I do *have* a lot of attorneys."

"Not ones in Bitterroot Valley. What's up?"

My brother frowns, looks down the street, and then back at me. "Keep this between us for now, okay?"

"Are you in trouble, Ryan?"

"No." He shakes his head. "It's nothing like that. I was speaking with a family law attorney. I'd like Jake to be placed with me, permanently."

That word seems to be going around a lot lately.

"Wow." My brow lifts in surprise. "It's going that well?"

"It really is, and I'm as surprised as anyone, but he's so great with my animals, and he just seems to fit in there, you know? His attitude is mellowing out with time and patience. He's been staying with me on the weekends because the assholes who have custody right now don't give a shit about him, and I *like* having him there. He's not a little ass with me; he's respectful, and he's just a good kid."

"And you want to adopt him?"

"Yeah." Ryan raises his chin, almost defiantly. "I do. He deserves a hell of a lot better than what he's gotten in the past year, and I can give him a damn good home."

"You can give him a life that most people only dream of," I reply. "Let's not sugarcoat it."

"I haven't talked to Jake about it yet. I wanted to talk it over with the attorney and stuff before I talk to the kid and see if it's what he wants. If the attorney told me that it couldn't happen, I didn't want to get his hopes up and then stomp all over them."

"I can't imagine the state not giving you custody, Ry."

"That's what I was told today. Looks like I should get

immediate custodial custody while we wait for the adoption stuff to go through. He won't have to stay in that shithole anymore."

"I'd say that's damn good news." I pat my brother on the shoulder, so fucking proud of him. "Is he coming to your place after school for the weekend?"

"Yeah. He started keeping some things at my house. He's claimed a bedroom, for fuck's sake." He grins like a loon. "That way, he doesn't have to go to the foster home for anything after school."

"I've done some digging since that day at your place," I say and nod at Jeannie as she hustles past with a delivery from her deli. "There have been a few reports from previous placements of bad conditions in that house, but nothing could be proven. It's pretty obvious to everyone that Wally and his wife only take on the fosters for the money from the state every month, but there's such a shortage of foster homes in Montana that nothing has been done about it."

"Fuck," Ryan mutters. "What assholes."

"You're right on the mark there. So, I'm glad that you're getting him out of that house."

"Only to free up a bedroom for the next victim." Ryan's face is grim as he stares at me, and the radio on my belt sounds.

"Wild, you're needed at 983 O'Brien Avenue. Domestic dispute, minor involved."

Ryan and I scowl at each other as I speak into a radio on my shoulder. "Isn't that the Wally Beck residence?"

"Confirmed."

"Fuck," Ryan says again.

"On my way, ETA five minutes."

"I'm coming with you."

"Ryan—"

"I can come with you or follow you there. Either way, *I'm fucking coming*."

I don't argue when he climbs into the passenger side of my car, and I hit the siren and lights as I speed through town and come to a screaming stop outside of the residence.

It's a small, white house with peeling blue trim. The yard is overgrown, and nothing about this place has been maintained at all.

"*This* is where he's been living?" Ryan demands.

"You didn't know?"

"Fuck no, I didn't know. Jesus, I should have checked it out."

"You stay out here." I point a finger at his chest. "I mean it, you stay here. I don't know if anyone is armed inside."

The neighbor comes running out, her face ashen. "I'm so glad you're here. It's been going on for at least an hour, and I just know that someone's hurt in there."

"Stay back," I tell her and move for the door.

I can hear the yelling and swearing. The crash as things are thrown, and I pull my weapon and approach the door just as backup arrives behind me.

Knocking on the door, I try to look through the window.

"This is Officer Wild of the BVPD. I need you to open the door, please."

Everything inside the house goes silent, and I narrow my eyes as the door is flung open and a woman, eyes wild and full of fear, stares up at me.

"There's nothing wrong," she says, but she's breathing hard, and she's holding her shirt closed in front of her where it's been torn.

"Janice, I heard the yelling and crashing from out there. I need to come in and make sure everyone is okay."

"No." She steps in front of me, her eyes even more wild now. "No, please. Everything is *fine* here."

I can hear grunting behind her, and then the sound of flesh hitting flesh, and she winces.

"Back up," I tell her and push past her, to find Wally beating the hell out of Jake. "Back away from the boy."

"Fuck you," he growls, his fist cocked back to strike again, and my blood runs cold. Jake's face is swollen, blood running down his right cheek. He's missing a tooth, and his left arm hangs loosely to the side, as if the shoulder is dislocated. Immediately, I lunge for Wally and knock him to the ground.

"Call for an ambulance," I manage to call out to backup as I punch Wally in the face, knock him around, and get his arms behind his back and cuffed, then pull him up off of the floor. "You're under arrest, you worthless sack of shit." I read him his rights, then turn to Janice. "How badly are you hurt?"

"Oh, I—"

"How bad?"

"Tried to rape her," Jake says, his voice coming in a whisper. "Pulled him off."

"Jesus," Ryan says as he rushes inside and hurries over to Jake. "My God, buddy."

"He wouldn't stop." Jake finally sees that Ryan's here, and his eyes fill with tears. "He just wouldn't stop. Gonna kill me."

"No," Ryan says, gently brushing his hand over Jake's hair. "He won't. You're safe, and we're getting you to the hospital."

"My kids," Janice whimpers. "They're hiding in their rooms."

"They'll be taken care of." I can hear the ambulance on the way. "We'll need two ambulances."

"Two are on the way," I'm assured, and I nod, then turn my attention back to Ryan, who's holding Jake against him.

———

SIX HOURS LATER, with my shift finally over, Wally and Janice's kids placed in foster homes—oh, the irony—and all of my reports written and filed, I make my way into the hospital and find Ryan at Jake's bedside. The kid's asleep, with a brace holding his arm in place and bandages on his face.

"He's a fucking mess," Ryan says without looking up at me. "Dislocated shoulder, broken cheekbone, and the asswipe took out a tooth."

"Jesus." I sit on the other side of the bed from him

and lean my elbows on my knees. "Has he said what started all of this?"

"Wally was going for Janice, and Jake pulled him off of her. Wally turned on Jake, and the rest, we know. Apparently, it's not unusual for such things in that house, but this is the first time Jake felt confident enough to step up and do something about it."

"Don't make me go back," Jake whispers. "Please, don't make me go. I'll do whatever you want."

"Hey, you're not going back there, buddy," Ryan assures him. "You'll be coming to stay with me."

"Until they find me another home?"

"No." Ryan shakes his head and smiles softly at the teenager. "For good. If that's okay with you, that is."

"You're not shitting me?"

Ryan winces. "We need to work on your mouth, but no. I'm not shitting you. What do you say?"

Rather than answer, Jake looks away and gives in to the tears that he's been fighting back.

"Y-you don't h-have to," he says and wipes away the tears with his good hand. "I know you feel bad for me, but—"

"Hey, look at me, Jake." Jake's head turns so he can look at Ryan. "I'd already started looking into it. I spoke with my attorney this morning, in fact."

"He's not lying. I saw him walk out of the office myself."

Jake glances my way, hope gleaming in his swollen eyes. "You did?"

"Yeah. I figure we make a good team, and I like

having you at my place. So, I'd already set things in motion. When you were sleeping, I spoke with child services, and they've agreed that you can go home with me when you're released. I've been given emergency custody."

"So, I'll be your foster kid until I'm eighteen?"

Ryan looks down at his hands and then back at Jake. "If that's how you want it, sure. We can do it that way. But I'd really rather officially adopt you. If you want to take my name, you can. If you want to keep your dad's name, that's cool with me, too. I want you to have a solid home with a good family, Jake."

"Can I think about the name thing?" Jake asks quietly.

"You can think about all of it," Ryan assures him. "For now, just know that you'll be safe with me."

"Thank you." Jake's lower lip quivers. "Really, thank you."

"You're very welcome."

"I think the medicine is making me sleepy again," Jake says, wiping at his tears. "I hope I didn't dream this."

"I'll remind you when you wake up," Ryan assures him, and then sighs when Jake falls back to sleep. "Well, that went pretty okay."

"I'm really proud of you."

Ryan's head comes up at my words, and he nods. "Not surprised?"

"Oh, I'm surprised as hell. I was just hoping you'd give the kid a weekend job and keep him out of trouble. I had no idea that you'd fall for him and want to be his daddy."

"I'm not—" He pauses the denial and then lets out a shaky laugh. "I guess that's the short version of it. I know it won't be easy or a walk in the park, but it's a chance for him, you know?"

"Yeah. Not everyone gets the amazing life we had growing up, and the fact that you're giving Jake one hell of a chance at that amazing life is pretty damn great. Mom and Dad are going to shit their pants. A new grandkid to fuss over? Mom will have his Christmas stocking made by the end of the week."

Ryan's grin is as bright as the sun. "Yeah. That's pretty great, huh?"

"Pretty great. For everyone."

CHAPTER NINETEEN
SUMMER

Today has been a ton of work and so much *fun*. We're all so excited about this cocktail party, and I have to say, the whole bar here at the resort looks *amazing*. I knew that they'd let us use the space, especially since the women gathered here aren't shy about ordering drinks and food. I've set out little bouquets of pink, red, and yellow dahlias and ranunculus on all eighteen of the four-top tables scattered around the room and on the end of the bar. Twinkle lights are strung around the room, and we have an amazing view of the ski runs—still without snow—and a good part of Bitterroot Valley, since the bar sits up high.

"These flowers are gorgeous," Charlie Lexington says with a grin. "So bright and fun. A great way to cheer up a dreary fall day."

"Thanks. You know, it's a misconception that fall flowers have to be drab and boring. I don't know what I'll do with them later. I hate to throw them away."

She turns shrewd brown eyes my way. "I have an elopement tomorrow, and they didn't plan for flowers. Could I buy these from you?"

"Of course. I'll give you a steal of a deal, and I'll even take them back to the shop tonight and put them in the cooler so they're fresh for tomorrow."

"Now you're going to make me cry." Charlie grins at me and nudges my shoulder with hers as we gaze around the full room. More women than we expected came out for our first party, and I'm relieved that so many people are excited. "I love this whole idea, by the way. The lifting up women in business idea. It's not easy being a business owner, and I can't wait to trade ideas with everyone."

"Networking is highly underrated," I reply with a nod. "There's room for everyone to do well."

"I'll drink to that." She lifts her flute of bubbly champagne and clinks it to mine just as Billie Blackwell joins us, a huge grin on her pretty face. "Hey, Billie."

"Hi." Billie shuffles self-consciously as Millie also walks over to join us. "I appreciate you including me tonight. I don't own my own business. Yet."

"Are you thinking of starting one?" Millie asks.

"Well, yeah. I was telling Brooks about it the other day, and he suggested I come to this tonight. I hadn't even heard about it because I *hate* social media, and I'm so glad my brother mentioned it because you have London Ambrose speaking."

"I can't wait to hear her," Millie agrees.

"What kind of business are you planning to start?" I ask Billie.

"Oh, a bookstore." She smiles and shrugs a shoulder. "I'll call it Billie's Books, I think. Maybe Blackwell Books."

"You could go for Double B Books, after your family's ranch," Millie suggests, but then shakes her head. "No. Call it Billie's Books. Make it about *you*. It's your vision."

"I agree," I add. "Also, I'll be your first customer."

"You know," Millie says, tapping her chin in thought. "I have it on good authority that the business next to the coffee shop might be going out of business soon. What's more perfect than a coffee shop and a bookstore, right next to each other?"

Billie's eyes light up in excitement, and I see Erin gesturing for me to join her from across the room.

"Excuse me, ladies. You keep talking about this because it's *brilliant*. I have to run over this way." I cross to where Erin's standing with London. "Hey, London, thank you for coming."

"Oh, it's completely my pleasure. Thanks for inviting me. I didn't really prepare a speech, because I thought I would just give a little background on myself and then take questions. Is that okay?"

"Works great for me," I assure her as Polly rushes over to join us.

"We're ready when you are," Polly announces.

"I'm ready," London says and straightens her gray Chanel jacket. "Let's inspire some women, friends."

"May I have your attention?" Polly calls out, and the

room immediately quiets. "Please, take your seats, and we will get started."

There's shuffling and some chatter as the women grab their seats. I see that Marion, the former owner of the coffee shop, is here. We have massage therapists and real estate agents and attorneys in attendance.

Abbi is almost vibrating with excitement as we join Polly.

"Thank you all for coming to our first Iconic Women's Collective event," Polly says, and we all smile as everyone erupts in applause. "I'm Polly Allen, the owner of Pocket Full of Polly, and I'm one of the five creators of this amazing collective."

"I'm Summer Quinn," I continue. "I own Paula's Posey's."

"You may not have heard," Millie picks up the introduction torch, "but I recently bought Bitterroot Valley Coffee Co from Marion. Oh, and I'm Millie Wild."

"Hi, everyone," Abbi says with a wave. "I'm Abbi Kastella. I own Bitterroot Valley Housekeeping Services."

"And she's an angel," Charlie calls out. "My house has never been cleaner."

"I need your number," someone else calls, making Abbi grin.

"I happen to have business cards with me," she says. "Hit me up later."

"You should," Erin says with a nod. "And last but not least, I'm Erin Wild. I'm a bookkeeper, and I'm in the process of getting our event space up and running out at Wild River Ranch. The five of us were having drinks together not too long ago, and with the courage of a little tequila, we decided that there is a need in our community to work together to build up other women entrepreneurs."

"Agreed," I put in as the others around the room nod. "I'm so tired of society telling us that we should be in competition with each other. Since when? There's room at the table for *all* of us."

"We all have strengths and weaknesses," Polly continues. "And this is a wonderful way for us to network and help each other. The five of us are open books, and we're happy to discuss just about everything."

"Our goal is to bring in amazing guest speakers to talk to us as a group about what has worked for them or what hasn't. To tell us their stories." I smile over at London and gesture for her to join us. "At this inaugural meeting, I'm so delighted to introduce a powerhouse of a woman to all of you, London Ambrose-Montgomery. In case any of you have been living under a rock, London is the co-owner of Seattle's professional football team, she owns a podcast, an amazing clothing boutique in New York, and does so much more than I can run down for you here. So, without further ado, please welcome London Ambrose-Montgomery."

The five of us take our seats, mixed in with the other ladies in the audience, and for the next half hour, we listen raptly as London tells us all about her childhood, where she comes from, and how it was important to her to set herself apart from her billionaire father. To make her own way in business.

I have to check with Libby, the manager of the bar, to make sure we're okay to run over our allotted time because there's no sign of anyone wanting to leave by 8:00 p.m.

In fact, London is still answering questions at nine, and I step in to save her.

"Let's give London the chance to catch her breath," I suggest and pass the woman a glass of wine. "I suspect that we'll be able to talk her into coming back another time to speak with us again."

"You got it," London confirms after sipping her wine. "I have a condo here at the resort, and I would love to come back. I'd also like to speak with some of you individually. Based on what I've heard, you all have some incredible business ideas."

I move off to the side with her and hug her tightly.

"Thank you." I hold her hands in mine. "You're welcome every month, if you want to come, and we won't make you be a speaker. Just come for fun."

"OMG, do it!" Erin hops on her toes with excitement. "Bring all the girl cousins with you. Okay, maybe that's a bit aggressive, but you know what I mean."

"I'll take you up on coming often," London promises. "And you know as well as I do that many of the cousins are entrepreneurs. I'll bring them."

"Excuse me," Stephanie Miller, a local photographer, says with a shy smile. "I know you have to be tired after we all railed you with questions, but, London, do you mind if I pick your brain for a few minutes?"

"Of course not. Stephanie, right?"

The two walk off to talk in a quiet corner, and I turn to my cohorts with a grin. "This was a *huge* success."

"And it's just the beginning," Millie reminds me. "We need to do this every month, like you said. We can do themes and poll the women to find out what they want to learn more about. We can do workshops, too."

"I'm so glad it worked," Abbi says with a relieved sigh. "Everyone had fun, the bar had a good amount of business, and London *rocked* it."

"She really did," Erin says with a proud nod. "She's awesome."

———

WITH POLLY and I being the last to leave, we walk to our cars parked just outside of the bar.

"I'll see you later," she says with a tired wave. "I'm going to go sleep for about a week now. You'd think we've just partied all night long."

"I know. Instead, we stayed up past our bedtime, talking business with some super-smart girls."

Polly's grin is wide and smug. "It was *awesome.*"

I get in my car, and before I leave, I shoot Chase a text. I've been in contact with him throughout the evening, especially when I realized we'd be here much later than we first thought.

Me: We're done here! I'm going to drop these flowers off

at the shop so they stay cold. Charlie wants them for a wedding tomorrow. Then I'll be home.

The three dots bounce on my screen as Chase types out his reply.

Chase: Just drive safely. Need anything?

I grin at the question. That's Chase, always ready to make sure I'm taken care of.

Me: No, I'm good. I had food. Can't wait to tell you all about it!

Chase hearts my message, and I start the car and head back into the heart of downtown, which isn't very far. I would usually park in the alley, behind the shop, to unload my car, but it's dark, and I don't like being back there by myself after dark. Even in Bitterroot Valley.

So, I pull up to a stop at the curb out front and unlock the door first, move to disable the alarm, and then realize that it's not set. With a frown, I stare at the keypad. I could have sworn I set it when I left earlier.

Shrugging, I return to the car and grab four bouquets at a time, transferring them from my vehicle and into the walk-in cooler of my floral shop. When I've moved the last few bouquets, I pause and sniff the air. Something smells...hot.

"Smoke," I mutter with a scowl as I round the glass counter toward the back room, and then I see the haze of smoke in the air. "Oh, shit. There's a fire."

I run back to the sink and fill up a pitcher, but when I round the corner again, I see flames reaching up to the ceiling, and I know my little pitcher of water isn't going to do the trick.

"Oh, shit. Oh, Jesus." I take a deep breath, trying to calm down, but all that does is make me cough as I pull my phone out of my pocket and call 9-1-1.

"9-1-1, what is your emergency?"

"Fire," I cry out. "My shop is on fire. Paula's Posey's."

"Are you inside, ma'am?"

"Yes." Panic fills my chest as I watch the flames grow. "Oh, God, it's spreading."

"I need you to get out of that building. We have trucks on the way, along with law enforcement, but you have to get out right now. Can you do that?"

"Yes." I hurry away, back to the front of the shop, but I don't want to leave. "Isn't there something I can do? This is my aunt's legacy. It's all I have."

"You can get out of the building, ma'am. Do you hear the trucks?"

I push through the glass door and breathe in the clean air. "Yes, I hear them."

"They see you," she says. "Are you okay if I hang up now?"

"Yes, yes, okay."

I lower the phone and feel almost numb as the firetrucks pull up, along with several police cars. Has anyone called Chase? Will he come?

Shoving my phone into my purse, I turn and gasp. The flames are already in the front of the store, licking against the glass.

"You can't be here," someone yells at me, pulling me away, into the middle of the street. "Those windows will explode."

Sure enough, there's a loud crash, and glass rains down around us. I cover my face and shriek, and I'm passed to someone else.

"Summer?" I look up into a familiar face. "My God, Summer, are you okay?"

"Evan?" I swallow, and my throat feels hoarse and sore. "Evan, my shop. Your office! Oh God, how did this happen?"

"Hey, come on. Let's get out of the way."

He leads me fully across the street and down just a bit so we're not in anyone's way, but we can see what's going on. It's so *loud*. I didn't realize that fire was so loud.

"The flowers are gone," I murmur softly, thinking of Charlie, and how I won't have the flowers for her tomorrow. I feel bad. I should have let her take them with her tonight. "It's all gone. I have to call Aunt Paula."

"Take a minute," Evan suggests and wraps his arm around my shoulders. "Just take a minute, Summer. You're shaking."

"I am?" I look down at my hands and realize he's right. And they're dirty. My teeth are chattering. "I wonder if I'm in shock."

"You're okay," he croons softly. His phone pings with a text, and he checks it, frowns, and then shoves it back into his pocket. "I promise, it'll be okay. Take a minute and then call Paula."

"Yeah, okay." I lean into him and look at my sweet shop, thinking about all the memories I have tucked inside there. Helping Aunt Paula in the summer, coming here when I had nowhere else to go, and finally, buying it for my own. How proud I was on that day. It's been my safe place for all these years, and now, in a matter of minutes, it's just...*gone*.

The men rush about. There are ladders in the air, hoses spewing water. Yelling voices, giving orders. But it's too late to save it.

"Summer!"

CHAPTER TWENTY
CHASE

"Are you guys good here?" I watch as Ryan helps Jake into bed. We brought Jake home to Ryan's place just a little while ago after he was discharged from the hospital, and I wanted to stick close by, in case they needed anything.

Not to mention, it's fucking interesting to watch Ryan's father instincts kick in with the boy. I honestly had no idea that we'd end up here when I suggested he hire Jake to help him with the horses, but I have to admit, they look natural together.

"I think so," Ryan says and props his hands on his hips as he gestures for me to leave the room with him. "He's on some good meds, and he'll just take it easy for a while."

We walk down the stairs to the kitchen, where Ryan passes me a bottle of water and takes a beer out of the fridge for himself.

"When are you going to fill the family in on all of this?" I ask him.

"Mom and Dad were out here last weekend. They met Jake and hung out for a while." He leans his hips against the countertop. "Mom winked at me. It's like she has a sixth sense for these things."

"Oh, I get it." I think back to Rem's rehearsal dinner and the looks she was shooting me regarding Summer. "Mom knows everything. So, it won't be a surprise to them, then."

"I don't think so. But, like you said earlier, they won't mind."

"None of us will mind a bit. It might cramp your bachelor style, having a kid underfoot."

Ryan scowls, staring down at his untouched beer.

"What is it?"

"Nothing."

"Come on." I sit on a stool at the island the size of Massachusetts and grin at him. "Talk. Tell Uncle Chase everything."

"You're an idiot," he says with a half laugh and then sets the bottle on the counter and crosses his arms over his chest. "It's really nothing. I've been kind of interested in a woman here in town, but it doesn't look like that'll pan out."

"Who?" I narrow my eyes at him, mind whirling, wondering who it could be. "Spill it."

"It doesn't matter now. You just pointed out that I have a kid; I can't be canoodling with a woman."

"I mean, I think you can find the time to canoodle if

you put your mind to it, and you're a fairly intelligent guy. Who is she?"

He sighs. "This stays in this kitchen, Chase. I mean it."

"Who am I gonna tell?"

He stares at me as if to say, *"Really?"*

"Okay, I won't tell. I promise. I'm a vault. Who's the broad?"

"Would you be okay with me calling Summer a *broad*?"

"For fuck's sake, Ry, just tell me."

"Polly." He swallows hard, shakes his head, and reaches for the bottle again, and I stare at him in shock.

Of all the women in town, she might be the last person I would have guessed. Not because she isn't pretty or smart or even successful. But she's not the type that's usually photographed on Ryan's arm. He usually goes for the super tall, super blonde, super...model type. Polly can't be five feet two in her sneakers, and she's got curves for days. Not to mention her fiery red hair. She's just the opposite of what Ryan's known to date.

"I hear what you're thinking, you know."

"I didn't say a word."

"You don't have to." He takes a pull on the bottle and sets it aside. "She's smart and funny, and she...well, it doesn't matter. I have other things on my mind."

"Let the dust settle," I suggest, but then the hair on the back of my neck stands up. "Whoa. You already slept with her."

His eyes whip up to mine, and he doesn't deny it.

"You did."

"We're both consenting adults, so I don't think we broke any laws or anything. At least, not in *this* state." His grin is smug and satisfied, and I can't help but laugh.

"Yeah, let the dust settle, then see what's what. Polly's great."

My phone pings with a text, and I glance down to see Summer's name.

Summer: We're done here! I'm going to drop these flowers off at the shop so they stay cold. Charlie wants them for a wedding tomorrow. Then I'll be home.

"Looks like the girls are finished with their first meeting," I inform my brother as I type out my reply.

Me: Just drive safely. Need anything?

"I hope it went well," Ryan says. "London came to town to speak to them, which I think is pretty cool. I liked chatting with her at the wedding. She and Drew are great."

I nod in agreement as I watch the three dots bounce with her reply.

Summer: No, I'm good. I had food. Can't wait to tell you all about it!

"How are things with you and Rem?" I heart her reply and shove my phone back into my pocket. "They seem better, but how are they really?"

"Fine." He shrugs a shoulder. "I'd say they're just fine, compared to how it's been the past few years."

"I don't know what went down between you two, and it's none of my business, but I hope you figure it out. I'm going to head out and meet Summer at home."

"Yeah, I need to check on the kid. I don't think I'll get much sleep tonight."

"Just call any of us if you need anything. You know we'll help."

"I know. I'll probably call Mom after you leave to fill her in, but I don't think there's anything anyone can do. Except give me five minutes alone with that asshole in his cell and turn off the fucking cameras."

I blink at him. "You know I can't do that."

He lifts an eyebrow. "I'm sure the department could use an anonymous million-dollar donation."

"Fuck, Ry." I push my hand through my hair. "I want that as much as you do."

"No," he interrupts, his voice hard and cold. "You don't. I want to fucking kill him. I want to take him apart slowly, painfully, but I'll settle for five minutes of beating his fucking face in."

I lick my lips and shake my head. I understand the rage. That boy upstairs is in terrible shape, and it'll take him a while to heal from all the injuries.

Wally deserves to have his ass kicked big time.

"This isn't the wild west," I reply softly. "I can't just hand him over to you so you can bloody him up."

"Think about it," he suggests. "The donation stands."

"Man, if I could afford to give a million dollars as a donation just to kick someone's ass, well...I don't know what I'd do."

"I'm telling you," he says as he follows me to the front door. "Let me help—"

"With my investments. Yeah, yeah, I know. You can't do much with my measly police pension."

"Oh, you'd be surprised." He tugs me in for a manly hug, pats my back, and then I head down to my truck. "Thank you for today."

"It's what I do, as a cop and as a brother." I wave and start the truck, then pull out of the driveway and onto the highway into town. Ryan isn't as far out as our family ranch, so it doesn't take quite as long to get back into Bitterroot Valley.

I'm still ten minutes out when I get a call.

"Wild," I say.

"Chase, you need to get downtown," Bridger Blackwell, the fire chief, says. "Now, man."

"What's up?"

"Summer's shop is on fire. She's—"

I hang up and press my foot on the gas as my heart hammers with adrenaline. I *just* heard from her, and she was fine. But she took the flowers back to the shop. Jesus, is she inside? Is she hurt?

The last few miles feel like they take forever, and when I reach downtown, I can't get near the shop because of the emergency vehicles, so I pull to a stop two blocks away and jump out of my truck, running as fast as I can. The smoke is intense, and there are still flames coming out of the roof of the flower shop as well as the office next door. I scan the area, looking for Summer, and then spot her across the street.

And motherfucking Evan Spencer has his arms around her.

Seeing red, I yell out, "Summer!"

Her head whips up, looking for me, and when she sees me, her eyes fill with tears.

"Chase!"

Evan's arms tighten around her, and Summer scowls as she shrugs him off. When I reach her, I frame her face in my hands and take her in.

"Are you hurt?"

"No." She shakes her head. "No, not at all. Evan—"

I turn on the man and punch him square in the jaw. "You're going to learn to keep your fucking hands to yourself."

"Hey!"

I get closer to him, intending to get right in the asshole's face, when I smell the gasoline on him, and the fury that rolls through me is all-encompassing.

"You son of a bitch." I swing again, this time knocking him to the ground. Fisting my hand in his shirt, I pull him to his feet and hit him again. And again.

"Chase!" Summer yells behind me, but I don't stop. I *can't* stop. "You need to stop this, Chase."

I shake my head and hit him again, satisfied when blood spurts out of his broken nose.

"Wild!" Someone grabs my arms from behind, and I'm pulled off of Evan. "Stop it, man."

It's Bridger and Brooks, and I shake my head, trying to shake the two brothers off.

"Let me fucking go."

"No," Brooks says. "You can't kill him, man."

"He smells of gasoline," I inform them, and Bridger scowls down at Evan. I hear Summer gasp.

"I didn't smell it," she says.

"You were in the building," Bridger reminds her. "You probably just smell smoke. You son of a bitch."

"Hey!" Evan cries out, dabbing at his nose with his sleeve. "You can't prove that."

"You idiot," I growl. "You fucking *reek* of gas. You set this fire."

"Evan set the fire," Summer says as I turn to her. She's staring at the man in shock. "Evan, *you* set the fire?"

"You're a fucking whore," Evan erupts as rage takes over the pain he's in. "You're a goddamn worthless piece of shit. I did *everything* right. You were supposed to come running to *me* for help, not this asshole." He gestures to me, and as more police join us, I let the man hang himself.

"You tried to break into my house," Summer says as realization dawns. "You spray-painted it, broke my window. Why?"

"I'm the one you're supposed to be with." He's breathing hard, and blood continues to spill onto the sidewalk from his nose. "We were going to live an amazing life in Helena. I'll be a senator. It's what I've always wanted, and if I just did a couple of small things to scare you a little, you'd come to *me* for help. It never would have escalated to this, but you just wouldn't follow the goddamn plan, so your mom and I came up with this. If there's no shop, you have nothing to stay here for. And now look what you've done!"

His phone rings, and he answers it before I can wrestle it away from him, but then I hear a woman's voice say, "Is it done?"

Summer takes the phone and puts it on speaker. "Who is this?"

"Summer?"

"*Mom*?" Summer's eyes fill with tears. "Mom!"

"You'll come home now. It's for the best, sweetheart."

"I'm pressing charges," Summer says as her mother starts to yell on the other end of the line. "Have her arrested."

Summer passes the phone to me, then rage covers her face, and she shoves forward and decks Evan right in the jaw. I can't hold back the proud grin that spreads over my face. "You son of a bitch, you vandalized my home. You scared me to the point where I didn't feel *safe* in my own home. And you conspired with my *mother*!"

"I would have protected you," Evan cries.

"Against *you*! Do you know how absurd you sound right now? For fuck's sake, you're crazy!"

"I am *not*." Evan lurches forward and pushes his face into Summer's. "I'm *not* crazy. We can still make it work. I won't tell your dad about this. Your mom didn't involve him, so he never has to know, and he'll still support me in my campaign. You and I can still be together."

"You're delusional," Summer says. "And you're going

to jail. You can campaign for head yard worker or something in prison, but you won't be a senator."

Evan howls with rage and reaches for Summer, his hands in claws, but I get to him first and push him against the wall.

"Say one more word," I murmur into his ear, "make one more move toward her, and I'll fucking kill you right here. Think I won't?"

I hold his eyes with mine and snarl.

"Try me, you bastard."

"I think he just peed his pants," Bridger says from behind me as Evan starts to cry.

"Take him in," I say, passing Evan off to the other officers, and Summer walks right into my arms, holding on tightly. "Hey, it's okay, baby. It's okay."

"It was *Evan*," she says, shaking her head. "This whole time, I thought he was my friend. A nuisance, but my friend, and he had this weird fantasy that he could *make* me want to be with him if he scared me. I can't even think about my mother."

"That's the Cliff's Notes version," I agree and kiss the top of her head. She smells like smoke and a little like gasoline after being near that asshole. "When all of this is over, we really need to have a conversation about you letting other men put their hands on you."

"I was in shock, and he was there," she says with a frown. "And I didn't question it because his office is right next door. It didn't feel out of place. God, I'm stupid."

"Hey." I tip her chin up with my fingers and shake my head. "You're *not* stupid. I didn't suspect him either, and

I can't stand the idiot. I should have. It's over now, babe. You don't have to be scared."

"Thank God." She sighs and then pulls her phone out of her pocket in a frenzy. "I haven't called Aunt Paula."

"Summer! Where's my girl? Summer!"

"There she is," I tell Summer, pointing to our right.

"Aunt Paula!" She runs to the older woman and is swept up in a fierce hug.

"Oh, my baby," Paula cries. "Are you hurt?"

"No, I'm not hurt. I'm so sorry, Aunt Paula. Your beautiful shop."

Paula holds Summer by the shoulders. "It's *your* shop, my love, and it will be rebuilt. You have insurance. But I can't replace *you*, so as long as you're okay, that's all that matters."

"I'm okay," Summer assures her. "Is Lily at your house?"

"Yes, darling, she's safe at my house. Don't worry about her."

IT'S BEEN A LONG FUCKING night. The first thing I did was contact Helena PD to have Summer's mom arrested, and as far as I know, she's in custody and denying everything.

Summer refused to leave. She wanted to be here, for her shop, until it was done. Word spread through town almost as quickly as the fire did through that building, and my family—minus Ryan, who is home with Jake— came to support us. I couldn't believe it when Rem arrived, along with my parents and Brady. Erin stayed back with the kids, but she promised to come check on things today.

Millie's here, and she opened her coffee shop early so everyone could have some caffeine and a little comfort that a warm drink provides.

It's six in the morning when the last of the fire is out. The firemen did a great job of keeping the fire contained to just the flower shop and Evan's law office next door. None of the other businesses on the street were impacted at all.

"The fire's out," Bridger says as he approaches us. "There's going to be smoke for a little while yet, but there are no more hot spots that could flare up. I'm sorry, Summer, but it's a total loss."

Summer nods and bites her lip as tears fill her pretty blue eyes. "I know. I'm just glad that no one else lost their businesses. Thank you, Bridger, for everything."

"Here's my card," the fire chief says, and passes a card to Summer. "Call me anytime. I'll be happy to work with your insurance company, as well."

"You're the best," Summer says with a smile. "I really appreciate it."

"I think it's time to go home and get some rest," my dad says and pats Summer on the back. God, she looks tired. "There's nothing more to do here, my dear. But there will be plenty that need your attention later. Go home."

Summer nods and then smiles at everyone. "Thank you all for coming. You didn't have to stay all night."

"That's what family does," Brady says with a wink. Everyone takes turns hugging us both, and then they start to disperse, walking several blocks away to find their vehicles to head home.

"I'll come by later," Polly promises as she pulls Summer in for a hug. "I'll bring liquor and food. Because I'm your person, and that's what *I* do."

"Thank you," Summer says, holding on just a minute more. "I'll take it. But go catch some sleep first, then we'll wallow in food and liquor."

"Sounds like a plan," Polly says before walking away.

"Everyone came," Summer murmurs as I take her hand in mine and lead her to where I abandoned my truck last night. "Even though it was the middle of the night, they just...*came.*"

"You've lived here long enough to know that this town bands together, especially when something like this happens. They *want* to help, in any way they can, even if it's just to stand by and be moral support."

She chews her lip and stares out the window as I drive her to my place.

"I want Lily," she says and turns to me. "Can we go get her? Or have someone get her and bring her home?"

"I'll go get her, baby. Let me get you home first."

"Okay." She sighs and relaxes into the seat, and just when I think she's fallen asleep, she reaches for my hand and holds on tightly. "Thank you."

I DIDN'T WANT to leave her. She was just out of the shower, finally washing away the smoke and soot from the fire, and I wanted to just curl into bed with her and hold her.

But she wants Lily home with us, and I'm not about to deny her anything right now.

"I'm sorry, I know you wanted to sleep," I say to Paula as she opens the door of her cottage. "I think Lily will be a comfort to Summer today."

"Of course, she will," Paula says with a kind smile. "Lily should be home with you two."

I squat down and pick up the dog, and when I stand, Paula's still grinning at me.

"You're going to marry her."

It isn't a question, and I grin back at her. "How do you know that? Are you a fortune teller?"

"I know true love when I see it. Go on now. Take care of our girl."

CHAPTER TWENTY-ONE
SUMMER

"It's so nice of your family to include Aunt Paula today." I grin over at Chase, who's driving Lily and me out to the ranch for Thanksgiving dinner at Remington and Erin's house. "That way, I didn't have to try to choose between the two or spend half the day at one place and then race over to the other."

"We all love Paula," he says and reaches for my hand, lifting it to his lips. "Always have. And we all love you, so it makes sense that we would all spend the holiday together."

"You're sweet." He brushes his thumb over the back of my fingers, pausing over my ring finger, and lets go so he can pull off of the highway and onto the ranch road. He keys us through the gate, but rather than turning toward the farmhouse, he takes a right at the fork in the road and drives us around the lake, on the fresh dirt road that was recently made, to where his house will be.

The shop is done now, thanks to the help of so many

of Chase's friends. They put in time on their days off to help him get it done before any snow fell for the season.

The past two months have gone by quickly. The insurance company finally paid me to rebuild the flower shop, and I'm in talks with an architect on the design. Hopefully, it'll be finished before wedding season next year. My house sold, and Lily and I officially moved in with Chase less than a week after the fire.

And Evan is in jail, about to go on trial for a whole list of charges, including attempted murder, because I was in the building when he set the fire. He's in a lot of trouble. And my mom? Well, my dad got her off, which didn't surprise me at all, but I'll never speak to either of them ever again.

"What are we doing out here?" I ask with a frown. "Do you need to get something?"

"Something," he says with a wink and pushes out of the truck. Lily wiggles on the seat next to me. She *loves* being out on the ranch. Chase walks around to open my door, and when I'm out, he lifts Lily out and sets her on the ground, taking her leash.

She's *never* off of her leash when we're out here, even though she's a good girl and comes when called. There's too much wildlife, and I don't know what I would do without this little dog.

"Isn't your family expecting us?"

Chase smiles down at me as he leads me toward the dock. "They'll wait. Brady can hold off on eating all the goddamn turkey for twenty minutes."

"I don't know...Brady can put the food away."

Chase chuckles, and when we reach the end of the dock, he turns to me and pulls me into his arms for a long, tight hug.

There is nothing in this world as fabulous as this, as being in Chase's arms in the place that means so much to both of us. I *love* it out here. I hope, one day, Chase might ask me to live here with him.

"I love it out here," I murmur as I gaze out over the lake and to the mountains beyond. The tops of those mountains are covered with snow now, and it won't be long before we'll have snow that sticks in the valley, as well. "It just feels so good."

"Does it feel like home?" he asks and pulls away to watch me with serious hazel eyes.

I look back to the lake, to the trees and mountains, and nod. "Yeah, it does. I think it has since that first day you brought me out here and showed it to me. Are you going to ask me to live here with you when the house is done?"

He grins and tucks my hair behind my ear.

"Well, that's part of it, absolutely. But I want more than that." He looks around us, at the property behind us, and gestures.

I turn to look where he's pointing and gasp. "An eagle."

We watch as the bird circles and then sits on an evergreen tree, watching.

"It's not after Lily, is it? For lunch?" I look down at the dog sitting at our feet with concern.

Chase laughs. "No, Lily's too big, but it might be

looking for fish." He wraps his arms around me from behind and kisses my neck. "The house will be right there, hopefully by the end of summer."

"But I thought you were going to build it yourself, and that takes time. Are you thinking of hiring a contractor?"

"I've already hired one. I'm impatient," he says and kisses the top of my head. "I want to be out here sooner rather than later. I built the shop, and that's good enough for me. We'll also build that greenhouse you talked about, right over there."

"And a vegetable garden next to it," I add, picturing it all perfectly in my head. "I'll want lots of flowerpots on the porch. It's a wraparound porch, right?"

"Of course. We have to be able to sit out and look at the view, and there are views all around us."

I grin and nod in agreement. A deer wanders out of the woods and looks our way, chewing on his food. Chase and I stay still, watching as he continues back into the forest. Lily didn't even notice him, otherwise, she would have barked. "Oh, my gosh, I didn't even realize that there are huckleberry bushes about twenty feet away from where the house will be. You're not planning on taking those out, are you?"

"Uh, that's sacrilegious," he says with a chuckle. "No, I plan to put a grassy yard in on the other side for Lily to run around and do her business. And kids, of course. I'll put in swings, maybe a trampoline."

"Kids?" I lean back so I can gaze up at him in surprise. "*Kids*?"

"Two or three." He nods, still looking at the property, as if it's already happening, right before his eyes. "We don't have to go crazy and have five like my parents did. But if you have your heart set on a big family, I can live with that."

"Chase, we haven't even built the house yet."

He turns me around once more so he can look down into my eyes, and now his face sobers, as if he's about to get down to serious business.

"When I think of all of these things, the house, the yard, the view, the kids...you're in every picture, Summer. I can't envision any of this without you. You're the center. You're the reason for everything, including every breath I take. I love you so much."

He bends his knee and kneels in front of me. Lily wags her whole body and lifts her front end up to kiss Chase on the face.

"Whoa, girl, I need a minute," he says with a laugh and rubs her side. "One minute, okay? I have an important question for your mom."

He reaches into his pants pocket and pulls out a shiny diamond ring.

"Summer, will you do me the honor of being my wife? Will you live with me here, make a home and a family with me? I promise, I'll live the rest of my life making sure you're happy and taken care of. You won't ever question how much I love you."

I have to swallow over the lump in my throat. "Of course, I'll marry you and have babies and make a life with you, Chase Wild. I love you, too."

He slides the ring onto my finger, and then he catches me up in a kiss so full of passion and heat, it takes my breath away.

He *always* takes my breath away.

I can hear Lily's nails clickity clacking on the dock with excitement, and Chase picks her up so she can get in on the happy snuggles.

"We'd better head over to Remington's and tell *our* family," Chase says with a happy smile as he leads me off of the dock, but I stop for a moment, looking out over the lake, and back to where the house will be. To where the eagle is still perched on the tree, and I take a deep breath as a chilly breeze blows over my face and through my hair.

Yes, I can picture it all. The gardens, the flowers, the view every night from our bedroom as the sun sets behind those snow-capped mountains.

I'm going to sit on that porch, rocking my babies to sleep as I watch our other children play in the water or fish off the dock or run in the yard. We're going to invite our friends here, for food and laughter.

We're going to make a beautiful life here, in this gorgeous place on Wild River Ranch.

"You okay?" Chase asks and reaches for my hand.

"I've never been better," I assure him. "I was just picturing it, that's all."

He raises an eyebrow, those hazel eyes full of love.

"And?"

"And I can't wait to get started."

EPILOGUE
RYAN WILD

"Congratulations, Mr. Wild." My attorney, Dan Meeks, grins and shakes my hand. "You have a court date for next month, and then the judge will officially sign off on it, and you'll have yourself a son."

A son.

I don't think I've truly wrapped my brain around that yet.

Tomorrow is Christmas, and I plan to tell Jake in the morning when it's just the two of us and I give him his present. A horse and a truck.

Because he has to have transportation to and from the ranch, *and* he just passed his driving test.

I'm damn proud of him.

With a nod, I step out of the attorney's office and into a freaking blizzard.

"Holy shit," I mutter, pulling the collar of my jacket up around my neck, just as I walk right into a woman who's hurrying through the snow and wind.

"I'm sorry," she says, and then her green eyes widen when she sees it's me. "Ryan."

"Hi, Polly." Wanting to chat with her, I glance around, take her hand, and pull her into the doorway of a business so we're out of the worst of the weather. "How are you?"

"Busy," she says with a happy little laugh that makes my dick sit up and take notice. "And I *hate* that answer, but tomorrow's Christmas, so the shop is bustling and full of gift-buying people, and that makes me happy. How are *you*?"

I love her smile. That whole night with her, she grinned at me. When I was inside of her, when I was touching her, telling her *exactly* what I wanted to do to her.

"Ryan?"

"I'm good." I swallow hard and nod. "Yeah, I'm really good, thanks. You look fantastic. Why don't you have any gloves?"

She frowns down at her bare hands.

"Oh, I must have left them somewhere. I'm always doing that." She pushes her hand through her snow-covered hair self-consciously. "I'm a little frazzled today."

"No, you look beautiful."

I stand at least a foot taller than her, and everything in me wants to kiss her, but I don't. I pull my own gloves off and pass them to her. "Put these on. It's too cold to be without them."

"But what about you?"

"I'll be fine," I insist and smile with satisfaction when she tugs the gloves on. They're way too big for her, but she'll be warm.

"I'll get them back to you."

I laugh and shake my head. "Don't worry about it. Really. I won't keep you out in this cold."

She looks like she wants to say something, but then she shakes her head and offers me another big smile. "I hope you have an excellent Christmas, Ryan."

"You, too, Polly."

She hurries off, and I watch her go, hunched against the wind of the storm, and feel my gut clench.

I want her. I've wanted her for a long time, and I had her for one incredible night that has seemingly ruined me for all other women. Chase told me to let the dust settle, and with Jake's adoption almost finished, I think it's time to give some energy to the gorgeous redhead.

I've just slipped inside my new truck and started the engine when a call comes in from my security team at my property.

"This is Wild," I answer.

"Sir, it's Adams. We have a situation."

I scowl out of the windshield as I put the truck in gear and ease out onto the roadway.

"What kind of situation?"

"You need to get home, sir. We need eyes on you."

"I'm on my way."

. . .

ARE you excited for Ryan and Polly's story? Keep reading for a preview of Wildest Dreams. You can get more information on Wildest Dreams here: https://www.kristen probyauthor.com/wildest-dreams

WILDEST DREAMS PREVIEW

Prologue

Ryan

Her thick, red, *fucking amazing* hair is like silk between my fingers where my hand is fisted at the nape of her neck as I plunder her luscious mouth. She tastes like strawberries and champagne and absolute *sin*, and I can't get enough of her.

"Jesus, God, yes," she moans against my lips as I pluck at a nipple. At the rate we're going, we'll make it through the box of condoms before sunrise because I have no intention of sleeping tonight. "It's so *good*."

I've known her for *years*, have been attracted to her for just as long, and thanks to a few drinks at my brother's wedding and some serious flirtation, I've got her in my bed, naked and writhing beneath me.

"You're so fucking beautiful." Nibbling down her neck, I make my way to her small, round breasts and tug a nipple into my mouth. Polly Allen is petite, at least a foot shorter than me, and she has curves so damn amazing that, once they finished creating her, the gods wept with joy.

My hand glides down her belly, and I slide two fingers inside of her, only to have her grind against me and moan with anticipation.

"You're soaking." I kiss down her belly, needing to taste her. So, I reverse our positions and lie flat on the bed. "Sit on my face."

Polly's green eyes go wide, and then she laughs. "Yeah, right, I'll smother you."

"Not a chance." I hook my arm around her waist and pull her up my body and settle her right over my face, then grab on to her ass and urge her down over me so I can lick and suck and devour her.

"Oh, my God," she moans, leaning against the dark leather headboard. Her hips move, back and forth, as she rides my face, and when I push my fingers inside of her again, I feel her already contracting with her impending orgasm.

She comes hard and fast, grinding down over my face, and I lap up every delicious drop of her, and when she's finished, I wiggle out from under her, tuck a pillow under her hips to keep her ass in the air, and once I've protected us both, I tease her with the tip of my cock.

"For fuck's sake, Ryan," she breathes, pushing back, urging me to slam inside of her.

"What?" I fist that glorious hair once more, loving the way it feels in my hand, and lean in to press my lips against her ear. "What do you want, Polly? Use your words."

"I want—" She licks her lips. "I want you to fuck me."

I grin, biting her earlobe. "Good girl."

Taking it easy, I push inside of her, not wanting to hurt her, but she's so fucking wet she takes me easily, and we both groan with the pleasure of it.

"God, you're snug," I growl and push up to drag my hand down her spine to the small of her back as I push in and out of her. My thumb tickles her tight little pink anus, and she yells out as she comes again, all over me.

It's the most beautiful thing I've ever seen in all of my thirty-three years, and her pussy tightening around me sends me over the edge with her.

I lean in to press my forehead against her back, then kiss her spine, right between her shoulder blades before I pull out and collapse to the side of her.

Polly's face is buried in a pillow, but she turns to suck in a breath and opens one emerald eye to watch me.

"That was fun," she says, her voice still breathless.

"That's one word to describe it."

I'd use life-altering.

"I should go," she says with a frown.

"It's one in the morning." I brush a lock of hair off her cheek and hook it behind her ear. "Where could you possibly need to be at this time of the night?"

"Well, you probably didn't plan to have an overnight guest."

"No, I didn't plan it." I grin and push over to kiss her soft, swollen lips. "It's a happy surprise. You're staying here, Polly. I'm not done with you yet."

She lets out a strangled laugh. "You're trying to kill me."

"But what a way to go."

***

I wake the way I always do: quickly and fully alert. But I don't open my eyes yet. I can smell the sex and Polly's perfume, and I could swear the sound of my name on her lips as she succumbed to that last orgasm still hangs in the air. I grin, remembering how amazing she looked, spread out like a feast before me, and I'm not ashamed to say that I took full advantage.

That couldn't have been more than an hour ago.

I crack one eye and glance over at my phone on the bedside table, surprised to see that it's already eight a.m. I'm always up by six.

Of course, I don't usually go a half a dozen rounds of sex with no sleep in between in just one night. I blame Polly.

She's fucking irresistible.

Deciding to snuggle up to her for a few before I make my way downstairs to make breakfast for her, I turn over to pull her against me but find an empty bed. Scowling, I run my hand over the sheets and find it already cool.

Maybe she went downstairs looking for coffee and food. I climb out of bed, brush my fingers through my hair as I locate a pair of jeans, put them on, and then go in search of one stunning redhead.

But when I walk downstairs, the house is quiet, and there's no scent of coffee in the air. I check the rest of the house and the bathrooms, and then run to the front door and swear ripely when I find that her car is gone.

She fucking left.

Chapter One

Polly

It's the first day of glorious summer.

Stepping out of the front door of my shop, Pocket Full of Polly, I take in a long, deep breath. I can smell new leaves and grass in the air, and the birds are chirping with excitement, as if they know, too. The sun is out, and I don't have to try to remember my damn winter jacket anymore.

In this part of Montana, the seasons are literally like clockwork. We had a small snowstorm just last week, and now it's a warm spring day with just a hint of a cool breeze, and I'm walking down the sidewalk in Bitterroot Valley toward the coffee shop that my friend, Millie Wild, owns.

"Good morning," I announce with a smile as I sashay into Bitterroot Valley Coffee Co. "It's *spring!*"

"Hell to the yes," Millie returns as she smiles back at me from where she's making magic at her ginormous coffee-making contraption behind the counter. "And it's a pretty day. I've had enough gloom and cloud cover to last until...well, next winter."

I laugh and walk to the counter, and every hair on my body stands up as the door opens behind me, and in walks Millie's older brother, Ryan.

The man I've had a crush on since I was old enough to know what that means.

The man who rocked my world last September for an entire night.

The same man who never called me afterward.

"Polly," Ryan says with a wide, happy grin. "It's good to see you."

"Hey, Ryan." He hugs me, and my damn nipples betray me by going instantly hard. "How are you?"

"I'm great." He smiles down at me as he pulls away and stuffs his hands into his pockets. He's fucking *delicious* in a simple black T-shirt and jeans, and he's wearing his signature baseball cap, backward. "And yourself? Your brother tells me that you've closed the shop for the week."

"I have." I nod and then smile at Millie when she passes me my favorite coffee. I don't even have to order; she just whips it up and keeps a tab for me. "I'm doing some rearranging, replacing old stock with new, and cleaning. I do it every spring before the summer rush starts."

And I freaking *love* it. Touching all the clothes and styling them to look trendy and attractive is my favorite. But freshening the place up, deep cleaning, and showing my business love is also rewarding.

"Mac also mentioned that he'll be helping you today?" Ryan asks as Millie also passes him a cup of coffee.

As more customers shuffle in behind us, Ryan and I move off to the side to get out of their way.

"He is," I confirm with a nod. "I have some heavy

things that need to be moved, built, and all that good stuff, and Mac's coming to do most of that for me."

"I can help," Ryan offers immediately, and I want to say no. When I'm around him, which isn't often, all I can think about is how good it felt when he gave me some of the best orgasms of my damn life. *But* I'm sure Mac could use an extra pair of hands, and I know from experience that Ryan has the muscles. "I'll bring Jake, too."

"Are you sure?" I shift my feet, thinking it over. "I can bring in lunch for everyone as a thank-you."

"Are you kidding? Jake will do just about anything for a sandwich. The kid eats anything that isn't tied down."

That makes me laugh. Last winter, Ryan took Jake in after Jake had been brutalized by his foster dad. Earlier this year, Ryan officially adopted the teenager, and I am *so* happy for the two of them. From what I hear, they get along great, and Jake loves working out on Ryan's ranch with the horses and other animals.

"Jake is absolutely welcome to come help. Are you sure you're not too busy? I know you must have your own business to see to."

His lips tip up on one side, and he shrugs a shoulder. "The best part about being the boss is, I can make my own hours."

"Well, that's true. I'll be at the shop all day, if you and Jake want to pop in for a while. I'd really appreciate it."

Ryan nods and walks with me to the door. "I'll go kick the kid out of bed. Since school got out for the summer, all he wants to do is sleep after he goes out to do his morning chores."

"That sounds pretty normal to me. I'll see you later."

With a wave, I head back to the shop. Is it a bad idea to have Ryan around to help out today? Probably. But I could use the extra hands, and I'm an adult. I can curb my lustful thoughts when it comes to the sexy billionaire cowboy.

Probably.

***

While Mac loads boxes of new product onto a dolly to bring into the newly cleaned showroom, I'm shifting older stock to clearance racks in the back of the store. Loaded down with about fifty pounds of clothes, I try to lift the hangers onto the tall rack, but I'm just not tall enough.

"It sucks when you're a tiny leprechaun," I mutter to myself.

"Prettiest leprechaun I've ever seen," Ryan says from behind me, startling me. He reaches around me to take the hangers out of my hands and easily lifts them to the rack, his body pressed against mine, and the spicy, woodsy scent of him surrounds me.

I could eat him with a spoon.

"Thanks." I smile up at him as he steps back. "I was too impatient to grab the step stool."

"Now you don't have to." He gestures over to Jake with his head. "The kid and I are here to help. Are you filling these racks with clearance?"

"Yes." I turn to Jake with a smile. "Thanks for this. I know it's probably not how you planned to spend summer vacation."

"It's one day," the handsome teenager says. "And I hear I get a sandwich out of the deal, so it's all good."

With a laugh, I turn back to Ryan. "Mac's in the back, loading up new product to be unboxed. I'll have Jake help me with the rest of the clearance."

"I have my marching orders," Ryan says with a wink, and off he goes to help out my brother.

"I'm so glad you're tall," I say to Jake as I lead him to the racks of clothes that I have sorted by size. "In fact, I think you've grown about six inches in the past year."

"About that," he confirms. "Ry says it's because of all the food I eat, and claims I'm eating him out of house and home, but he can afford it." His grin is a happy one, and that makes *me* happy. It was just last year that I found the boys he was hanging out with shoplifting from my store. I'm so glad that he's turned his life around.

"Things at Ryan's are good, then?"

"The best." He sighs, props his hands on his hips, and looks out the window. "Sometimes I don't know if I deserve everything that he's done for me, you know? It's a lot. Just letting me live with him is enough, but I have the horses, and he bought me a truck for Christmas. Shit, he *adopted* me. Oops, sorry for the shit."

"No problem, I've said it myself." I pass him some more clothes to move. "These can go right behind the others up there. You know, I don't think that a man like Ryan does much of anything that he doesn't *want* to do. And he absolutely wouldn't do it for someone who doesn't deserve it. Powerful men like that are successful for a reason."

Jake turns back to me after placing the clothes on the rack, and we walk back to gather more. "I know. It's so weird to think about how much money he has. Especially because he's just a regular guy. Mostly normal."

I laugh and pass him more clothes and then follow him loaded down with more of my own, and before long, we've transferred everything to where they need to go.

I'm pleased to realize that there's less left over from last season than I planned for, so I can use more racks for the new stuff.

Ryan and Mac come strolling in with dollies loaded with big boxes of clothes that I can't wait to get my hands on.

"Jesus, clothes are heavy," Mac says with a scowl. "I thought summer clothes are supposed to weigh *less*."

"I can just get *more* in the boxes," I reply. "I have hangers set up over there, with my steamer. I'll get started on that if the three of you want to start putting my new shelves together."

"Power tools," Jake says with a grin. "Manly stuff."

Ryan laughs, and the three of them return to the back, where my big storage room is, to start assembling the furniture. I unlock my phone and turn on my favorite playlist, pairing it to the Bluetooth speakers in the shop, and then set it aside. As Harry Styles starts to sing about watermelon sugar, I dive into boxes, slicing them open with my box cutter, and then I start to hang them on hangers, sort by size, and then steam.

It's a long, laborious process, but I love it. I have four employees who all offered to come in and help today, but they've been here all week, cleaning and sorting, and they've put in long days. So, I told them to take today off, and I'd work on this part alone. It'll take me through the weekend to get it all unpacked, pressed, and set out, but it'll be worth it.

I've just moved on to my fifth box, and Ed Sheeran is crooning about dancing in the dark when I'm suddenly swept up in Ryan's arms, and he dances me around the mostly empty showroom.

I'm laughing when, still singing along, he dips me back and then brings me back up and hugs me.

"I couldn't resist," he says and kisses me on the cheek before pulling away. "We're about ready for the furniture."

"That was fast."

"It's good furniture," he says. "Not particle board that you have to put together piece by piece. Do you want to show me where you want it?"

"Sure." Pleased that he approves of what I chose, I show Ryan where I want each piece, and then he disappears into the back again, and I have to take a deep breath.

Being around that man is...well, it does things to me. And he doesn't seem to be affected *at all*. Which is a bit of a blow to the ego, but oh well. Before long, the men have everything placed exactly where I want it, and the four of us stand back, admiring it.

"I like the colors," Jake offers. "They're not boring brown."

"I wanted to brighten the space up," I agree. "The

only windows are the ones in the front, and dark furniture would make it feel like a cave in here. So, I got pieces that were painted in bright colors. I think it looks great, guys. Thanks. I'll go order those sandwiches."

I take their order and call it into the deli down the street.

"They'll be here in about twenty minutes."

"What can we do in the meantime?" Ryan asks.

"I have to hang some mirrors in the dressing rooms," Mac says. "You can help me with those heavy fuckers."

"Mac!" I gesture to Jake. "Really? There's a kid here."

"Oh, I've heard it all," Jake assures me. "It's fine. I can help lift a mirror."

"He's a good kid," I say to Ryan when the other two are in the back, measuring for the mirrors."

"Yeah, he is. We've had a few bumps here and there, but he'll be sixteen next month, and I suspect that's normal."

"I would guess so," I agree with a nod. "Well, I'd better get back to hanging these clothes."

"You know," he continues, not taking the hint at *all*, "you do a lot of avoiding me these days."

I frown down at the pair of white jeans I'm holding. "I don't think that's true."

"At Summer and Chase's wedding last month, you didn't even *look* at me."

"I was busy," I remind him. "I was the maid of honor, and I had a long list of duties."

"Polly."

I stop at the sound of his voice and turn to look at him, raising an eyebrow.

"I don't want things to be weird between us." He reaches out and tucks a stray strand of my hair behind my ear.

"You didn't call." I feel my eyes widen. I did *not* mean to say that out loud. "Uh, never mind. That was—"

"You left," he says, interrupting me. "If you wanted me to call, you sent me a mixed message with that move."

I bite my lip, thinking it over, and then let out a gusty sigh, but the other guys return to us, looking smug.

"All done," Mac says and high-fives Jake. The door opens, and Jeannie, the manager of Mama's Deli, walks in, carrying two big brown bags full of food.

"Delivery," she calls out with a smile. "Oh, it's already so *different* in here, Polly. I can't wait to see it when you've finished."

"I reopen Monday morning," I inform her as Mac takes the bags off her hands, and I pass her the cash to cover the order. "I have some new things that I think you're going to love."

"Now I *really* can't wait. I'm so grateful that you carry inclusive sizes for us curvier girls," Jeannie says with a happy smile.

"Every woman is gorgeous and deserves to wear clothes that make her feel confident," I reply. "No matter her size. Definitely come see me next week, and I'll help you shop."

"I can't wait. Have a good day, all of you. I'd better get back."

She hustles out the door, and I turn to find Ryan watching me intently.

"What? Do I have something on my face?"

"No." He shakes his head and takes a bite of his sandwich. "You're a good businesswoman."

Coming from the likes of Ryan Wild, the owner and CEO of Wild Enterprises, a multi-billion-dollar company, that's a *huge* compliment.

"Thanks." I raise my sandwich to tap it to his in *cheers*.

NEWSLETTER SIGN UP

I hope you enjoyed reading this story as much as I enjoyed writing it! For upcoming book news, be sure to join my newsletter! I promise I will only send you news-filled mail, and none of the spam. You can sign up here:

https://mailchi.mp/kristenproby.com/newsletter-sign-up

ALSO BY KRISTEN PROBY:

Other Books by Kristen Proby

The Wilds of Montana Series
Wild for You - Remington & Erin
Chasing Wild - Chase & Summer

Get more information on the series here: https://www.
kristenprobyauthor.com/the-wilds-of-montana

Single in Seattle Series
The Secret - Vaughn & Olivia
The Scandal - Gray & Stella
The Score - Ike & Sophie
The Setup - Keaton & Sidney
The Stand-In - Drew & London

Check out the full series here: https://www.
kristenprobyauthor.com/single-in-seattle

ALSO BY KRISTEN PROBY:

Huckleberry Bay Series

Lighthouse Way
Fernhill Lane
Chapel Bend
Cherry Lane

The With Me In Seattle Series

Come Away With Me - Luke & Natalie
Under The Mistletoe With Me - Isaac & Stacy
Fight With Me - Nate & Jules
Play With Me - Will & Meg
Rock With Me - Leo & Sam
Safe With Me - Caleb & Brynna
Tied With Me - Matt & Nic
Breathe With Me - Mark & Meredith
Forever With Me - Dominic & Alecia
Stay With Me - Wyatt & Amelia
Indulge With Me
Love With Me - Jace & Joy
Dance With Me Levi & Starla
You Belong With Me - Archer & Elena
Dream With Me - Kane & Anastasia
Imagine With Me - Shawn & Lexi
Escape With Me - Keegan & Isabella
Flirt With Me - Hunter & Maeve
Take a Chance With Me - Cameron & Maggie

Check out the full series here: https://www.
kristenprobyauthor.com/with-me-in-seattle

The Big Sky Universe

Love Under the Big Sky

Loving Cara

Seducing Lauren

Falling for Jillian

Saving Grace

The Big Sky

Charming Hannah

Kissing Jenna

Waiting for Willa

Soaring With Fallon

Big Sky Royal

Enchanting Sebastian

Enticing Liam

Taunting Callum

Heroes of Big Sky

Honor

Courage

Shelter

Check out the full Big Sky universe here: https://www.
kristenprobyauthor.com/under-the-big-sky

Bayou Magic

Shadows
Spells
Serendipity

Check out the full series here: https://www.
kristenprobyauthor.com/bayou-magic

The Curse of the Blood Moon Series

Hallows End
Cauldrons Call
Salems Song

The Romancing Manhattan Series

All the Way
All it Takes
After All

Check out the full series here: https://www.
kristenprobyauthor.com/romancing-manhattan

The Boudreaux Series

Easy Love
Easy Charm
Easy Melody
Easy Kisses

Easy Magic
Easy Fortune
Easy Nights

Check out the full series here: https://www.
kristenprobyauthor.com/boudreaux

The Fusion Series

Listen to Me
Close to You
Blush for Me
The Beauty of Us
Savor You

Check out the full series here: https://www.
kristenprobyauthor.com/fusion

From 1001 Dark Nights

Easy With You
Easy For Keeps
No Reservations
Tempting Brooke
Wonder With Me
Shine With Me
Change With Me
The Scramble
Cherry Lane

Kristen Proby's Crossover Collection

Soaring with Fallon, A Big Sky Novel

Wicked Force: A Wicked Horse Vegas/Big Sky Novella
By Sawyer Bennett

All Stars Fall: A Seaside Pictures/Big Sky Novella
By Rachel Van Dyken

Hold On: A Play On/Big Sky Novella
By Samantha Young

Worth Fighting For: A Warrior Fight Club/Big Sky
Novella
By Laura Kaye

Crazy Imperfect Love: A Dirty Dicks/Big Sky Novella
By K.L. Grayson

Nothing Without You: A Forever Yours/Big Sky Novella
By Monica Murphy

Check out the entire Crossover Collection here:
https://www.kristenprobyauthor.com/kristen-proby-crossover-collection

ABOUT THE AUTHOR

Kristen Proby has published more than sixty titles, many of which have hit the USA Today, New York Times and Wall Street Journal Bestsellers lists.

Kristen and her husband, John, make their home in her hometown of Whitefish, Montana with their two cats and dog.

Printed in the USA
CPSIA information can be obtained
at www.ICGtesting.com
LVHW091018070724
784807LV00008B/327

9 781633 501812